I would like to dedicate this book to all my family members and friends.

Rick Weeks was born in Albany, NY, in 1950 and grew up in South Troy, NY. He attended St. Joseph's School, Troy High and Hudson Valley Community College. He then joined the United States Marine Corps in 1967 and got wounded in Vietnam in 1968. He retired in 2005 from the NYS Education Dept. after 36 years of service. Rick has been married to Melody Rivenburgh for forty years and they have six children: Stacy Vazquetelles, Robert G. Berry III, Jamie L. Weeks, Jeremy R. Weeks, April Dawn van Wagner and Michele Harris. They moved to Kentucky in 2008.

Rick Weeks

STATUES IN THE DARK AND THE CELEBRATION

PART TWO

AUSTIN MACAULEY PUBLISHERS™

LONDON • CAMBRIDGE • NEW YORK • SHARJAH

Ordering Information
Quantity sales: Special discounts are available on quantity purchases by corporations, associations, and others. For details, contact the publisher at the address below.

Publisher's Cataloging-in-Publication data
Weeks, Rick
Statues in the Dark and the Celebration

ISBN 9781645753100 (Paperback)
ISBN 9781645753094 (Hardback)
ISBN 9781645753117 (ePub e-book)

Library of Congress Control Number: 2020924346

www.austinmacauley.com/us

First Published (2021)
Austin Macauley Publishers LLC
40 Wall Street, 33rd Floor, Suite 3302
New York, NY 10005
USA

mail-usa@austinmacauley.com
+1 (646) 5125767

First, I would like to thank God, He guided me through this entire book. When I started writing this book, I knew what the ending would be. After the first page, God took over, and what you read was inspired by God. I would also like to thank my wife, Melody, who always encourages me.

Part One
Statues in the Dark

Prologue

This book is complete fiction; it's a story about an old black man named Buck who can talk with statues. The question is why? Who can give someone this ability?

In 1938, Buck Thompson was born. His father (Mathew) was a share cropper in a small town in North Carolina, his mamma (May) helped worked the crops and did all the domestic chores.

Buck grew up with no more than a 5th grade education; he could read some and write some. As a child, he worked the fields picking fruit and rolling wheat. He did anything his father asked him to do. His father passed away when Buck was eleven. As a child, he took over for his dad and did what he could to help his mamma. When he was 19, his mamma passed away. Buck tried to enter the military, but was rejected because of flat feet.

When his mamma passed, he seemed to lose all his vigor. He decided to move north and try to create a new life. He heard stories that blacks were treated a lot better and you could make an honest wage for an honest day's work. In 1958, he left North Carolina for up-state New York. He had a cousin Willy who lived in Albany and he worked for the State of New York as a cleaner. When Willy would go back home to visit his family, he would stop by and see his cousin Buck and Aunt May.

Willy explained that there were some people who hated black people, but most people were very kind to him. He liked his job and told Buck he met the perfect woman. Buck got word he married her two years earlier.

Buck managed to work and save for his trip; going by bus was the cheapest way to travel. Buck was amazed that when he left North Carolina, he had to sit in the back of the Bus. But when he reached New Jersey to change buses, he was allowed to sit wherever he wanted. This made him feel a lot better about his decision to move north. When he changed buses in New York City, a white woman sat next to him. At first, he was very scared and waited for someone to say something. The woman broke the ice when she asked Buck where he was from.

"North Carolina, mam," was his answer.

"Is this your first trip to New York?"

"Yes, mam."

"Where are you headed?" she asked.

"Albany, mam," was his reply.

It seemed they talked all the way to Albany, the woman stayed on the bus; her destination was Utica.

When Buck exited the bus, he was met by his cousin, Willy, who was standing next to this very pretty woman.

Willy introduced his wife, Olivia. Buck would be staying with them until he got settled. Olivia taught Buck how to dance; they frequented a couple of clubs on Northern Boulevard. She also introduced Buck to the woman who would steal his heart, Rose Budder, of course, Buck referred to her as his little Rose Bud.

Buck got a job as a cleaner with the New York State Education Department. He never missed a day.

Buck and Rose dated for a year before Buck popped the question. Buck had to make sure that they would have their own apartment. He rented a flat two doors down from Willy's apartment on North Pearl Street. There wedding was small, but their life together was larger than life itself.

Two weeks before the wedding, Rose told Buck that she couldn't bear children. She broke down and cried, telling Buck if he wanted to change his mind, she would understand. Buck put his arm around her and squeezed.

"I could never live without you," he said. This made Rose feel a whole lot better.

Buck never thought about having children. He would light up whenever he saw Rose. To Buck, this only meant all of his love would go to Rose.

Rose worked at Woolworths as a cashier when Buck met her. Buck talked her into taking a job with the State of New York. She took the Beginning Office Worker's test. She was one of the top ten. She got a job a few months after taking the test. She worked as a clerk. Together, they had a great life and no money problems. Rose took care of all the bills and even bought Bucks clothes. She was also a great cook; she made all of Buck's favorites.

Buck and Rose retired after thirty-six years of service. Rose actually retired two years before Buck. Buck retired in 1997. Five years later, they would celebrate their fortieth anniversary. Three weeks later, Rose passed away. Buck had her buried at the Albany Rural Cemetery in Menands, N.Y., which was a six-mile walk from Bucks house. Buck would visit her every Sunday and spend the afternoon with Rose; he would keep her up to date on anything that was happening.

Chapter One

After Rose passed, Buck had his credit union pay his rent and utilities and phone bill out of his account every month. This way Buck wouldn't forget or have to make a late payment. Every Monday, he would go to his credit union and withdraw $35.00, this was for food and personal items for the apartment. If he had five dollars left over at the end of the week, he would treat himself to breakfast at the Miss Albany Diner on his way to visit with Rose.

His visits to Rose were the only thing that kept him going. He still visited with his cousin Willy and Olivia. They would worry about Buck walking the twelve miles in the middle of the winter. Buck never thought about it, all the way, he would think of what he would tell Rose. In the winter, he would dress warm and had a scarf to protect his neck and face. On his hands, he wore mittens that were made of wool. His hands never got cold.

His life wasn't complicated. At night, he would listen to music or watch TV. He would get lonely at times, but he knew Rose was with him, the loneliness would drift away. He would remember things that he and Rose did. Most of the time, you would see a smile appear on his face; sometimes, he would laugh out loud. They had so many great times together and his mind was strong and he remembered most everything. Every now and then, he would look toward heaven and thank God for the life he shared with Rose.

It was in the early spring on a visit to Rose that his life would change forever. He walked the six miles after a great breakfast at Miss Albany Diner. As he entered the cemetery, he walked up a small hill towards Rose's grave. He would always notice the grave next to Rose; it had a marble base and a bronze statue of a little girl. The little girl's name was Elizabeth Harnett. He read the base and she died when she was only ten years old.

This visit, he brought a light blanket that he placed on the ground. As he sat there, he told Rose about everything he was involved with this week. He told her that Willy was the same old Willy, but Olivia wasn't feeling very well. He told her even about his breakfast, how his eggs were done just the same way Rose always made them. He would bring up thoughts he had of his life with Rose and he would laugh out loud at some of their adventures.

After three hours, it was time to leave to head back home. Buck picked up the blanket and adjusted it inside his jacket. He looked down at Rose's grave and said, "I will see you next week, I love you so much."

He turned to Elizabeth's statue, he tipped his hat, and said, "I hope you have a blessed week, Missy."

"And the same to you, sir," he heard the voice come from the statue, but stood there stunned.

Buck stepped in front of the statue, "Did you say something, Missy?"

"Yes, I said the same to you, sir."

Buck thought he was losing his mind. He knew statues couldn't talk. He heard the voice but didn't see the lips move. He decided to say something else, "Missy, are you really talking to me?"

"Yes, sir," was the reply.

"How can you talk, you're a statue?" Buck asked.

"When I died from the flu, my father cried for weeks. He had this statue made of me from a picture he carried in his wallet. Whenever I want to see this world, I just come to this statue and I can see out of these bronze eyes and can hear anyone talking who is close."

"Can all statues talk?"

"I don't know, sir. No one has ever spoken to me before. My father would come and sit and cry; my mother would walk away because his sorrow was too much for her to handle."

"How come I never heard you talk before?"

"When you would show up, I would leave to give you the privacy you needed."

"Why were you here today?"

"I knew you would be leaving about this time. Really, I thought you were gone. When you spoke to me, I felt I should reply. I didn't know you could hear me."

"Can my little Rosebud hear me?"

"Yes! She smiles every second your here."

"Can you talk to her for me?"

"No, sir, I can only see her smiling."

Buck really couldn't understand what was happening. He excused himself and headed home. His journey home brought more questions than he could get answers for. After getting home, he sat at his kitchen table and thought of what he thought he heard today. He shook his head in a no motion and headed for bed. He thought he would never get to sleep. But his twelve-mile walk forced the sleep upon him.

The following morning, Buck got up and fixed himself a cup of coffee. When Rose was alive, she would make a pot of coffee every morning. Buck switched to instant, because he couldn't drink an entire pot of coffee. After his cup of coffee, Buck took a shower. He then got dressed and fixed another cup. From the time his eyes opened, he kept thinking about talking to the statue of the young girl at the cemetery.

Was he going crazy or did that really happen? Where Buck worked before he retired was the State Education Department on Washington Avenue. In front of the building were two statues. The right side of the steps had a blooming center with children sitting on the base. Each child had something to do with education, reading a book, looking at a globe, playing a violin. On the left side of the steps was the same blooming center with children sitting at the base. Each child had something to do with playing; one held a tennis racket, there was a boy with a baseball glove and bat. There was a little girl holding a doll.

After his second cup of coffee, Buck decided to visit the statues to see if anyone was there that would talk. When he reached Washington Avenue, he saw the statue of Philip Schuyler in front of Albany's City Hall. He thought about stopping but decided to head up the hill to the Education Department.

It was near lunch time and there were a small number of people sitting on the steps soaking in the early spring sun. One man, sitting there, waved at Buck, he remembered Buck as a cleaner. Buck waved back and then headed for the statue on the left side. He sat down next to it and looked at the girl holding the tennis racket.

"Can you hear me, Missy?"

There was no reply. Buck heard laughter coming from a group on the steps behind him. He turned and noticed a young girl pointing at him and laughing. Buck knew he must look crazy talking to a statue. He turned back, towards the statue, "I'll come back tonight," he said. A few moments later, he got up and walked across the street to a park that sat between the State Capital Building and the Alfred E. Smith Office Building. He noticed a statue of George Washington toward the end across from the Alfred E. Smith Office Building. A thought came to mind, *If statues could talk, what a thrill it would be to talk to George Washington.*

After a while, Buck decided to walk home and wait for it to get dark. It was early spring and it got dark about seven o'clock. When Buck got home, he fixed a ham sandwich and heated the water for another cup of coffee. He looked at the clock and it was approaching three o'clock. He decided he would leave about six thirty. He knew that at seven o'clock, downtown Albany was deserted.

He remembered the girl pointing at him and laughing, she must be telling everyone about the crazy old man talking to statues. Mr. Potter, who lives downstairs, would leave the newspaper on Buck's steps when he was through with it. Buck thumbed through the paper for something to do. He hated reading about the street gangs and blacks killing blacks. There was one article where gang members in a car drove up to kill another gang's member. The gang member sitting on a step with his girlfriend, he pulled his girlfriend in front of him and she was shot and died. *So terrible*, Buck thought, *Kids killing kids, how stupid.*

Buck could hear music coming from the downstairs apartment. He thought of Rose and the great times they would have dancing. Buck remembered a time when another man walked up to Rose to ask her to dance. Rose started shouting at the man. "I am married to the greatest man ever," she said and then slapped the man. "You should never ask a married woman to dance," then she walked away. So many times, Rose said, "I am a married woman." She was proud, but Buck was more than proud, he was astonished that a woman as beautiful as Rose could love him so much.

Chapter Two

Buck thought of having another coffee, but he didn't need to have to go to the bathroom when one wasn't present. At 6:30 p.m., he left his house to head up to the Education Department. As he walked, he thought about what he would say if the statue answered him. The streets were deserted as he thought they would be.

As he reached the steps, he walked up to the statue on the left and sat down. At first, he didn't know what to say.

"I really didn't think you were coming back," he heard the girl holding the tennis racket say.

"Missy, what is your name?"

"I am Jamie Teal. What is your name?"

"I am Buck Thompson."

"How did you know I was here?" Jamie asked.

"I didn't, I spoke to a statue at a cemetery and she answered me."

"I didn't know anyone could hear me," Jamie said.

"I didn't know I could talk to statues," he said and heard Jamie giggle.

"This opens a whole new world for me," she said.

"Me, too!" Buck answered and then asked, "How long ago did you pose for this statue?"

"It was 1910, I was twelve years old."

"Then you've been looking out of those eyes for a real long time."

"Well, yes and no, I guess."

"What do you mean?" Buck asked.

"I died when I was 99 years old. It was 1997."

"Well, I have to tell you, you sound like a young lady."

"That's a wonderful thing to hear," She said and giggled again.

"Did you work or were you a house wife with children."

"I did work as a teacher for thirty years. I was married and had four children. My husband died in World War II. Our children were small at the time. So, I didn't start teaching until my youngest went to school full time. How about you, Mr. Thompson?"

"Please, call me Buck. I grew up in North Carolina, my father was a share cropper, so I worked the farm with him until he passed. I was eleven. I still worked the farm until my momma passed and I was nineteen. I decided to move to New York. I worked right here at this building for 36 years. My wife, Rose, passed a number of years later."

"You seemed to have a rough life."

"Not really, I enjoyed my life as a child and I enjoyed working the farm, but when I moved here and met Rose, life became five hundred percent better."

"She must have been a great woman."

"She was, but why would you say that?"

"Any person who can make another person's life one hundred percent better is a great person, but someone who makes another person's life five hundred percent better has to be a real, real great person."

"I guess she really was."

"You see the boy with the baseball bat?"

"Yeah, I use to play a lot of baseball when I was a boy. To this day, I have never held a real bat."

"His name is Peter Todd, sometimes, he comes here. You should check now and again. He had a very interesting life. You will stop back, won't you?"

"Yes, mam. I'll be back later this week."

"I will enjoy talking to you again, Buck."

Buck tipped his hat and said, "Have a blessed week."

"Thank you and I hope you have a blessed week also."

With that said, Buck walked down the stairs. The park across the street was lit up, so Buck decided to see if George Washington was there. As he approached, it dawned on him that he didn't know what to say. He stopped and stared at the statue. *I'm not going to ask him about the cherry tree*, he thought. Buck thought that the statue was small in size for such a great man. He approached slowly, "Mr. Washington, I mean President Washington, are you here?" There was no reply. He asked again, still no reply. *He must not be here today*, Buck thought. He decided to head home. He thought of telling Willy and Olivia, but didn't want them to think he was losing it.

As Buck walked home, he felt there was something he had to do. He figured he could think about it tonight. To Buck, there was a blank page that needed to be filled. But with what was the question. As Buck reached Pearl Street, he saw two men arguing. He shut his ears and kept walking until he reached his apartment. He looked back and they were gone.

As Buck headed up the stairs, he thought of Rose. She would say, "It's time to climb the wooden mountain." It was something her mother would say to her when it was time to go upstairs to bed. Rose had the ability to remember her entire life. Buck was so grateful she shared it with him. One story Buck liked was the one where Rose went on a fishing trip with her grandmother and a male friend of hers named Matt. Matt caught the first fish and her grandmother caught the second. Rose didn't even get a bite. Matt looked at her and said, "If you don't get a fish, you're going to have to walk home." Rose panicked, it took over two hours to get here and that was by car. She had no idea which way to walk. She thought it would take her all night. She was only ten, she always believed adults when they said something. As she sat there, she began to cry.

Her grandmother came over to ask her, "Why are you crying?"

She blurted out, "I don't know the way home."

Matt walked over and knelt down in front of her and took her hands in his, "Little darling, I was only joking, I would never have you walk home." He smiled and said, "Except if you catch a bigger fish then me," immediately followed by, "I'm joking, I'm joking."

Her grandmother said, "Matt jokes a lot, don't believe anything he says."

Matt heard that and said, "Then I won't tell you about the snake that is behind you."

Rose's grandmother jumped up so quick she knocked down Matt trying to get away from there. Rose saw there was no snake and started laughing. Her grandmother had a few choice words for Matt.

Buck laughed out loud thinking of that episode in Rose' life.

As he sat at the kitchen table, his mind turned towards the statues. He looked across the kitchen as if he would find something that would solve his problem. He saw a pad of paper sitting by the phone. He walked over and picked it up. He wore a puzzled look on his face, but then a light went on. He sat at the kitchen table and began to write down questions he had.

1. How come I can talk to statues?

2. How come I can hear statues talk?

3. How many statues are in Albany?

4. Need to learn about History of Albany.

5. Learn about statues in Washington, D.C.

Buck's mind started to think of statues all over the world and wished he and Rose could see them together. He also thought, *I wish I was younger.*

He kept the pad on the table and started getting ready for bed. He needed a shower for sure. He walked to the bathroom and noticed the hamper by the door. He looked inside, it was empty. *Need to wash my clothes, too,* he thought.

Chapter Three

The next morning when Buck got up, he turned on the kettle to make a cup of coffee. While the water was heating, he sat at the kitchen table and looked over his notes.

He decided to go to City Hall to see if they had any booklets on the Statues in Albany. A man there told him that they did, but they were out of them. He said, "You should check the Albany Public Library." As Buck walked up Washington Avenue, he had the urge to stop and say hi to Jamie. But he saw people sitting on the steps and decided against it. When he reached the Albany Public Library, he entered and went straight to the main desk. The woman there greeted him with a smile.

"Can I help you, sir?" she asked.

"Do you have any books on statues in Albany?"

"We do, I think we have one that covers the Capital Region. Would that work?"

"Yes, mam," Buck replied.

"Do you have a library card?" she asked.

"No, mam," Buck said with disappointment in his voice.

"Would you like to apply for one?"

Buck knew he only had a few dollars in his pocket, "How much does that cost?"

"Are you a resident of Albany?"

"Yes, mam."

"Then just fill out this card and it doesn't cost anything."

Buck took the card from the lady's hand and sat at a table close by. He noticed all they wanted on the card was his name and address. He filled out the card and handed it back to the woman. Within a few minutes, he was holding his first library card ever.

"You can take a seat, I will have someone bring the book to you."

"Thank you, mam," was Bucks reply.

A few moments later, a young woman placed the book in front of Buck, "This is what Mrs. Burke had me retrieve for you."

"Thank you very much."

The title was Monuments of the Capital Region. When Buck opened the book, he was staring at the monument in Washington Park of Moses. Buck knew all about Moses, he read his bible from cover to cover. He also knew he wasn't ready to try and talk with Moses, he turned the page and saw the statue of Uncle Sam in the City of Troy. He began to read the caption under the picture. This really wasn't Uncle Sam, but a tribute to him. According to what Buck read, Samuel Wilson was a meat packer who sold barrels of meat to the United States Army during the War of 1812. He would stamp the barrels U.S. The soldiers receiving the allotment would say, "Just got a ship load from Uncle Sam." So that is how Uncle Sam got started. It was 1813 when the United States got the nick name Uncle Sam. In 1961, the U.S. Congress recognized Samuel Wilson as the progenitor of America's symbol of the United States. "Learn something new every day," he would hear Rose say in his mind. Buck wasn't a fast reader. He got up and approached the main desk.

"Can I help you?" the woman asked.

"Mam, would I be able to take this home for a few days?"

"Sure, hand me your library card."

Buck did as the woman requested. She opened the book to the back inside cover and stamped a date, "You have two weeks, if you want to renew it, just stop back and we will lend it to you for another two weeks."

"Thanks so much, mam," Buck said and took the book and left the library. He headed home.

He knew he had to stop by sometime today and see Willy and Olivia. Buck walked up the wooden mountain and placed the book on the kitchen table and headed out to see Willy and Olivia. As he started up the outside steps, he heard Willy yelling something. He rang the bell and Willy opened the door.

"I just yelled to Olivia that if you didn't stop by today, I would go to your apartment to make sure everything was okay."

"I'm sorry I didn't stop by sooner, I really didn't mean to cause you and Olivia any worry."

"We promised Rose we would look out for you."

At that moment, Olivia yelled from the kitchen.

"Who was at the door?"

"It's Buck!"

Olivia walked into the parlor, "What have you been up to? I stopped by your house twice and you weren't home. I even stopped the other night and you were out. I want to know everything."

"Sorry, Livy, I didn't mean to make you worry any. As far as the truth, I feel I really need to be honest with you two. You're my best friends and closest relatives. But I don't know if I can," Buck hesitated and began again, "I don't know if I can be honest with you. You will think I'm nuts. But I really ain't."

Willy looked at Olivia. Olivia took a seat next to Willy. "We're all ears, fess up," Willy said.

Buck looked at the floor and shook his head, "Hear me out before you say anything."

"We love you, Buck, we are here for you. You can tell us anything," Olivia said.

"Well, I really do need to tell somebody," Buck said and began his tale of woe, "I was visiting Rose Sunday and you know that statue of the little girl next to Rose's grave?"

Willy and Olivia nodded.

"As I was getting ready to leave, I told Rose I would see her next Sunday, and I tipped my hat at the statue of the little girl and said, 'I hope you have a blessed week, Missy.' Then I heard a voice say, 'And the same to you sir.' I thought I was hearing things. I asked the statue, 'Did you say something Missy?' And she replied, 'Yes, I said the same to you, sir.'"

Willy and Olivia looked amazed, but not shocked. Then Buck proceeded to explain about the statue on the steps of the State Education Department and how he went back later that night and talked with Jamie, the child holding the tennis racket. He explained about going to the Albany Public Library when he was done. He waited for Olivia and Willy to tell him he was crazy. But they just sat there. Willy broke the silence, "Can anyone hear them?"

"I don't know. But I can hear them."

Olivia asked, "What did the girl on the steps say?"

Buck explained that she said she posed for the statue back in 1910, she was twelve at the time. But she didn't die until 1997, she was ninety-nine when she passed. But she sounded like a young girl.

"Has these statues talked to anybody else?" Willy asked.

"According to Elizabeth, that's the name of the girl next to Rose. She tried to talk with her father but all he did was cry, he never heard her. Elizabeth also said that whenever she wants to see this world, she can go to her statue and look out from her bronze eyes. And Jamie at the State Education Department said the same thing. Jamie has never talked to anyone, because no one ever talked to her before."

"Would you let me go with you sometime to see if I can hear them?" Willy asked.

"Yeah, I would like that. But what if I am the only one who can hear them."

"Can they hear other people talk?" Willy asked.

"According to Elizabeth, she can hear anyone who is close."

"Then I can ask a question in her ear and she would be able to hear it."

"I think so," Buck replied.

"Maybe I can go with you Sunday when you go to visit Rose."

"It would be better if you came about two o'clock. Elizabeth won't be there until I'm ready to leave. She wants me to have private time with Rose."

"That's so sweet," Olivia said.

"I'll be there about two o'clock. This is the most excitement I have felt in a long time," Willy said. Olivia gave him a watch out stare. "You know what I mean honey," Willy said and gave Olivia a light squeeze.

"You know I thought you both were going to say I was crazy."

Willy looked at Olivia and said, "I believe him, do you?"

"Of course, I do. I have known you for a real long time and I never heard a lie come out of your mouth. God has given people all kinds of abilities. He must have done this for a reason. So, we must pay attention to what happens."

"Well, I feel a hundred pounds lighter sharing this with both of you," Buck said as he stood up to leave.

"We are always here for you," Willy said as he walked Buck to the door.

Wow, they believed me, Buck thought as he walked home. When he reached his apartment, he turned on the water for a cup of coffee, then it dawned on Buck that he never ate today. He opened up the fridge and saw some cold cuts in a plastic bag. "Baloney or turkey," Buck slipped out the turkey. It wasn't a week old. He smelled it and it smelled fine. He made a thick sandwich and had his cup of coffee with it.

Buck felt so relieved that Willy and Olivia believed him. He wasn't alone anymore. As he ate, he thumbed through the book. He saw the statues of Washington and Sheridan. There were many that Buck never heard of, but he would read up on them. He felt tired and decided to go to bed and get to sleep. He would continue his journey tomorrow.

When he got up on Wednesday morning, he tried to remember the name Jamie said about the boy with the baseball bat. He thought on it and couldn't remember. He would have to ask Jamie when he went to visit her again. He fixed a cup of coffee and began to go through the book again. He saw one that he remembered, Philip Schuyler, the statue out in front of City Hall. He decided he would approach him tonight, but first, he would read about him.

As he read, he learned that Schuyler served in the N.Y.S. Assembly and then the N.Y.S. Senate. He was elected to the U.S. Continental Congress in 1775, he also served in the U.S. Senate, and he fought in the French and Indian War. Buck read all he could read, but couldn't think of a question for him. He was the father-in-law of Alexander Hamilton. He also read that his health interfered with many of his accomplishments.

Buck would have to think about what he would say. He thought he might want to visit the Schuyler Mansion. Then he could tell him about what he saw. This could lead to an interesting discussion. As he looked at his notes, he saw (U.S. Continental Congress in 1775), he could talk to him about Washington, Franklin, Jefferson, and many others that he had served with.

Buck decided to deal with one statue at a time. He closed the book and pushed it away. Tonight, he would try and talk with Philip Schuyler. There was no telling if Schuyler would even be there. He also wanted to stop by and see if Jamie was there.

He left his apartment at 6:30 p.m. It was a twenty-minute walk and it was all up-hill. As he reached the statue of Philip Schuyler, the area was deserted. He stood in front of the statue, remembering the last office he held was United States Senator and asked, "Senator Schuyler, are you here?"

There was no answer. Buck heard a car approaching behind him. It was the Albany police. "Can I help you?" the policeman asked.

"No, I'm trying to educate myself with Senator Schuyler here."

"He served in the New York State Senate?" the policeman asked.

"Well, yeah, and the United States Senate also."

"I didn't know that, thanks for sharing your education," the policeman said and drove away.

Buck asked again, "Are you here, Senator Schuyler?" only to be greeted by silence. Buck decided to walk up Washington Avenue and see if Jamie was there. As he approached the steps to the Education Department, he thought he heard someone talking. He looked around and saw no one. As he approached Jamie's statue, he heard her say.

"You came back?"

"I told you I would be back later in the week."

"I thought I would come here every night until you came," Jamie said.

"What was the name of the boy with the baseball bat again?"

"His name is Peter Todd."

"Can you talk with other statues?"

"Only those who are near-by, like Peter."

"Is he here tonight?"

"No! He was here last night and I told him about you. I know he has some questions for you."

"I hope I have the answers. I'm not from Albany. Though, I have been here for over fifty years."

"When I was a young girl, I read about Peter in the newspaper. His mother was killed in their house. Peter slept through it. His father was a traveling salesman, he was not home at the time,"

"How old was Peter when that happened?" Buck asked.

"He was thirteen, the story doesn't stop there. He told the police that he was asleep. When he woke up, he could smell his father. He went to see if he was home and that is how he found his mother. She was stabbed five times. According to Peter, blood was everywhere."

"How terrible for a boy to witness such a gruesome mess," Buck said.

"Because of what Peter told the police, they arrested his father when he came home two days later. His father confessed, it seems he had another family in Buffalo. Peter was taken to Social Services and they placed him with a couple that couldn't have children. Peter was in shock for a long time, with counseling and his new family support, he worked his way through it."

"Oh my, how awful."

"You know how some people say God works in mysterious ways?"

"Yes, I heard that in the Sargent York movie."

"He really does. Peter is a graduate of Yale, he has three degrees and spent most of his life helping the less fortunate. He turned out to be a great man. Admired by all that knew him."

"Wow! God does work in mysterious ways," Buck added.

"Have you talked with any other statues?" Jamie asked.

"I tried to talk tonight with Philip Schuyler, but he wasn't there. I will try again."

"I remember reading that he was heroic on the battle field, but was afraid of the dark. You may have to try him when its daylight."

"In a few weeks, it will be light until eight o'clock. I'll try again then."

"Will you come back again?" Jamie asked.

"I will be back Monday night."

"What is today?" Jamie asked.

"It's Wednesday."

"We have no sense of time."

"Are you in heaven?"

"Yes!"

"And God lets you come down to earth and see out of your bronze eyes."

"If I were stone, I could do the same thing."

"What about all the people that don't have a statue that they can use."

"Those people only have to look down and they can see their loved ones, they can get this close."

"You mean my Rose can be right in front of me?"

"Yes, but I don't think they have a voice to talk with."

"Why is that.?"

"Until you, we didn't know anyone could hear us. But I remember before I knew I could come here, I would go to my daughter's house and I try to talk. She never responded."

On his way home, Buck thought about what Jamie told him. When he reached his apartment, he felt really tired. He sat on the sofa and leaned back and fell asleep within minutes.

He slept through the night. When he woke up in the morning, he went in and took a shower. After his shower, he fixed a cup of coffee and made four pieces of toast.

Chapter Four

As Buck had his coffee and toast, he remembered that he forgot to go to the credit union to take out his money for the week. He laughed at himself, but was pleased to know on Sunday, he could stop at the Miss Albany Diner and have his favorite breakfast.

He made the forty-minute walk to the credit union. He filled out his withdrawal slip and waited in line. There were always a lot of people at the credit union, then again, over ten thousand people worked in the Empire State Plaza.

After he received his money, he took the forty-minute walk back home. He wanted to look through the book again, but had no plans on trying to talk with a statue today. He did plan on going out for dinner. On the way back, he would stop at the store. He sat at the kitchen table and pulled the book to him. He opened the book and saw the statue of George Washington, he then thought he forgot to stop over to see the statue last night after talking with Jamie. At this point, the doorbell rang. As Buck approached the door, he heard someone climbing the stairs. He opened the door to see Olivia trying to catch her breath.

"Come in, Olivia, take a seat on the sofa," Buck said and then he went to get her a drink of water. He handed it to her and said, "Take small sips." Olivia did and within a few moments, she was her same old self again.

"I stopped by an hour ago and you weren't home."

"I went to the credit union to take out some money. I need to pick up a few things at the store."

"Willy and I were wondering if you would like to come by for dinner tonight."

"Sure, why not, you're a great cook."

"Well, thank you. I'm making up some of my fried chicken with biscuits and gravy."

"I can smell them now," Buck said.

Olivia smiled. "We plan on eating at 5:00," she said. Buck assured her that he would be there at 4:30.

After Olivia left, Buck still had to head to the store. He went to a small mom and pop place on Clinton Ave. He picked up everything he could think of that he needed. After getting back home, he put everything away.

Again, he sat at the kitchen table and began to go through the book. He began to read about Sheridan. Something made him look at the clock. It was ten minutes after four. He pushed the book away and went into the bathroom to clean up a bit. He needed to shave. When he was done, he looked at the clock again, it was four twenty-five. He left for Willy and Olivia's apartment.

Buck was greeted by his friends and discussed what had happened over the past couple of days.

"Olivia, you were born here right?"

"Yes, April 20th, 1936. Why?"

"Did you ever hear of a person named Peter Todd."

"Everybody heard of Peter Todd, if it weren't for him, many of us wouldn't have had a Christmas."

"What do you mean?" asked Willy.

"Back in the forties and fifties, Mr. Todd played Santa Claus. He would come to the poor sections of Albany with a car full of toys. Around Thanksgiving, he would come with a car full of turkeys. I don't know how to explain it, but I swear he had a twinkle in his eye. Whenever he handed me a toy, I always saw a twinkle in his eye."

"Do you know what happened to him when he was a kid?"

"No, not really, what?"

"Did you know his mother was murdered by his father. It was Mr. Todd who found her body. He told the police when he woke up, he could smell his father. He checked their bedroom to see if he was there. He was a traveling salesman. He wasn't there, but according to Jamie, when he returned two days later, the police arrested him. He did confess."

"Oh! My Lord, how terrible. For a boy to witness such a thing," Olivia said.

"My thoughts exactly. I will be talking with him soon, I hope."

"I didn't know they made a statue of him, here in Albany."

"He was a boy when he sat for the statue that Jamie's in on the left side of the State Education Department steps. He sits next to her, he is holding a baseball bat and glove."

Willy sat there stunned as he listened to Olivia and Buck talking about this man.

"Jamie said that he worked through the shock with counseling and family support he received from foster parents who adopted him. She said he turned out to be a great man."

"When did he die?" Olivia asked.

"I don't know, I will ask him when I talk with him," Buck replied.

"What's your plans for Saturday?" Willy asked.

"I'm going to take it easy, read, I guess. Want to make notes so I can share all this with Rose on Sunday."

"I can't wait until Sunday," Willy added.

"I would like to walk over to the Education Department Building and take a look at that statue," Olivia said.

Willy looked at Buck, "Well, I guess I know what we'll be doing Saturday."

"Say hi to Jamie," Buck replied.

"Let's eat," Olivia said and everyone headed to the dining room.

As Buck bit into his first piece of chicken, the juices ran down to his chin. Buck grabbed his napkin, wiped his face, and said, "Olivia, you always make the juiciest chicken I've ever had."

"Thank you, Buck," she replied.

"I didn't marry her because she is a great cook. I married her because I knew our life together would be fun and it is."

Olivia smiled at Willy as he finished his fourth piece of chicken. After dinner, they all helped to clean up and sat back down for a cup of coffee.

After Buck had his coffee, he stood up and thanked them both for a great evening and to Olivia for a great dinner.

"If I don't see you tomorrow, I'll see you Sunday," Willy said as he walked Buck to the door.

"See you then," Buck said, then headed home. Buck thought that it must be all the excitement that is making him so tired. It was seven thirty when Buck looked at the clock. He turned on the television and sat there in hopes of finding a show that he would like: Gun Smoke, that's the one he decided on. Within a view minutes, he began to doze off. He woke up at two o'clock in the morning. He got up and went to his bedroom. Before he turned on the light, he swore Rose was there lying in bed. As the light went on, the room was empty.

After he disrobed, he got in bed, he hugged his pillow, and said aloud, "I love you, Rose."

The following morning while having his coffee and toast, he started to make notes of things he needed to share with Rose. He planned on resting all day Friday. He did laundry and cleaned up a bit around the apartment. He decided he would go to McGeary's for dinner. Everybody there always seemed to be happy. That could be because they all just got out of work. He left for McGeary's at four thirty, it was Friday and it looked to be crowded. As he walked in, the people there always parted. He thought that was because he was probably the oldest person there. He sat at a small table for two in hopes the waitress saw him. She did and walked right over.

"Hi, Buck, haven't seen you in a while."

"I don't go out much in the winter, now that spring is here, you will see me more."

"What can I get for you?"

"A mug of beer," he hesitated, "Do you have fish?"

"Yes, we always have fish. We have fried haddock platter that comes with fries and coleslaw. Or we have fish fries."

"I'll take that haddock platter."

"What kind of beer?"

"Wet and cold," he said with a smile.

"I'll put your order in and bring back a mug of wet and cold beer."

Buck enjoyed watching the young people talking and laughing. It seemed that no one had a care in the world.

After Buck had dinner and a beer, he headed home. Tomorrow was Saturday and it was supposed to rain. He thought how Olivia and Willy wanted to visit the statue with Jamie and Peter Todd at the State Education Department. *Maybe it will only be a light rain,* he thought. Sunday was going to be warmer and sunny. That sounded great to Buck.

He had been compiling notes to share with Rose. As he reviewed what he had written, he thought of a few other things that needed to be added. He heard someone coming up the stairs and then he heard them go back down. He opened the door and saw his mail sitting on the top step. It must have been Mr. Potter from downstairs. As he glanced at the envelopes, he noticed one was from his credit union. He received statements that he really never looked at. This looked like a letter. He opened it and began to read,

'Mr. Buck Thompson,

We have reviewed your account and would like to discuss a certain matter with you. At your convenience, please contact me to set up an appointment. It has been a pleasure having you as a member for so many years.

With Best Regards,

Simon Z. Templar, Credit Union Manager.'

Buck, at first, got worried; did he take out too much money, was there enough money to pay his bills? Buck had direct deposit and so did Rose. He would deal with this next week. He had no idea how much money went into the account each month. He only knew how much was spent on bills and how much cash he would withdraw each week from his account. "Yeah, I will deal with this next week," he said aloud as he stuck the letter to the fridge with a magnet.

The other envelope was from a company that said he could apply for a free hearing aid. Buck thought of calling the number and every time the other person said something, Buck would just yell back, "What!" At that thought, Buck had to laugh at himself.

Buck thought of looking at the book on monuments, but decided against it. He would watch some T.V. and then go to bed.

When Buck got up Saturday morning, it was pouring rain. He thought of Willy and Olivia again and thought that they would not attempt to go out in it.

Looking at the rain pouring down through one of his front windows. He thought of Rose again and how she talked Buck into going out for a walk in the pouring rain. He could picture her swirling around with her face aimed at the sky. They got drenched, but it was all worth it. It seemed anything would remind him of Rose.

Tomorrow was Sunday and the thought of talking to Rose filled him with a certain type of joy. Buck never pictured his life without Rose. Now she has been gone a long time, but to Buck, she was always here. He gathered up his notes and placed them on a blanket he planned on taking with him. He spent most of Saturday reliving old times. When he got in bed that evening, he said, "I'll see you in the morning, Rose."

Chapter Five

When he woke up Sunday morning, he washed up and got everything ready that he wanted to take. He placed his notes in his jacket pocket and the blanket he slipped inside his jacket. He didn't fix himself any coffee. He would get that at the Miss Albany Diner. He left his apartment about eight-thirty. He arrived at the Miss Albany Diner about nine o'clock.

"How are you today, Buck?" a man named Sam Greaten asked. Sam knew Buck was on his way to visit his departed wife. Sam saw Buck every week. He knew sometimes Buck didn't stop in. It was Sunday and Buck was going to visit Rose.

"I am doing fine, thank you for asking," Buck replied, "How are you doing, Sam?"

"I don't know if I have new pains or if these are the ones I have every day. At our age, we have to expect this sort of thing, I guess."

"I've been blessed I don't have any pain. I walk a lot maybe that's the trick."

"I get the urge to take a walk, but I usually sit down and wait for that to pass," Sam said.

Buck heard someone laugh at Sam's remarks. At that moment, the man behind the counter placed a cup of coffee down in front of Buck, "You want your usual?"

Buck nodded and poured some cream in the cup. In all the years that Buck came to the Miss Albany Diner, he never saw another black man in there.

Buck enjoyed every bit of his breakfast. He loved dunking his toast into the yoke of the eggs. The bacon and home-fries were perfect. This was a treat that he truly loved. After breakfast, he paid his bill and stopped at the restroom. As he left the restroom, Sam said, "Say hi to Rose for me."

"I will Sam, thank you," he tipped his hat and left. It took another hour of walking before he would be with Rose. It was a little after eleven when he reached her grave site. He knew Elizabeth wouldn't be there until he was getting ready to leave. He spread out the blanket and sat down, "Rose, I have so much to tell you about." As he took his notes from his jacket pocket, he held them up, "I had to make notes to remember everything that happened this week."

He first proceeded to tell about all the good times he remembered he had with Rose. He then told her all about Jamie and this man named Peter Todd. He told her about getting a library card and how it doesn't cost anything to take books out of the library.

He told her about how Willy would be stopping by to see if he can talk with Elizabeth. He told her that he explained everything to Willy and Olivia. They didn't think he was crazy either. He talked about Schuyler and George Washington. He talked non-stop for almost three hours.

He looked at his watch and it was approaching two o'clock. He told Rose that Willy would be here about two o'clock. He also told Rose that Jamie told him that as a spirit, she could be right in front of him. He thought he heard something behind him; he saw nothing, as he turned back towards Rose, he felt a light touch hit his cheek.

Then, he heard, "She kissed you."

Buck looked at the statue of Elizabeth, "Was that you, Missy?"

"Yes! It looked like you felt her kiss."

"I did feel a light touch to my cheek."

"She always gives you a kiss before you leave."

"I never felt it before," Buck placed his hand on his cheek. "Rose, I love you so much," he said.

"She knows you do," Elizabeth said.

"I have a cousin coming to see if he can hear you. Is that alright?"

"Yes, that would be fine," she answered.

Buck looked towards Rose, "I will keep notes of the coming week. I will share them with you next Sunday."

"She nodded yes," Elizabeth said.

Buck looked to see if Willy was coming, but he saw no one.

"Have you tried to talk with any other statues?"

"Yes! I did talk with a statue named Jamie."

"You heard her and she heard you?"

"Yes! I have talked to her twice so far. There is another statue named Peter Todd, I hope to talk to him this week."

At this point, Buck heard Willy walking towards them, "Here's my cousin Willy."

Buck stood up and waved to Willy. Willy seemed to be out of breath.

"You shouldn't have walked all that way," he said.

"I didn't, I took a cab to the main gate. That small hill kicked my butt."

"Watch your language, we are among women," Buck said.

Willy stepped in front of Elizabeth, "So, you are the one who talks with my cousin, Buck?"

"Yes, I am," Elizabeth said.

"Did you hear what she said?" Buck asked.

Willy looked at Buck and asked, "What did she say?"

"When you asked if she was the one who talked with me, she said, 'Yes, I am.'"

"I didn't hear that. Ask her to say it again."

Buck heard Elizabeth giggle, "She can hear you."

Willy looked at the statue. "Will you say that again?" Willy listened and heard nothing. "I didn't hear anything," Willy said. Willy then moved closer to her ear and whispered, "My wife's name is Olivia."

Buck didn't hear what he said.

"Ask her what did I say and then tell me."

Buck didn't move, "Missy, what did my cousin say?"

Elizabeth said, "My wife's name is Olivia."

Buck Looked at Willy, "She said, 'My wife's name is Olivia.'"

"She can really hear me? And you can really talk with statues?"

"You really didn't believe me?"

"No, I did, but to see it, set me back a few steps," Willy had an amazed look on his face, "I guess only you can talk with them, and hear what they say."

"Yeah, but why me?"

Willy shrugged, "I don't know, Buck."

Buck looked at Rose's grave. "I'll be back, to see you Sunday," he said, then he turned to Elizabeth and said, "You have a blessed week, Missy."

He heard Elizabeth giggle again, "And the same to you, sir."

Buck stepped in front of Elizabeth and said, "Do you have any questions for me?"

"Thank you, Buck, I really don't. But if I think of anything, I will bring it up next week."

"I'll see, I mean I'll hear you then."

Again, he heard Elizabeth giggle.

As Willy and Buck started to walk away, "What did she say?" Willy asked.

"She said she didn't have a question, but she would think about it and if she comes up with a question, she will let me know next week."

"So, it seems that only you can talk with statues and hear what they say," Willy said.

"I can't understand why it's happening to me. I felt Rose kiss me on the cheek. According to Elizabeth, she has done that every week. But this week, I felt it."

Willy looked at his watch as they reached the main gate. "I have a cab coming in fifteen minutes. You're going to drive back with me, right!"

"Sure, why not."

"What are your plans for this week?" Willy asked.

"I got a letter from the credit union; the manager wants me to call and make an appointment."

"What for?" asked Willy.

"I have no idea, I hope it's not because I messed up somewhere along the way."

"Maybe they want to talk to you about investing your money."

"We never made that kind of money."

"You want me to go with you?"

"No, I don't think so."

"If you change your mind, let me know."

Buck thanked God for having a friend as loyal as Willy.

"Here's the cab!" Willy said as the cab approached with its blinker on to turn into the entrance of the cemetery.

"This will be the earliest I have been home on a Sunday for a long time," Buck said.

"Do you want to stop by for a bite to eat?" Willy asked.

Buck thought about it for a moment and said, "I can't pass up Olivia's cooking."

"Rose was a good cook, too."

"Yes, she was, but she's not here now. Olivia will carry that title for me until I pass."

"Or until we pass," Willy said.

"I do realize that we really don't have many years left, but I'm fine with that. I'll be with Rose."

"We will all be together in heaven," Willy added.

"What do you think Heaven is like?"

"It's Heaven. I picture it as being everything we want. We will be reunited with our families that have passed before us. You really won't want anything, because in Heaven, you will have everything."

"That sounds really nice. Of course, I can't wait to see Rose, but it will be great to see my mamma and dad again, too."

"Yeah! Heaven's going to be Heaven."

At this point, the cab pulled up in front of Willy's apartment. Buck and Willy got out of the cab. Buck pushed Willy back and paid for the cab ride himself.

"You didn't have to do that. I'm the one who had the cab come back."

Both men headed for Willy's apartment. As they reached the steps, Buck smelled something good. Willy unlocked the door and they both walked in. Olivia yelled from the kitchen, "Willy, is Buck with you?"

"Yes, he is," was Willy's reply.

"Hi, Buck!" Olivia yelled.

"Hi, Livy," was Buck's response. Both men sat at the dining room table.

"Do you need any help?" Willy asked.

"No, just sit down, I'll be in, in a moment."

When Olivia walked in, she was holding a Honey Suckle Ham. Buck's mouth started to water. As she placed it on the table, she asked Willy to start slicing it. While Willy did that, Olivia returned from the kitchen holding a bowl of mashed potatoes and a gravy boat filled with gravy. She placed them on the table and went back to the kitchen again. This time she returned with some black-eye peas and French style green beans.

"You sure you don't want any help?" Buck asked.

"The only thing left are the biscuits."

She went back into the kitchen and returned with the steaming biscuits. She placed them on the table and held out her hands for Willy and Buck to take one. When they did, Olivia began to pray. She thanked God for the day, and the food that he supplied for them.

"Let's dig in," Willy said.

As the men began to pile their plates, Olivia asked, "Willy did you hear her?"

"No, but I whispered something in her ear. She repeated it to Buck. I couldn't hear her, but she did hear me. Oh yeah, Rose kissed Buck on the cheek and he felt it."

Olivia looked at Buck, "She did and Elizabeth said she kisses my cheek every week. Today, I felt it."

"Wow," was Olivia's response.

"Did Willy tell you that we did go over to the steps of the Education Department, so I could see the statue of Peter Todd. Do you know why all the children holding something to do with games don't smile, while the children doing things with educational objects are smiling?"

"I never noticed that before," Buck said.

"I did tell Jamie that you said Hi! I didn't hear her say anything though."

"Buck and me think only Buck has that gift," Willy said.

"I told Jamie that I would be back Monday evening," Buck added.

As Buck took his last bite of his biscuit which filled him up completely, Olivia left the table, went into the kitchen, and returned with an apple pie. "Who would like a piece of pie?" Olivia asked.

Both Willy and Buck declined the offer, "You are going to be taking a piece home with you and I don't want to hear no."

Buck smiled and said, "That would be fine."

Buck and Willy had to adjust their belts before they stood up. "You want to stay and watch T.V.?" Willy asked.

"No, I think I'm going to settle on the sofa and watch some T.V. at home."

As Willy walked Buck to the door, he said, "If you want me to go with you, let me know."

After Buck left, Olivia asked Willy, "What was that about?"

Willy explained about the letter he got from the credit union.

Chapter Six

Buck watched T.V. for about an hour, then fell asleep. He dreamed about him and Rose walking the path along the Hudson River, which they did all summer long. In his dream, he watched Rose smile and laughed. He loved every minute of that dream.

He woke up at eight twenty-two, according to the clock on the wall. He smiled thinking of the dream he had of Rose. He very seldom ever dreamed. He turned on the water for his cup of coffee and then entered the bedroom. He took off the clothes from yesterday and put on his robe. After his coffee, he would take a shower.

He sat at the kitchen table waiting for the water to boil. He saw the letter from the credit manager and decided to call to make the appointment.

"S.E.F.C.U.!" he heard the woman who answered the phone say.

"I'm Buck Thompson, I received a letter from Mr. Templar, he wanted me to call and make an appointment."

"Can I have your account number?" the woman asked.

Buck gave her his account number and she asked if she could place him on hold for a minute.

"Yes!" was Buck's reply. He was still a little worried about receiving a letter from Mr. Templar.

"Mr. Thompson, what would be a good time for you. Mr. Templar said he is open pretty much all week."

Buck wanted to get this over, "Would today be good?"

"Yes, how about eleven-thirty?"

"That would be fine. You don't know what this is about, do you?"

"No, if you want, I can call Mr. Templar and ask him."

"No, that's alright. I'll be there for eleven-thirty."

"Thank you, Mr. Thompson," she said and they both hung up.

The water started whistling while Buck was getting ready to hang up the phone. He turned it off and got his cup ready. He never looked at his statements from the credit union. He thought about digging them out, but decided against it. He really wasn't any good in math.

After his shower, he put on his Sunday suit, which he used to put on every Sunday when he and Rose went to church. He really hasn't attended church since Rose passed. His Sundays were spent visiting Rose. He did talk to God a lot. But it wasn't like going to church. He decided to find out what night his church had services. He thought it was Wednesday, he wasn't really sure. After Rose passed, Deacon Roger would stop by every once in a while for religious support. Buck hasn't seen him in about five years. Buck picked up his phone and address book. He searched for Deacon Roger's number. He didn't fine it, but he did fine brother Robert's number. He was the pastor of their Baptist Church. He dialed the number and then listened to a recording. It was very helpful, they did have Wednesday night services at seven o'clock. He marked that down on the pad he had sitting on the kitchen table. He didn't think brother Robert was still at that church.

At ten-thirty, he decided to take the walk over to the credit union. He thought of Willy, but didn't want Willy there in case he made a big mistake, he didn't want everybody to know.

He arrived at eleven-fifteen. There was a woman sitting at a desk on his right. He walked over and said he had an eleven-thirty appointment with Mr. Templar. The woman asked him to take a seat. As soon as he sat down, the woman said, "Mr. Templar can see you now." She then pointed to an office in the back.

"Thank you, mam," Buck said and started to walk to the back. He saw two offices and noticed Mr. Templar's name on the office door to his left.

Before he reached the office, the door opened and a gentleman walked out. He held out his hand, "Mr. Thompson, it is a real pleasure to meet you." Buck shook his hand and Mr. Templar guided him to a seat in front of his desk.

"Did I mess up with my account?" Buck asked.

"No, not at all. Do you check your monthly statements?"

"Not really, I'm not good with numbers," Buck answered, "My wife always took care of that stuff."

Mr. Templar looked at the papers on his desk, "She passed about fourteen years ago, right?"

"Has it been that long," Buck shook his head.

"You both had a joint account, you both had direct deposit."

Buck nodded his head.

"Mr. Thompson, you have almost eight hundred thousand dollars in your account."

Buck couldn't comprehend what Mr. Templar was saying. He placed a sheet of paper in front of Buck. He pointed at a number $797,657.78.

"Mr. Thompson, I called to see if you wanted to invest your money or just let it sit. As it goes now, only two-hundred and fifty thousand is insured with F.D.I.C. We could invest seven-hundred and fifty thousand, which you would get thirty-six thousand a year in interest."

"Can you put together everything you told me, so I can ask a friend about it."

"I can do that right now. You really need to trust the people you ask. People can swindle you really quick."

"I'm not worried, this is family. They have helped me since my Rose passed."

Mr. Templar called his secretary and asked her to fix a portfolio for Mr. Thompson.

Buck looked at Mr. Templar, "I thought I messed up and owed money."

"I see here that you only withdraw thirty-five a week. If you were to take out a couple hundred a week, your money would still grow."

At this point, a woman entered the room and handed Buck a thick folder.

"That is all your recent records, please be careful with who you share it with. Can I suggest that we give you a couple of hundred dollars and freeze your account until you make up your mind."

Buck thought about what Mr. Templar said, "okay, let's do that," Buck said.

"Good, your making me feel a whole lot better."

With that said, he asked Buck to sign a withdrawal slip. After Buck signed, Mr. Templar called his secretary again. She came in took the withdrawal slip and left. She returned a minute later with two hundred dollars in an envelope, she handed it to Buck. "Thank you, Missy," Buck said and then left to head home.

Holding all of his papers close to his chest as he walked. He thought about what Mr. Templar said about someone trying to swindle you out of all your money. Buck decided to head to Willy's house instead of his. When he reached Willy's house, he started up the stairs. Willy noticed him, he was at the door before Buck could knock.

"It looks like you're ready to head to the credit union."

"No, I'm on my way back."

Olivia entered the room from the kitchen, "Did I hear you right, you're on your way back from the credit union?"

"Yeah, I need to talk to both of you if it's okay?"

"Have a seat," Willy said, "Did you mess up like you thought?"

"No!" Buck started to take the papers out of the folder. He handed Willy the paper that showed the amount he had in the credit union.

"Oh my," Olivia said.

"You have close to a million dollars in this account," Willy said.

"I really don't know how I could have that much money. I think that they made a mistake."

"Can I see the other paper work?" Willy asked.

Buck handed him the folder and watched as Willy went from page to page, "How long has Rose been gone?"

"Fourteen years," Buck answered.

"According to this, you have twenty-two hundred dollars deposited every month from retirement. Rose has twenty-six hundred from retirement. You have your social security check deposited that's another fourteen hundred dollars a month. Rose had six years of her social security deposited while she was still alive, that was another fifteen hundred a month. You should have switched over to Rose's social security. You would be getting fifteen hundred instead of fourteen. This looks totally accurate. You only take out eighteen hundred a year for pocket money. They take care of your rent, utilities, and phone bill."

"I don't know how we could have so much money."

"You actually deposit over six thousand dollars a month, that's seventy-two thousand a year. Yes! This is right."

"Mr. Templar wanted me to invest seven hundred and fifty thousand. He said I would collect thirty-six thousand a year in interest. He said the credit union only insures the first two-hundred and fifty thousand."

"I know what you can do with some of that money," Olivia said.

"What?" Buck asked.

"Have a bronze statue of Rose made up."

Bucks eyes lit up, "I remember Elizabeth saying her father had hers done up from a picture he had."

"We have pictures of Rose," Willy said.

"I do, too," Buck replied.

"Let me ask my nephew to look up a company that makes bronze statues on his computer," Olivia said.

"Wow! That would be great," Buck added.

Buck felt an unbridled energy surge through his body, "I really want to do that as quick as I can."

Olivia walked over to the phone and dialed her sister's number, "Betsey is that you?" Buck heard her say, "I need Louie to look up something on his computer for me."

She could hear Betsey calling Louie, she heard her sister say, "Aunt Olivia needs you to find something on your computer."

Betsey handed the phone to Louie.

"Hi Aunt Olivia, what do you need?"

"Louie, I would like you to look up companies that make bronze statues. I'm helping a friend."

"I will call you back in a few minutes," Louie said.

"He said he will call back in a few minutes," she said to Buck and Willy.

"That's a great idea, Livy. Thank you for thinking about it."

"Maybe you should get one done for each of you. When you pass, you and Rose could be together whenever you want to look out of those bronze eyes," Willy said.

"Another great idea," Buck said.

"I'm a little worried about you having so much money. People who find out will want to steal it," Olivia said.

"My account is frozen until I tell Mr. Templar what I want to do."

"That's a great idea," Willy added.

It took about two minutes for Louie to find what Buck needed. Olivia answered the phone. Before she could say hi, Louie was explaining that he found what they needed. The closest one was only fifty miles away. Louie told his Aunt Olivia that he would drop off the list in about an hour. Olivia thanked him, then hung-up.

"He will drop off the list of companies in about an hour."

"I want to treat you both to dinner tonight," Buck said, "Oh! I told Jamie that I would visit tonight."

"We can do dinner some other night," Willy said.

"No, I'll go after dinner."

"I prefer an early dinner myself," Olivia added.

"Where would you like to go?" Buck asked.

"Do you have enough money on you to afford dinner?" Willy asked.

"Oh yeah."

"How about Chicago?" Olivia said and everyone laughed.

"Not tonight, but let's not take it off the list of places we want to go for dinner," Buck added, they all laughed again.

"How about JACK'S Oyster House?" Buck said.

"That might run about seventy-five dollars," Willy mentioned.

"I got it covered," Buck added.

"They sell other stuff besides oysters, right?" Olivia asked.

"Don't know, never been there," Buck replied.

"They must," Willy said.

It was only forty minutes later that Louie dropped off the list of the bronze casting companies.

They all reviewed the list. "How much do you think it will cost?" Willy asked.

"Don't care," was Buck's reply.

"Tomorrow we will get all of the pictures out of Rose and you bring yours Buck," Olivia said.

Buck looked at the clock it was two-thirty, "You want to go to dinner about four?"

"Sounds good to me," Olivia and Willy said in unison.

"I want you both to be a part of this. Will you keep these papers and names of the companies?" Buck asked them both.

"Yes!" again in unison.

"I'm going home to change, I'll meet you here about a quarter to four. Then we will call a cab. I want to go in style."

Willy walked Buck to the door, "I am really happy for you."

"Thanks, Willy, see you in a little bit."

Buck headed home, he felt like jumping up and kicking his heels together. He knew if he did that, he would fall on his face. *I'm going to be able to talk with you Rose*, he thought. When he walked into his apartment, he went to the bathroom and washed up. Then to his closet, he hung up his Sunday suit. He took out a black pair of pants and a white shirt. After getting dressed, he thought, *Looking good, Buck.*

At a quarter to four, he knocked on Willy and Olivia's door. Willy opened the door, he had a black pair of pants and a white shirt. They both laughed. "Now if we were girls, one of us would have to go and change," Willy said. At that moment, Olivia walked into the room, she had a beautiful black and white dress on.

"We should start a black and white dress code club," Willy said and they all laughed.

"Let's call the cab," Buck said.

"I did the moment I heard you knock on the door," was Olivia's response.

They all headed outside. As Willy shut the door, the cab pulled up. When they pulled up to JACK's, Willy said, 'I'll get this, you got the bill inside.' Buck smiled. To all of them, everything at Jack's was elegant. The menus were classy.

"Remember, order anything, I got this."

Buck had them also order a glass of wine to toast their new life. "You mean your new life Buck," Olivia said.

"No, I mean our new life. You will see what I mean."

Willy and Olivia looked at each other with a puzzled look. What they were unaware of was that Buck checked out the wanted-ads and noticed the house between them was for sale at one hundred and twenty thousand dollars. Buck would bring that up tomorrow.

Buck had them toast their new life. Then they placed their order. When the check came at the end of the meal, Willy glanced at it and saw it came to seventy-five dollars and eighty-seven cents.

Buck pulled the envelope out of his pocket and took out ninety dollars and placed it on top of the bill that sat on a small tray. When the waitress came by Buck handed it to her and said, "Thank you and keep the change."

"You gave her half of your weekly allowance for a tip," Willy said.

"And it feels good, too," Buck replied.

Olivia elbowed Willy in the ribs and said, "Mind your own business."

As they were getting ready to leave, Buck stopped the waitress and asked, "Is there a phone that I can use to call a cab."

"I'll call one for you, where are you going?"

"North Pearl Street," was Bucks reply.

"Please take a seat. I'll be right back," the waitress said.

They sat back down. A few moments later, the waitress returned, "It should be here in a few minutes." Buck thanked her and they headed outside.

As they all got outside, the cab pulled up. Willy gave him their address and off they went. Before Willy could get his wallet out. Buck handed the driver a ten-dollar bill.

"Will this cover it?" Buck asked.

"It only comes to seven dollars," the cab driver said.

"Keep the change," Buck said.

"You can't keep giving your money away like that," Willy said, only to feel an elbow in the ribs again.

"Mind your own business," Olivia said again. "We had a wonderful time Buck," Olivia said.

"Yeah, that really was classy," Willy added.

"Believe me, we will be doing that again," was Buck's answer.

"What time you going to visit Jamie?" Olivia asked.

Buck looked at his watch, it was five thirty, "In about an hour."

They all headed to their own apartments. Buck eyed the 'For Sale' sign in the window on the first floor. As Olivia and Willy entered their home, Buck took out a pen and wrote down the phone number that was on the 'For Sale' sign. When he got upstairs, he went immediately to the phone and dialed the number.

"Hello!" a woman answered.

"Hi! I'm Buck Thompson, I'm calling about the house next door which you have for sale."

"Can I get your phone number and I will have my husband call you when he gets home. He's at the house now cleaning up."

"I'll go down and see if I can catch him before he leaves," Buck said. He hung up and headed down stairs. He knocked on the door, it opened immediately. The owner was just getting ready to leave.

"Can I help you?" the owner said.

"Yes! I'm interested in buying this building,"

"Then come right in," he said.

As Buck walked in, he saw the beautiful staircase that led to the second floor.

"I'll show you the first-floor apartment first."

He led the way, when he opened the door, Buck noticed all the woodwork was beautiful, quarter, sawed oak. The walls were freshly painted. Buck looked at the living room and the dining room. There was a small bedroom off of the dining room. He walked into the kitchen and saw the quarter, sawed oak made up all of the cabinets. Off of the kitchen were two more bedrooms and a large bathroom. The owner unlocked the back door and opened it. Buck saw a beautiful yard, well -maintained. The owner started up the back stairs and took out his keys and unlocked the door. Buck walked in to see a mirror image of the first-floor kitchen.

"The only thing different between this apartment and the one down stairs is this has one more bedroom off of the living room."

"How much you asking?" Buck said, he knew the price in the paper of a hundred and twenty thousand.

"I'm asking a hundred and twenty thousand. But I'll take a hundred and ten."

"I want to say I will take it right now. But I need to show someone. Can I meet you back here in the morning say about ten o'clock?"

"Sure, I'll meet you then. What's your name?"

"Sorry." Buck put out his hand to shake the owner's hand. "I'm Buck Thompson."

"I'm Fred Willis," The owner replied.

"See you in the morning," Buck said and left.

Chapter Seven

At six thirty, Buck left to go and see Jamie. He reminded himself to check on George Washington. When he reached Washington Avenue, he glanced over at the Philip Schuyler Statue. It was starting to get dark and he remembered what Jamie said about Philip Schuyler being afraid of the dark. He would check on him in a couple of weeks.

As he approached the steps to the State Education Department, he glanced over at the Statue of George Washington. He walked up the steps and asked, "Jamie, are you here?"

"Yes, I am, this must be Monday."

"It is Monday and I told you I would be here."

"Buck, let me introduce you to Peter Todd."

"I heard a lot of great things about you, Mr. Todd."

"Please call me Pete, I have heard a lot about you also."

"My cousin's wife, Olivia, said if it wasn't for you, many poor children wouldn't have had a Christmas."

"I tried to do what I could afford to do."

"I was told that you passed out turkeys to the poor around Thanksgiving."

"Like I said, I only did what I could afford to do."

"I was also told that anyone who met you, respected you. I was told that most people thought of you as a great man."

"I'm glad I'm a statue, because you would make me blush."

"I'm just repeating what I heard."

Jamie spoke up, "You had some questions for Buck, didn't you?"

"Yes, I passed away in 1962. How did President Kennedy do in his first term?"

"I am sorry I have to tell you he was assassinated after a thousand days in office."

"That is sad to hear, who did it?"

"It was Lee Harvey Oswald. It happened in Dallas, Texas. Jamie, you knew all this, why didn't you tell him?"

"My memories could have been of history or family. I chose family."

"That is a choice you have to make in Heaven?" Buck asked.

"You have heard of Adam and Eve and the tree of knowledge."

"Yes, and the snake that was Satan."

"That's not exactly right, Satan was dressed as a beautiful angel. That is why Eve believed him. It wasn't until Adam took a bite before the beautiful angel, turned into a snake, and slithered away. But to get back at the question about having to decide on family or history. I didn't have to choose. I sacrificed my knowledge in support of what Jesus sacrificed for us. I am very happy with my choice."

In Buck's mind, he heard Rose say, "You learn something new every day." Buck turned back toward Mr. Todd, "I am willing to answer any questions you might have."

"I had a lot of faith in President Kennedy when he said we would go to the Moon   by   1970."

"We went to the moon in 1969. Eventually, we built a shuttle to go back and forth."

"That is great to hear, what about now? What year is it?"

"It's twenty sixteen, Mr. Todd, I mean Pete. I read that N.A.S.A. has already sent an exploring device to Mars. They plan on developing a colony, sometime in the future."

"I would have thought that everyone would have their own space vehicle by now, I never saw one from this site. I sort of thought of this area as a no-fly zone with all the people here."

"No, we haven't advanced that far."

"Johnson became President after Kennedy, who came after Johnson?"

"Richard Nixon."

"He was the Vice President under Eisenhower. He ran against Kennedy. I never liked him."

"You remember the actor Ronald Reagan."

"Yeah, he wasn't a great actor."

"He was President for two terms in the eighties."

"They elected an actor; did he act like a President?"

"All I remember is he cut our taxes and then had to raise our taxes three times to make up for the mistake."

Jamie broke in again, "Buck, ask him how he died."

"Is that okay to ask you how you died?"

"Yeah, I loved trout fishing, it was April 13th. I was fishing in a stream called the Little Hoosick. I was doing pretty good, too, I had three nice size brown trout in my side sac. Then I heard someone yelling. When I looked back, a fisherman was in the water flowing in my direction. The current was strong, the water was only thirty-six degrees. I reached for the man and was pulled into the water. He grabbed a branch on the other side of the stream and was saved. The cold water caused me to have a heart attack. I died before anyone could help me."

"You are a great man, you knew that the water temperature could cause a heart attack."

"Yes, I did, but I had to try and save that guy."

"It is a real honor talking to you," Buck said, then added, "If you think of any more questions, I'll be back on Friday."

"I have really enjoyed your conversation," Jamie said.

"That goes for you too Jamie, if you think of any questions, I'll be back on Friday night."

As Buck started to leave, he remembered that he wanted to see if George Washington was in his statue. He headed across the street and stood in front of George Washington. "Mr. President, are you here tonight?" he asked, he heard nothing, he repeated the question. Still no reply.

"I'll keep trying, I hope sometime you will be here."

Buck started heading down the hill. On his walk home, he felt a surge of joy, knowing he would be talking with his Rose Bud again. He had no idea how long it would take to make her statue. It really didn't matter how long it took. He would be talking with Rose and hearing her voice. He hasn't heard her voice in fourteen years.

Then he thought about the house between him and Willy. He hoped Willy and Olivia would like it, too. He would buy it outright, own it from day one. Willy and Olivia would never have to pay rent again.

This was the least he could do for his closest friends and relatives.

When Buck got home, he climbed the wooden mountain to his apartment. He looked at the clock on the wall in the kitchen, it was nearing nine o'clock. *What an exciting day this turned out to be*, he thought. He turned on the T.V. to fill the silent void. He then went to the hall closet and took out the box marked pictures. He placed it on the kitchen table and removed the lid. On top was the most beautiful picture of Rose. He thumbed through and found others that show her from head to toe. He started separating the pictures in order to fine the ones that showed Rose entirely.

Tomorrow, he would look for the statue makers with Willy and Olivia. He didn't think he would be able to sleep, he was so excited. When he finally went to bed, he was asleep in minutes.

He woke up at a quarter to seven. He actually hopped out of bed. Went to the kitchen to put the water on for his coffee. He waited to eight o'clock before he called Willy. Olivia answered. Buck asked her and Willy if they could meet him out front.

"For what?" Olivia asked.

"It's a surprise."

"Buck, you're going to have to slow down soon."

"I have everything under control, please believe me. Just meet me out front at nine forty-five."

"Okay, Buck, see you then."

Buck was overjoyed at the thought of what he was about to do. In his mind, he could hear Willy saying, "No! You're wasting your money."

He thought of a reply, "If I died tomorrow, all that money would be lost. I have no will." Buck couldn't imagine Willy would have a comeback.

At nine forty, Buck looked out his front window to see Mr. Willis heading to the front door of the building that was for sale. He went downstairs to meet Willy and Olivia. They were leaving their front door as Buck was leaving his.

"So, what's up?" Willy asked.

"I want to show you something." was Bucks reply. Buck headed for the front door of the building that was for sale. Mr. Willis opened the door and greeted Buck with a friendly hello,. Buck had Olivia walk in first, then Willy.

"This is Mr. Fred Willis, he is selling this building."

Willy tried to say something and Buck told him to stop.

"I want you two to check this out before you say anything."

Mr. Willis opened the front door of the first-floor apartment.

"This is beautiful," Olivia said.

Mr. Willis pointed at the living room and pointed out the bedroom off of the dining room. He guided them into the kitchen and pointed out the other two bedrooms, then the large bathroom. Willy and Olivia never said a word. He opened up the back door and showed them the yard. As with Buck, he led them upstairs. Willy also noticed it was a mirror image of the apartment downstairs. Mr. Willis repeated what he said to Buck, "The only thing different with this apartment and the one down stairs is this has one extra bedroom over the front stairway."

Buck looked at Willy and Olivia, "Would you share this house with me?"

"I don't think we could afford it," Willy replied.

"No! I would buy it and we would share it. No more rent."

Willy said, "Buck, your letting your money go to your head."

"Willy, if I died tomorrow, my money would be lost, I have no will made up. You are my only family. Please say yes."

Willy looked at Olivia, she nodded *yes*. Willy then turned to Buck.

"I have been informed not to question you about your money. Whatever you want to do is alright with us."

Buck looked at Mr. Willis and said, "I'll take it for the hundred and ten thousand."

Mr. Willis held out his hand to shake Buck's.

"Deal!" Mr. Willis said.

Buck moved away with Mr. Willis to discuss the arrangement. Mr. Willis would meet him Wednesday at eleven at the credit union.

Willy and Olivia discussed moving in, "At least, we don't have to hire a moving van."

Buck heard what Willy said as he approached them both.

"We are going to hire a moving company to cart all of our stuff from our apartment to here," Buck thought of the other day when Olivia went to his apartment and was totally out of breath, "The only thing I want to add is the stair lift for the front hall. So, you don't have to climb those stairs."

"I checked on that for my own house, they cost less than two thousand dollars," Mr. Willis said. Then added, "So I will only charge you one hundred and eight thousand for the house. I'll cover the cost of the stair lift."

As they left the apartment, Willy asked, "You sure you want to do this?"

Buck smiled, "It will be my pleasure."

Olivia leaned over and gave Buck a hug around his neck. And a peck on the cheek. "Love you, Buck," she said.

"And I love both of you," was his reply.

When Buck got up to his apartment, he called Mr. Templar at the credit union. He told him what he wanted to do. He mentioned he would like to invest half of his money. And he would like to buy that house tomorrow. He stated that he would meet him at eleven o'clock with Mr. Willis.

"Make sure he brings all the paper work," Mr. Templar added.

"I will, sir," he answered.

He then called Mr. Willis, "I talked to the guy at the credit union and he said to make sure you bring all your paperwork."

"You mean you will pay for it tomorrow?"

"Yeah! Is that going to be a problem?"

"Not at all, I will call my insurance man and have him call you. Insurance runs about twelve hundred dollars a year."

"Thank you, Mr. Willis, I look forward to talking with him. How much are the taxes per year?"

"School and property together are about twenty-five hundred a year."

Buck wrote all this down. He thought he would have the credit union handle all of this, "Then I will see you tomorrow at eleven o'clock at the credit union on the concourse of the Empire State Plaza."

"I'll be there," was Mr. Willis's response.

The next day, Buck showed up at the credit union at ten thirty, he needed to sign papers for his investment. And to get his new checking account and savings accounts in order. Mr. Templar was a great help and assured Buck that they would handle the insurance and taxes. Then Buck asked, "If I die, I want my money to go to my cousin, Willy, and his wife." Mr. Templar took out a piece of paper. The heading said 'Beneficiary.' Buck filled out the paper and slid it back to Mr. Templar who withdrew a stamp from his desk and stamped the paper.

"It needed to be stamped by a notary, which I am one."

He called in his secretary and asked her to sign it as a witness.

When they finished, Buck saw Mr. Willis waiting outside the door, "That is the man selling the house."

"Bring him in," Mr. Templar said.

Buck waved to Mr. Willis to come in, he was holding a thick folder. Buck did the intros and Mr. Willis handed the folder to Mr. Templar.

Mr. Templar checked out all the paper work and had his secretary make copies. He had to use his notary stamp on a few more sheets of paper and again had his secretary witness his signature.

He had Buck sign seven pieces of paperwork and had Mr. Willis sign six. He once again had his secretary make copies and had three folders; one would go to Buck and one to Mr. Willis and the third was the credit unions copy.

"Do you want to make out a check for Mr. Willis or would you like the credit union to issue one?"

"Can I have the credit union issue one."

Mr. Templar had Buck sign again to withdraw one hundred and eight thousand from his account. He had his secretary draw up the check.

Mr. Templar handed the check to Buck, who, in turn, handed it to Mr. Willis. Mr. Willis couldn't believe his eyes. He thought it would take months if not years to sell the house. He shook hands with Buck again and started to leave; he stopped in the doorway, reached in his pocket, and took out the keys. He tossed them to Buck, "These are yours now," then he left.

Mr. Templar sat there and said, "Buck, you need to get all the locks changed as soon as possible."

Buck remembered seeing a lock smith on Central Avenue.

"I will call and have that done as soon as possible."

Mr. Templar called his secretary in again, "Do you have Mr. Thompson's personal checks ready?"

"Yes, sir, and I also have his debit card."

"What's a debit card?" Buck asked.

"It's so you don't have to carry a lot of cash on you. What was the date of your birth?"

"3/12/38."

"Your secured pin number will be 0312. If you want to use your card, it will ask for your pin number, just punch in 0312. Then you will be all set."

Buck fully understood everything Mr. Templar said. He looked at the keys in his hand and thought, *I own a house.*

When Buck got home, he placed his checks in his dresser drawer. He had already placed his debit card in his wallet. He thumbed through the phone book and found the locksmith on Central Avenue. He called; they would be there tomorrow morning at ten-thirty. He decided to stop at Willy and Olivia's place to tell them the deal was done.

Olivia answered the door this time, "Hi, Buck, Willy's in the bathroom, what's up?"

"The house next door is ours."

"What do you mean ours?"

"I bought it this morning. All the paper work is done, here are the keys."

"Doesn't it take about a month to close on a house?"

"I don't know, but I didn't take out a loan. I just bought it."

With that said, Willy walked into the room.

"Buck already bought the house," Olivia said.

"How can you do that?"

"I met with Mr. Willis at the credit union. Mr. Templar took care of everything. I want to get that stair lift put in right away. Could you call them, Olivia?"

"Yeah! I guess I can."

"Do you have that list of those statue companies?"

"Yeah, there right here," Willy handed the papers to Buck, "Louie circled the closest ones."

"We have either Lake George or Newburgh. Newburgh is a little farther away. I'll take these homes and call them."

Willy looked at the keys on the cocktail table, "Are they yours?"

"There are three sets for next store."

"Why three?"

Olivia spoke up, "One for the first-floor apartment and one for the second floor. The third set belongs to the land lord."

"It doesn't matter. I am having all the locks changed tomorrow," Buck said. With that said, Buck stated he was going to call the companies on the list.

After Buck left, Willy said, "I think he is moving way to fast."

"Not at all," Olivia said.

"What are you talking about, Livy?"

"I think Buck wants to do this as fast as he can. He might be afraid that if he waits, he may die."

"Never thought of that, we all are pretty old."

"Buck has a plan, we should support him at every turn."

"I guess you're right, Livy. What am I saying? You're always right. That's another reason I love you."

Buck called the company in Newburgh, he laughed to himself after the man on the other end introduced himself as Harley Davidson. Buck explained what he wanted to do. Mr. Davidson was very helpful. He explained to Buck that it would take three to four months for one statue. He would need plenty of pictures of his wife in order to catch her likeness. He told Buck that with him, he would take the pictures himself and have Buck make a face mask. He then told Buck that they could cost up to fifty thousand dollars each.

Buck wasn't worried about the price. "How do we start this?" Buck asked.

"Where are you located?"

"I live in Albany."

"I have to go to Albany tomorrow to pick up some materials I ordered. If there is no problem, I can stop by and also show you pictures of my work."

"Give me a time and I'll be here," Buck said. He gave Mr. Davidson his address and they agreed to meet at two o'clock. All of this excitement was thrilling to Buck. He headed back over to Willy's to let them know what was happening.

As Willy opened the door to let Buck in, Olivia was hanging up the phone, "Buck, I called the stair lift place. They said they could stop by tomorrow morning around ten o'clock."

"That's great, thanks, Livy. I talked with the company in Newburgh. He is going to stop over tomorrow afternoon. I will need plenty of pictures of Rose, so he can catch her likeness."

"I took out a bunch that we have and placed them in this tote bag for you," Olivia said as she handed the bag to Buck.

"How much is it going to cost for the statues?" Willy asked to only receive another elbow in the ribs from Olivia. "Sorry, I asked," he said with a slight moan. Buck stated he was going to get his pictures out for Mr. Davidson, so he headed home.

As Buck looked at the pictures, he wanted the ones that were taken a couple of years before she died. He didn't want this young, beautiful girl standing next to an old man. Everything was going so perfect in Buck's mind. He settled on twenty-three photos of Rose.

He walked over to a pad he had on the table and marked down 'See Jamie and Pete, Friday night.' He figured if he didn't write it down, he would forget. Then he wrote down 'Stair lift and statues.' Wednesday! He needed to make a great effort keeping everything sorted out. That night, he slept like a baby. He woke up at seven-twenty, put the water on for coffee, and took a quick shower. He heard himself humming, which he hasn't done in the shower for years.

As he was getting dressed, he heard the kettle whistle. He poured the water for a cup of coffee. As he sipped his coffee, he checked his notes.

The guy for the stair lift company would be here at ten o'clock or was it ten-thirty, it really didn't matter. At this point, the phone rang.

"Hello!"

"Hi, Buck, this is Olivia, don't forget the guy coming for the stair lift at ten."

"I'll be over about nine thirty."

"See you then," Olivia said.

Buck felt he was forgetting something, but couldn't figure out what it could be. Then his door bell chimed. Buck had his slippers on, he headed down the stairs. When he opened the door, he saw the locksmith truck. *That was the other thing,* he thought.

"Hi! I'm Buck Thompson, I will go and get you the keys. Need new locks on all the doors in this house," he pointed to the house next door. At this time, Willy came out of his house jingling the keys.

"Willy, will you let him in? I'll be back down in a little bit."

Buck headed back upstairs to put his shoes on and to swallow the last of his coffee.

Willy was with the locksmith getting some stuff out of his truck. Then the stair lift company pulled up. Buck introduced himself and led the woman to the front hall.

"I would like to get the cost and when you could do the job."

The woman took out her measuring tape and got straight to work. The locksmith had changed the lock on the front door and Willy was taking him to the first-floor apartment door. The woman came back down the stairs and went to her truck to get a folder. Buck watched her do the paper work and she then turned to Buck.

"It would cost a total of twenty-two hundred, including tax."

"When could you do it?"

"When would you like it done?"

"The sooner, the better."

"I can do it now, if you want."

"That would be great," Buck said.

The woman returned to her truck and took out a box cart. She loaded four boxes on the cart and headed back to the house. Buck asked her what he could do. "I have this all under control, sir," she replied.

Buck watched as she pulled the box cart up the three stairs with ease. She unloaded everything and started to open all the boxes. Buck went to the front door of the first-floor apartment and that lock was also already installed, he walked to the back door. That one was also done. He saw Willy and the man doing the lower back door to the yard. He walked back to the front hall. The woman had half of the stairway done. *All these people are fast,* he thought.

He stepped back outside and saw Olivia heading his way.

"Is Willy in there?"

"Yeah, he is with the locksmith. They are almost done."

"What did the stair lift guy say?"

"It's a she and she's almost done, too."

"You're kidding me."

"No, these people are fast."

They talked a while about the statue and then Buck heard the woman from the stair lift company call him.

"Yes, mam."

"Do you want to try this out?"

"You're the one who will be using it, you should try it out," Buck said to Olivia. Together, they walked into the front hall. It took the woman less than an hour. The locksmith and Willy were coming down the stairs. "It's all done," Willy said. The woman then began to tell Olivia how the lift worked. Olivia sat down and with a smooth ease sort of floated up the stairs. The woman waved her back down. She explained how it would stop automatically if something were in the way. At that point, the woman placed a small box on the stairs and the lift stopped. She removed it and it began to run again.

Buck looked at the locksmith and the woman and told them to wait while he got his checkbook. The locksmith and the stair lift woman were taking boxes back to their trucks when Buck returned.

The locksmith handed him an invoice, Buck wrote out the check for three-hundred and twenty-six dollars and fifty-three cents.

The woman handed him her invoice.

"Would you like to finance this with payments?" she asked. Buck looked at the invoice; it came to two thousand and two hundred, even.

"No, I'll write you out a check, too."

He handed her the check and she handed him the guarantee and the directions. As Willy went around with the locksmith, the locksmith gave him three key chains; this way, Willy could separate the keys as they went along. He handed one set to Olivia and two to Buck. Buck handed him back the extra set.

"We all need a set and we all own this house."

"No, Buck, you own this house," Olivia said.

"You can check with Mr. Templar, you are my beneficiaries. Everything I have will go to you when I die."

Willy and Olivia just stood there stunned.

"You are my only relatives, all of Rose's relative have passed. Olivia, you have a sister and nieces and a nephew. You will have something to pass on."

Willy and Olivia still didn't know what to say. *Bless you, Buck!* is what Olivia thought. She stepped forward and kissed him on the cheek. Willy hugged both of them.

Chapter Eight

Buck left the stair lift paper work with Willy and Olivia. He went to his apartment and saw that he had a message on the phone. He listened, it was Mr. Davidson. He said he would be there about one o'clock. Buck looked at the clock on the wall, it was now twelve forty-five.

At one o'clock, he heard his door bell ring. He went down stairs and let Mr. Davidson in.

"Mr. Davidson, I have plenty of pictures of my Rose. I picked out these," he pointed to the pictures on the kitchen table.

"Mr. Thompson, if you choose me, we will be working together for three months, please call me Harley."

"Then call me, Buck."

The two men shook hands.

Harley placed the book he was holding on the table. He opened it to the first page, it was a beautiful statue of a woman, "This was Mrs. Snyder, she passed away a few years ago. Her family wanted me to make this for her grave site."

Buck looked at the beautiful statue and then Harley turned the page. Buck now was looking at the photos her family gave Harley. Buck thought, *He really captured her image perfectly*. Harley turned to the next page; it was a statue of a man sitting on a bench. This was Howard Dinkins. He turned the page again, there was a photo of the real Howard Dinkins sitting on a bench.

"You're really good!" Buck said.

"What are you looking for, standing, sitting?"

"Standing, for both of us," Buck replied.

"How tall was your wife?"

"Five foot, two."

"How tall are you?"

"Five foot, six."

Harley had a diagram that he was marking as Buck answered each question.

"Let me explain how this works, I will make a template of your wife in clay. I will spray it bronze, just to show you how it will look. Then I place the template in thin fine plaster which hardens faster than concrete and it's stronger. The clay sculpture is covered with a substance similar to Vaseline, I let it sit for a month. It takes that long for the inner plaster to dry. Then with a laser, I cut the shell into two pieces, length-wise. I then remove the template. Now I have the mold for Rose's statue. Then Bronze is poured into the mold. The statue will fill up, filling every nook and cranny. Then I remove a caster on the bottom. The extra bronze will leak out the bottom. It will set for another month. Then when I remove the outer shell. I will have to fill any air holes with lead. Sand down any over laps. This is why it takes three months."

"You will sculpture Rose' face and body first?"

"Her face, for her arms and legs, I use arms and legs that I have already used for other statues, they will go along with her body size, whatever dress you pick out and then shoes."

Buck looked at the book again, "You are really good."

"Now you are a different story, we can cast you in one day. Yours would take a couple of months."

"What do I need to do to have you start with Rose?"

"I would need to take the pictures back with me, I would also need a third down. That would be sixteen thousand and six hundred sixty-six dollars. After the sculpture is finished and you approve it, the same amount again. The last payment will be a few dollars more, that comes just before we install it."

"Who do I make the check out to?" Buck asked.

Harley placed his business card on the table. Buck made the check out to Davidson's Bronze Works. Harley quickly looked at the pictures of Rose and said, "These will work out fine. I will call you when the sculpture is finished, that could be about three weeks. Do you have a preference on what dress or shoes in these pictures you would like?"

"Any one would be fine," Buck said. Buck signed the agreement and handed over the check. This was the busiest day in Buck's life. At least as far back as he could remember. The inner excitement was still coursing through Buck's body. Another thought fell upon him, *Should he tell Rose this Sunday?*

It dawned on Buck that he forgot to eat again. It also occurred to him that he would have to calm down. Buck moved into the living room and sat on the sofa. He leaned back and placed his hands behind his head. The phone rang, Buck reached, and grabbed it, "Hello!"

"Buck, this is Olivia, you probably haven't eaten so I'm sending Willy over with some food."

"Thank You, Livy, I am a little hungry."

"You eat, then rest, this was a busy day for all of us."

"Will do, we did get a lot done today, didn't we?"

"Yes. After you eat, rest."

"I hear Willy coming up the stairs, see you tomorrow."

They hung up and Buck walked over and opened the door before Willy could knock.

"Olivia sent over dinner."

"Come on in, Willy, can I get you coffee or anything?"

"No, it has been a tiring day."

"I agree, but we got a lot done."

"How did it go with the statue guy?"

"Very well, there is a lot of work and high-level skill in order to make a statue. It will take three months. I will need to take a ride to Newburgh to get the cast done of myself."

"We can have Louie take you whenever you have to go."

Buck removed the small towel that covered the plate. "Southern fried steak, mashed potatoes, and peas," Buck started to cut up the steak.

"Buck, I really am so glad that this is happening to you. So, what's next?" Willy asked.

"We need to let our landlords know we're moving. We need to also contact a moving company."

"When are you going to visit Jamie again?"

"Friday night, weather permitting, it might rain."

"Yeah, I saw that on the weather this morning. At least were done with snow."

"I remember it was in the sixties, it snowed in late April."

"Thanks for ruining my peace of mind," both men laughed

"I am going to leave and let you eat, see you tomorrow."

"I will stop by sometime in the morning."

"See you then."

Willy left and Buck finished his dinner and decided to cap it off with a cup of coffee. He clicked on the T.V. The news came on, he immediately changed the channel. He eventually found a movie that he liked. He felt tired; he laid back on the sofa and fell asleep. Coffee didn't keep him awake any more.

Buck didn't wake up until the following morning. It was the phone ringing that woke him. He felt groggy, he answered the phone, and said "Hello."

It was Willy, "When you coming over, we need to pick a date for the moving company."

Buck looked at the clock it was nearing ten o'clock. "I'll be over in a half hour," he said. Buck knew yesterday was a busy day, but he slept for twelve hours; he never did that before. He put the water on for his cup of coffee. He didn't shower, he just washed up a bit. As he was finishing, he heard the kettle whistling. He noticed he left Olivia's plate from last night's dinner in the sink. He washed it and dried it. After his coffee, he took the plate back over to Olivia.

As he walked down the stairs, he still felt very tired. When he got to Willy's house, Olivia opened the door.

"Buck, are you alright, your color is off."

"I'm just tired, that's all."

"Didn't sleep good last night?"

"Really, I slept for twelve hours. I really don't know why I feel so tired."

"You need to see a doctor. I'm going to call and see if I can get you an appointment for today," Olivia said.

"No, I don't feel sick, just tired."

"That could be because you're sick," Olivia added.

"Where is Willy?" Buck asked.

"He had to go over to my sister's house, he should be right back."

Olivia walked over and placed the back of her hand onto Buck's forehead. "You don't feel warm," she said.

Willy came in the front door, "Betsey and Louie said to say hi to both of you. I talked with the moving company, they quoted a price of sixteen hundred for both of us. I was telling Betsey and Louie over heard and said he and three of his friends would move us for half that price. He also added that we wouldn't have to pack up everything in our dressers. They would move the dressers the way they are."

"Whatever you decide is good for me," Buck said.

Olivia picked up the phone and called Doctor Kristie's Office. She managed to get an appointment for one o'clock this afternoon. Buck reluctantly agreed to go. Olivia pointed at the kitchen, Willy and her went into the kitchen, Olivia explained to Willy about Buck being so tired.

They got to the doctor's office at a quarter to one. Buck filled out the papers they handed him. The nurse escorted Olivia and Buck to an examination room. When Doctor Kristie entered, he asked, "What seems to be the problem?"

"Been really tired lately," Buck said.

The doctor checked out Bucks breathing, listened to his heart, "Everything seems to be fine. I am going to schedule an appointment at Albany Med, run a few tests, and hope we can get to the bottom of this."

Buck nodded in agreement.

The doctor scheduled the appointment for Monday afternoon. Buck at least knew he wouldn't miss his date with Rose. He had so much to tell her. Olivia and Buck headed back to Olivia's house.

"I want you to slow down some. Do you understand me?"

"Yes, mam, I will."

"This could be caused by all the excitement your experiencing."

"You're right. I'll take it easy for a few days."

Buck knew he was going to see Jamie tomorrow night and likely Peter Todd, too. He decided in his mind that he would take a cab instead of walking up the hill. Sunday, he would take a cab to the Albany Rural Cemetery to see Rose. *I am seventy-eight*, he thought. "I do need to take it easy," he said in his mind.

Olivia made up some chicken soup for Buck to take home. He left their house at three o'clock. As he climbed the wooden mountain, the tiredness left his body and he felt wide awake. He really felt good. He thanked God for watching over him. Then he looked towards the Heavens. "God, why can I talk to statues?" he asked. Of course, there was no reply; Buck didn't expect one. "I want to thank you for all You have done for me. It was You who had made it possible for me to talk with my Rose and I am so grateful."

In this moment of spiritual meditation, Buck laughed to himself. What would he have done if God did talk to him?

Buck rested the rest of Thursday and all of Friday. He called a cab at six-fifteen, which brought him over to the Education Building. He still felt good. After he paid the cabbie, he waited for the cab to pull away before he walked up the stairs to see Jamie.

"Are you here, Missy?" he asked.

"Yes! Buck and how are you today?"

"A whole lot better than yesterday, I went to the doctor yesterday because I felt so tired, but today, I feel fine."

"I am glad to hear that," Peter Todd said.

"Hi, Pete, did you think of any questions?"

At that, he heard Jamie giggle.

"Is something funny, Missy?"

"Pete said he was afraid to ask more questions."

"One thing I did forget to tell you the other day, I don't know how you will take it, our president, we have now, is a black man named Obama."

"That is great to hear," Jamie said.

"It doesn't matter if your black or white. Is he a good president?"

"I really think he is. He is in his second term."

"Then I would think he is, also," Pete replied.

"Oh, I found out I have more money than I thought. I bought a house. I will be getting a statue made of my Rose and I will be talking to her."

"That is great!" Jamie said.

"I agree, Buck, this seems really important to you."

"It is, very important. It will take three months before the statue is done. In July, I will be talking to her."

"Do you know why you are able to talk to and hear statues?"

"No, I asked God today, but I haven't received an answer yet."

"It sounds like you expect an answer in the future," Pete said.

"I do, God gave me this ability. When He is ready, He will tell me."

"I believe that to be true, also," Jamie said.

"God does work in mysterious way," Pete said.

"I found that to be true with you," Buck said.

"Why me?" Pete replied.

"All you went through as a child. The higher education you received from your stepparents. Would, or should I say could, your parents have been able to afford to send you to Yale?"

"No, not at all. I understand what you mean. I never thought about it before."

"Jamie first thought of it and told me."

"Jamie, why didn't you ever say it to me?" Pete asked.

"You turned out to be such a great caring man, I would have thought you knew that."

"God did help me all the way. I guess you're right."

"I need to head back home, but I need to see if George Washington is at his statue across the street."

"Good luck with that," Pete said, "He must have a hundred statues all over the place."

"You're right but I think he may visit this one. He marched his troops through here. See you sometime next week."

"Be safe and take care of yourself," Jamie said.

"Thank you for everything," Pete added.

Buck started across the street knowing that what Pete said was probably right. As he approached the statue, he looked around to make sure no one was near. "Mr. President, are you here tonight?" Buck asked, there was no reply. He tried again, "Mr. President, are you here tonight?"

"Yes, I am, and who are you?"

Buck was in shock, "You are really here?"

"Who are you?"

"Mr. President, I am Buck Thompson. I don't know why I can talk to statues or why I can hear you talk. It is the greatest honor of my life to talk to you and hear you talk."

"I have never seen you here before."

"Mr. President, I have been here three times, but you weren't at this statue."

"I come here because I remember when this area was pastures and farmland. My troops and I traveled this way many times."

"That building in front of you is the New York State Capital."

"I have often wondered what it was. My statue was put here after the building was erected. At night, I can remember the trails we took by looking at the stars."

"On the other side of the Capital is Albany City Hall. In front of City Hall, there is a statue of Philip Schuyler. He was elected to the Continental Congress in 1775."

"Yes, I remember Philip, he was a good soldier. He helped us form this country."

"I have tried to talk to him, but he is not there. Someone told me he was a great soldier, but he was afraid of the dark. Do you know if that is true?"

"I have never heard that. During the revolution, he was charged with derelict of duty. He requested a Court Marshall to answer the charges and was vindicated. He was a member of the N.Y.S. Senate when I became President. He was a true patriot. He had a great love of God and country. Major General Marquis Gilbert Lafayette marched through here also."

"Over to your left, between the Education Building and the Capital, is Lafayette Park. I think a sign over there says he marched through that area with his troops."

"My last headquarters was in Newburgh, have you ever been there?"

"Not yet, but I will be going to Newburgh, I am having a statue made there."

"A statue of who?"

"A statue of my wife, Rose, who passed away fourteen years ago, also one of myself."

"Why?"

"I don't know why I can hear and talk to statues, I will be able to talk with Rose."

"That is understandable, but why one of you?"

"So, when I pass, we will be able to look out from our bronze eyes at the world together."

"I understand now."

"Do you know when you will be back here?" Buck asked.

"No, time isn't something we are aware of."

"I will be back about this time in a week."

"I have no conception of what a week is anymore."

"It is seven days."

Buck heard President Washington laugh a little.

"I have no idea what a day is."

"I truly hope I get to talk with you again."

"I do, too, this has been a pleasure. Do you only come at night?"

"Yes! If someone sees me talking to statues during the day time, they could have me locked up, thinking I am crazy."

"I guess you're right. I was caught talking to God a few times in the woods and some people wanted to label me a cracked pot."

"I will check to see if you are here, anytime I come this way. At night, of course."

"I truly hope to see you again."

"Me, too!" Buck replied and then left to head home.

Buck was thrilled, he got to talk with President George Washington. He looked forward to speaking with him again.

Chapter Nine

On the walk home, Buck thought of all the things he had to tell Rose. There was more than ever before. He would have to write all this stuff down or he would forget something, he knew he would.

The excitement of talking with George Washington was something he had to share with Willy and Olivia. When he got within a block, he checked his watch, it was nine-fifteen. He decided to wait until Saturday morning. He went up to his apartment and started getting his notes in order. What a busy week, he had. He looked forward to Sunday like never before. After getting his notes together, he looked up and threw a kiss to Rose.

Saturday morning, he awoke at eight-fifteen. He did his morning rituals and at ten o'clock, he decided to leave and go over to Willy's. Olivia answered the door. "Hi, Buck, Willy's in the bathroom, how did it go last night with Jamie and Mr. Todd?"

"I have a bunch to tell you about last night."

After saying that, Willy walked into the room.

"I spoke with George Washington."

"You're kidding?" Willy said.

"No! I asked are you here Mr. President and there was no answer. I tried again and he replied, 'Who are you?' I nearly fell over. We talked about Philip Schuyler and Major General Lafayette. He told me he lived for a while in Newburgh, his headquarters was there, and he had his last encampment in that area, too. He said that where the State Capital is, was pasture and farmland. He said he enjoyed talking to me and looked forward to talking again."

"Wow! I would be as excited as you if it were me," Willy said.

"I was so excited, I almost stopped by last night, but it was nine-fifteen."

"We are always up until about eleven," Olivia said, then added, "Was Mr. Todd there last night?"

"Yeah, he explained that when I say, I'll be back Monday, they have no understanding of time, here on earth. In Heaven, every day's a new day. There are no days of the week, weeks in a year, no months, time is non- existent. It's like every day is Sunday. President Washington said the same thing."

"You remember you have an appointment at Albany Med on Monday for some test," Olivia said.

"I forgot, but I'm blessed to have you to remind me. Thanks so much, Olivia."

"I plan on going with you," Olivia added.

"Did you contact your landlord to let him know you're moving?" Willy asked.

"Another thing I forgot to do, I will call him today. Did you call yours?"

"Yeah, he said because we didn't give him two months' notice, he would keep the security deposit."

"We will never have to deal with that again," Buck said, then added, "Do you have a phone book? I'll call Mr. Tilly from here,"

Olivia handed him the phone book, Buck found the number right away, and called. After a brief discussion, Buck hung up, "He seemed happy, he needed a place for his daughter, so it worked out fine. I need to be out by the first of the month."

"Louie and his friends are going to be moving us all on Wednesday," Willy said.

"That works for me," Buck added.

"We don't have to pack anything. Louie and his friends will move the dressers while they are full. They will place dishes, pots, and pans in boxes. We shouldn't have to do a thing."

"That sounds great. I need to go to the credit union and pick up some cash, I don't want to give them a check, cash would be better. How much?"

"Eight Hundred."

"I'll do that on Monday."

"In the morning, right? You have your appointment in the afternoon," Olivia reminded him again.

"I will do it on Tuesday; Monday, I will be with you all day. That way I won't miss that appointment."

Olivia nodded in agreement.

"I think you're going to need to buy some furniture, too. You only have a sofa and chair and a cocktail table. A kitchen table and four chairs. You have nothing for the dining room and you will need at least another chair for the living room and maybe some end tables," Willy said.

"And one of them big screen T.Vs," Buck added.

"Now you're talking, how about a T.V. for the bedroom?"

"I'll use the 19-inch from the living room."

"Buck, you shouldn't walk all the way to the cemetery until you get those tests done. Please take a cab."

"I planned on doing just that. A cab to the Miss Albany Diner and a cab to the cemetery."

"And a cab back home, right."

"Yes, mam," Buck said to Olivia

Buck stayed for lunch, then he headed home. He rewrote most of his notes that he planned on sharing with Rose. He placed the notes about George Washington on top.

Buck started looking around the apartment he and Rose shared for so many years. He wouldn't miss climbing the wooden mountain anymore. He never would have believed he would own his own home.

He decided to take a look at his new home. He took the keys off the table and headed down the stairs. He unlocked the outer door and went to the entrance to his place and unlocked that one, too. When he opened the door, he thought, *Willy was right.* I need more furniture. He checked out all the bedrooms and decided on the one off of the dining room for himself. The two bedrooms off the kitchen, he would buy beds and dressers for each.

Buck ordered Pizza for dinner and ended the night watching T.V.

He awoke Sunday morning very excited. He got everything ready and called for a cab. He would have his coffee at the Miss Albany Diner.

After reaching the diner, he told the cabbie that he would need a ride in about an hour. The cabbie checked out his tip and said, "See you in an hour." Buck hasn't tipped many people in his life. It felt good to be able to make up for lost time. After breakfast, the cab arrived. He took Buck to the Albany Rural Cemetery. "Can you come back in about three hours?" Buck asked. The cabbie nodded *yes*.

Another thing Buck learned from the Monument Book was that Philip Schuyler was buried here, too. As Buck approached Rose' place, it dawned on him that he didn't bring a blanket. The ground was dry, he laid his jacket on the ground and sat on it, "Rose, I have so much to tell you. It happens that we have saved a lot of money. I really mean a lot. I am having a statue of you made up and one of myself. We will be able to stand side by side right here. I will be able to talk with you and hear what you're saying. I bought the house next store, Willy and Olivia and I will be moving there this week. I have talked with George Washington this week."

Buck talked non-stop for over two hours. He covered everything in his notes. And added things he forgot to put in his notes. He explained how he was tired for a couple of days and Olivia made him see a doctor and he had to go for test tomorrow. But he said that the past few days, he felt great. When he was finished, he felt something touch his cheek again, he raised his hand and placed it on his cheek.

"She kissed you again and you felt it, didn't you?" Elizabeth said.

"Yes, Missy, I did."

Buck explained to Rose that he had a cab coming in about twenty minutes. Olivia didn't want him walking to the cemetery. He promised her he wouldn't until his medical test we're done. He closed his eyes and asked Rose to kiss him again. This time he felt her kiss on his lips.

Elizabeth said, "You two have more love for one another than I have ever saw."

"We do, Missy."

"What I see is a glow from both of you. Its amber in color and when you kiss, it forms a heart shape. I never once saw my parents' kiss. I know they loved one another, but not like you two."

Buck checked his watch and had to excuse himself. The cab was due any time. He said his goodbyes to Rose and turned to Elizabeth, "Missy, I thank you for all your insight. You have become a great asset to me and Rose. I hope you have a blessed week."

"The same to you, Buck."

This was the first time Elizabeth called Buck by name. He tipped his hat and then headed to the entrance. As he approached, the cab pulled up. When Buck got home, he reflected on the day and thanked God for letting him feel Rose' kiss.

This was the first time that he was home by three-thirty on Sunday since Rose passed. He called Olivia and Willy to let them know he was home. Olivia asked him to dinner, at first, Buck was thinking about having a couple of more pieces of pizza. But then, Olivia said, "We're having fried chicken." Buck could never pass up Olivia's fried chicken. He agreed and Olivia said that they would be eating at five o'clock. Buck spent the time thinking about what Elizabeth said about the amber glow. He could picture it in his mind.

His thoughts of the amber glow gave him piece of mind. At this point, the phone rang. He thought it was Willy or Olivia calling about dinner. Buck picked up the phone and said, "Hello!" waiting to hear Olivia's or Willy's voice.

"Hi, Mr. Thompson, this is Harley Davidson from Newburgh. I had a weird thing happen. I started sculpturing Rose' head last night from the pictures you gave me. I worked for six hours straight. I looked at it this morning and I think it's finished. Can you come to Newburgh this week and check it out, I could be wrong, but it's weird, that part usually takes a minimum of three weeks?"

"I have a doctor's appointment tomorrow, I'll see if I can make it on Tuesday."

"That would be great."

"Hope to see you then. If I can't make it, I will call."

"Thank you, Mr. Thompson."

Buck hung up and headed over to Willy and Olivia's house. Olivia opened the door and returned to her spot on the sofa next to Willy.

"You're not going to believe this, I just got a call from Mr. Davidson in Newburgh, he said he started on Rose' sculpture last night. He worked for six hours. When he got up this morning, he went to check out his work. He thinks the head may be done. He asked if I could come down this week and look at it. I told him I would try for Tuesday."

"How you going to get there?" Willy asked.

"I can't believe he did the sculpture in one night," Olivia said.

"He can't believe it either. He said this part takes about three weeks. He called the whole thing weird."

"Nothing you can say will make me think anything is weird anymore. You talk to statues," Willy said.

"I felt Rose' kiss again today."

"Like the brush against your cheek last week," Willy said.

"This week was different. First, I felt the kiss on the cheek and Elizabeth saw her do it again. Then I closed my eyes and asked Rose to kiss me on the mouth. I felt that one, too. Elizabeth said that when we kissed, there was an amber glow around our heads that turned heart shaped."

"And you think that guy doing a sculpture in one night is strange," Willy said.

"I'm with you, I don't think anything is strange about everything that has happened to me anymore."

"This is all happening because God wants it to happen," Olivia said.

"I believe that, too," Buck said.

"Now, is there anything that happened that I don't know about?" Olivia asked.

Buck and Willy looked at each other; they both shook their head *no*!

"At least I don't think there is," Willy added.

"Buck, I know you visit with Rose every Sunday. But you need to go to church and thank God for all he has done for you," Olivia added.

"You're absolutely right. I have been thinking about doing just that, I will go this Wednesday night," Buck said.

"Willy and I will go with you."

"I will need to go to the credit union tomorrow morning. I can't wait until Tuesday," Buck said.

"I'll go with you," Olivia said.

As they sat down for dinner, Olivia told Willy to say a prayer. He never prayed before a meal before and Willy fumbled through it.

"I will call Louie to see if he is available Tuesday. He seems to have a tight schedule lately, but I'll try," Olivia stated.

"I will pay him for his trouble," Buck added.

After dinner, Olivia called her sister Betsey and found out that Louie was out for the night with his friends. She would have him call tomorrow morning. "The move on Wednesday is still on, right?" Betsey asked.

"Oh yeah! Buck may need a ride on Tuesday, that's why I'm calling."

"I think he has plans for Tuesday, but I'll have him call."

"Thanks, Betsey, Love you."

"Love you, too, sis," was Betsey's reply.

After dinner Buck excused himself and headed back to his apartment.

Buck looked up towards the heavens and spoke, "Dear God, You, have done so much for me throughout my life. I know You're in charge. I know You are the one making all this happen. Why me, God?" Buck didn't expect an answer and didn't receive one.

This was the night Buck started to say a prayer before he fell asleep. He has done it ever since.

On Monday morning, when he woke up, it was seven-twenty; he fixed a cup of coffee and waited until nine before he called Olivia about the trip to the credit union.

"Buck, let's wait until eleven o'clock, from there, we can head up to Albany Med."

Buck agreed and decided to just take it easy this morning. He called Olivia at ten forty-five to let her know he called a cab. He would meet her out front in a few minutes. The cab pulled up and Olivia was just leaving her apartment. They both got into the cab and it was Buck who gave the cabbie their destination.

"I was on the phone with Louie, he was booked up for the whole day tomorrow. Then he got a call that all his plans were cancelled until Thursday. He will be able to take you to Newburgh tomorrow," Olivia said.

Buck knew this was God helping out again, he didn't say anything to Olivia, but he knew. Under his breath, he said, "Thank You, God."

When they got to the credit union, Buck noticed Mr. Templar wasn't in his office. He filled out a withdrawal slip and stood in line. Olivia waited just outside the door. When it was Buck's turn, he handed the slip to the teller and she placed one thousand dollars in an envelope. Buck asked for it in twenties.

They left the credit union and headed towards Madison Avenue from the concourse. As they reached the top of the steps. Buck saw a cab pull up to drop off a customer. Buck asked the driver if he could take them to Albany Med. The driver remembered Buck from Sunday. "Sure, hop in," was the cabbies reply. Buck remembered he had a ten-dollar bill left in his wallet. When they reached the Hospital, the driver said, "That looks like five bucks." Buck handed him the ten and asked for three dollars in change. Olivia had the information about where Buck was to go for the test. She retrieved it from her purse, "We have to go to X-ray, then to a heart doctor for an E.K.G."

"Lead the way," was Bucks reply.

It was twelve-fifteen when they got to X-ray. Buck's appointment was at one o'clock. After they checked in, a woman came out and called Buck in. Buck returned to the waiting room ten minutes later. They then headed to cardio for the E.K.G. The appointment there was for one-thirty. It was only twelve-thirty. Again, after they checked in, a man came out and called him in. After the E.K.G., Buck was asked to return to the waiting room and wait to be called in by Dr. Romeling. It was only a ten-minute wait when a nurse came out and said Dr. Romeling was ready to see Buck. Olivia looked at her watch and noticed it wasn't even one o'clock. Olivia asked the nurse if it was ok if she went in with Buck. "That's up to him," the nurse replied.

Buck waved to Olivia to follow. When they entered the office, Dr. Romeling was looking at the X-rays. Then he held up the E.K.G. sheets. "Please take a seat," he said. He looked back at the X-rays and then to the E.K.G. sheets again. He sat at his desk and asked, "What was the problem?"

"I felt very tired for a few days and then it just left."

"How do you feel now?"

"I feel good."

"Your X-rays show nothing and the E.K.G. came out fine. How have you been eating."

"I sometimes forget to eat."

"That's not a good thing." He looked at Olivia, "Are you his wife?"

"No, Doctor, I am married to Buck's cousin."

Then Buck interjected, "We all live in the same house now."

"You need to eat every day, at least two meals. You're not watching your weight, are you, Buck?"

"No, I just forget sometimes."

"I will make sure he eats every day," Olivia said.

"I think that would solve the problem," The Doctor added.

"How old are you, Buck?"

"Seventy-eight."

"Then you're old enough to follow my advice. Please put eating as a top priority."

"Yes, sir," Buck said.

"I will make sure, Doctor, I was unaware that he would forget to eat," Olivia mentioned.

"You both have a great day, if you have any problems, contact my office."

Buck and Olivia stood up, Buck shook the doctor's hand and thanked him again.

When they got to the lobby, Buck pointed out that they had direct lines to the cab companies. Olivia picked up a phone and then hung up.

"There are a few out front," the man said.

On the cab ride back, Olivia and Buck never spoke. When they got to Olivia's apartment, she asked, "How do you forget to eat?" Buck could tell she was upset, "I'm sorry, Livy. Last week, I had a lot going on."

"You're eating with us every day from now on," Olivia demanded.

"Yes, mam," was Bucks only reply.

Chapter Ten

When Willy got home from the store, Olivia told him everything and also informed him that Buck will be eating with them from now on. Olivia couldn't understand how someone could forget to eat. Willy did remind her of all that happened last week. He sided with Buck, because Willy has forgotten to eat during his life.

"Louie called and wanted to know what time you wanted to leave for Newburgh tomorrow?" Willy asked Buck.

"Anytime in the morning would be good," Buck answered.

"Not, anytime," Olivia said then added, "Not until you finish your breakfast."

"Before I call Louie back, what time are we having breakfast in the morning?" Willy asked.

"Eight o'clock, invite Louie to stop by for breakfast," Olivia said.

Willy called Louie. Louie passed up breakfast and said he would pick up Buck at nine o'clock.

Inside, Buck was laughing at all of this. He couldn't believe Olivia got so upset. He had never saw her act this way. She was becoming a mother hen watching over her chicks.

Willy sat next to Buck, "She feels guilty that she hasn't given you an open-door policy for meal time. She is worrying about your health."

"You got to love her," was Buck's reply.

"She has one of the kindest hearts of anyone I know," Willy added.

Buck stood up and walked over to Olivia, "I am truly sorry for causing you this grief. I promise I will never forget to eat again."

"That's for sure, because you will be here for breakfast and dinner."

"I am looking forward to it, you're a great cook."

This made Olivia smile and that made Buck feel good again.

After dinner, which was meat loaf, baked potato, and peas, Buck headed back home. He thought that he may want to set the alarm clock. This would ensure he would be next door for eight o'clock. Buck was a little afraid of what tomorrow would bring. He knew he want a complete and perfect likeness of his Rose. If it wasn't, he would have to disappoint Mr. Davidson. At fifty thousand dollars, he wanted it perfect.

He did decide to set the alarm for seven-thirty. The following morning, he woke up at seven-twenty. Clicked off the alarm and headed to heat the water up for coffee. He then went and took a shower. When he turned the shower off, he heard the kettle begin to whistle. He kept watching the clock to make sure he was next door at eight.

When he reached Willy's front door, he could smell bacon. Olivia was no longer mad at Buck, she returned to her jolly self.

"What do you expect to see in Newburgh?" Willy asked.

"I don't know. Mr. Davidson said he thinks he captured her image perfectly. But it has to be perfect to me before I agree."

"What time do you expect to be back?" Olivia asked.

"By dinner time," Buck said with a smile on his face. Olivia returned the smile. A few minutes before nine, there was a knock on the door; this alerted Buck that it must be Louie. Olivia opened the door.

"Hi, Aunt Olivia," Louie said, "You ready, Buck? I don't want to rush you."

"I been done for twenty minutes," Buck headed for the door.

"See you for dinner," Olivia said.

Buck and Louie got in the car. "Do you have the address?" Louie asked Buck.

Buck handed him Mr. Davidson's business card. Louie was holding a small box in his hand and began typing the address in.

"What is that?"

"It's a G.P.S. It will take us right to the front door."

"You're kidding."

"No, Buck. It will find us the shortest way to get there."

"Really?"

"I put in the address and its contacting the satellite. The satellite will take us there."

Buck then heard a woman's voice, 'Travel 2.3 miles and take the ramp to the New York State thruway.'

"It talks?"

Louie laughed, "Yes, it talks and if you miss your turn, it will recalculate for you."

"Wow, I never heard of such a thing."

"I have had this one for ten years."

"They've been around that long?"

"Longer really."

Buck was amused to hear the woman's voice, tell them every turn to take. Even when they reached Mr. Davidson shop, it told them, 'Your final destination is three hundred feet on the left.'

As they entered the shop, Buck didn't know what to expect. Mr. Davidson met him at the door and walked him and Louie to a room in the back. As Buck walked through the door, he saw a statue standing with the back facing them. Mr. Davidson stopped Buck and Louie and told them to stay there. As he walked to the wall and flipped a switch. The statue began to turn slowly. Then Buck became overwhelmed and ask to sit down. Louie stood there with his mouth opened.

"That is my Rose," Buck said.

"It looks just like Aunt Rose," Louie said.

"How did you get the body done so quick?"

"I have the parts here that I use over and over, I have to make sure that everything fits to the body size. This went together perfectly. This has never happened before. The best I can do is three weeks for the head alone."

"Looking at your book, I knew you were good. This is great."

"It cuts the time back to two months instead of three."

"I have goose bumps," Louie said.

"Me, too," was Buck's reply.

"Why you're here, can I take some pictures and cast your face?"

"How long would that take?"

"No more than an hour."

Buck looked at Louie, "Do we have the time?"

Louie was still looking at Rose, "Oh yeah! We have plenty of time."

While Mr. Davidson was getting things ready for Buck, Buck noticed a crane attached to the ceiling. Buck walked over and looked at Rose' hands. He knew that Mr. Davidson said they were parts he used over and over. To Buck, they were Rose's hands.

When Mr. Davidson was ready, he took about eight pictures of Buck and then applied a cream on Buck's face. He placed a square wooden crate in front of Buck. There was a small hose sticking up. He explained to Buck that this was fast setting plaster. He wanted Buck to put the hose in his mouth and place his face into the plaster. Buck did what he was directed to do. He could feel the plaster hardening in moments. Three minutes went by and Mr. Davidson said, "Just two more minutes."

At the end of the two minutes, Mr. Davidson told Buck that he would pull Buck's face straight up, as he did this, he told him to release the hose from his mouth at the same time. Again, Buck did as he was directed to do. Mr. Davidson handed him a towel to wipe off the rest of the *cream* on his face. He then directed Buck to the bathroom and advised him to wash with soap and water.

When Buck walked back into the room, he was in awe at the sight of his Rose. "Now what do you have to do?" Buck asked.

"We will take this entire sculpture and place it in the same type plaster you put you face in. It will be totally encapsulated. Then, in a month, we will cut the shell open with a laser and that will be the mold for the bronze."

"That plaster started setting immediately when I placed my face in it. Why does it take a month?"

"There isn't any air to force it to dry quicker. Without air is will stay soft for at least a week. From experience, four weeks guarantees it will be dry all the way through."

Buck understood what Harley was saying.

Then Harley added, "I can start on you after I get the mold set for Rose."

"Then I'll have to come back to approve that, also."

"Do you have a computer?"

"No!" was Bucks reply.

"I do," Louie said.

"When I am done, I can send you a picture. Which you will be able to see completely by moving your mouse in a circular motion."

Buck had no idea what Harley was saying to Louie. Louie's reply was "Cool!" Louie supplied Harley with his e-mail address and soon Buck and Louie were heading home.

"That sculpture of Aunt Rose was right on."

"Yes, it was very good."

"Almost scary," Louie added.

"He did that in three days," Buck said.

"Amazing," was Louie response.

Both men were thinking about what they saw, they had very little conversation on the way home.

Before they got back on the New York State Thruway, Buck had Louie stop at a Quick Mart. Buck forced Louie to buy a sandwich and he bought one for himself. He didn't buy it because he was hungry. He bought them so he could tell Olivia that they stopped and got something to eat.

Louie pulled up in front of Willy and Olivia's house at two fifteen. Buck handed Louie fifty dollars and asked him if that was enough. Louie didn't count the money, he just said, "Thank you."

Louie had to walk Buck inside to tell his aunt and uncle what he saw. "It was amazing. The sculpture looked just like Aunt Rose, right down to her fingers."

Buck smiled as he heard the excitement in Louie's voice. Olivia and Willy looked at Buck, "It's just like Louie said, it is a perfect image of my Rose. It's as if God made a duplication of Rose. It was perfect."

"What time are you and your friends coming over tomorrow for the move?" Willy asked.

"We would like to start at eight o'clock and we will stay until it is completely done," Louie answered.

"I will have sandwiches made up for you guys to have lunch and I'll have some sort of drink," Olivia said.

"Coffee would be fine, Aunt Olivia."

"Coffee it is," was her reply.

As Buck, Willy and Olivia sat down after Louie left, Willy said, "Oh no!"

"What is a matter?" Olivia asked.

"None of us have a stove or refrigerator, they came with the apartment."

"Let's buy them now," Buck said.

"Where?" Willy asked.

"Wendell's, over on Broadway. They advertise same day delivery. Let's check it out. I just need to get my checkbook," Buck added. Buck left to get his check book. Olivia said, "We can't have Buck buying us a stove and refrigerator, too."

"Maybe we can place a small payment down and pay weekly," Willy suggested.

"Why didn't we think of this before. We could have been better prepared," Olivia said.

Buck returned, "I flagged down a cab, its outside waiting."

Willy and Olivia followed Buck outside. The cab pulled up to Wendell's about five minutes later. Buck handed the driver some money and all headed inside.

Buck saw what he assumed to be a salesperson, "We're going to need two refrigerators and two gas stoves. And we would like them delivered today or tomorrow the latest."

The person turned to look over to the other end of the store.

"Let me get my dad," the young woman said. As she headed to the back of the store, Willy followed. "Would you have a credit plan?" he asked.

"Yes, we do, my dad will cover all that."

"My friend will want to pay for everything, my wife wants us to pay for our own."

The young woman approached her father, Willy saw her point at Buck and Olivia. The man started to head in their direction.

"Can I help you, my daughter just started and you took her by surprise. What can I help you with?"

Buck again said, "We need two refrigerators and two gas stoves. And we need them delivered today or tomorrow at the latest."

"Let's take a look at the refrigerators first," he guided them to three rows of refrigerators.

Buck saw a large side by side, "What do you think Olivia?" he asked.

"There beautiful, but I would want something cheaper," Buck looked at the man and said, "It's set we want two of these." Olivia leaned towards Buck and whispered, "We want to pay for this ourselves. A cheaper one would be better."

"Olivia, I told you and Willy this is our money. I wouldn't be able to spend it all on me. This is bringing me a great joy. If I die tomorrow, everything goes to you and Willy. So, lets enjoy this while I am alive."

Olivia agreed, she walked over to Willy and explained what Buck wants.

The gentleman said, "Do we want to check out the stoves?"

"Let's do it," Buck said.

Buck saw a large stove with a griddle in the center of the top, "Olivia, look at this, it's got a griddle in the center."

Olivia and Willy walked over; Buck opened the oven door, "Is it big enough?"

"It's perfect, Buck," Olivia answered.

"We will take two of these, too," Buck said. "When can you deliver them?" he asked.

"Tomorrow morning, if that's okay. One of the men delivering them will hook up the stoves for you."

"That would be fine, Willy, can you think of anything else we might need?"

"That should cover it," Willy replied.

The man started writing up the bill, "Oh, by the way. We guarantee these products for five years."

"That's great," Buck heard Olivia say.

The total was three thousand and five hundred and forty-seven dollars.

Buck wrote a check and handed it to the gentleman.

"Here you go," the man handed Buck all the paperwork and the guarantees, "We will have them delivered around nine o'clock."

"Thank You!" Buck said and handed all the paperwork to Olivia.

"Thank you, Buck," Olivia said.

"No thank you required. We're family and we take care of each other."

Buck walked to the door, he saw a cab pull up. "Our cab's here," he said.

"When did you have time to call for a cab," Willy asked.

"I didn't, I just told the cabbie if he is around in a half hour, stop back."

Willy and Olivia looked at each other and smiled, "He will always be a step ahead of us," Olivia whispered.

"Guess so," Willy said.

They were back home in five minutes.

"Buck, how much food do you have in your, fridge?" Olivia asked.

"A few pieces of pizza and some milk. I have two -minute steaks in the freezer, that's about it."

"You should bring that stuff over in the morning. I'll put it in our, fridge until the new ones cool up."

"Will do."

"You should also leave the refrigerator door open after you unplug it."

"What about the stove?"

"Louie will turn off the gas, don't worry about that."

After dinner, Buck headed back to his place. He spotted the monument book on the table. *I forgot to return this*, he thought. He looked inside the back cover. He still had three days. He will renew it like the librarian told him he could do.

In his mind, he could see the sculpture of Rose. *It's perfect*, he thought. He thought of what Harley said about it taking him three weeks on a sculpture, but that one took him six hours. One other thing he remembered was Harley saying he worked for six hours, it was the following morning he saw that it was done. He never thought it was done when he stopped the night before. Again, Buck thought, *This is God doing all this*. But the question was still *why*.

Buck went to bed early, so he would get up early. They were going to start at eight o'clock. He didn't want to hold them up. After his prayer, he felt a calm roll over his entire body, soon, he was asleep.

When he awoke, it was seven fifteen. He hopped out of bed, which he hadn't done in years. He collected everything out of the fridge and remembered to unplug it and left the door opened. He headed over to Willy's, hoping they had coffee ready. The door was opened a tiny bit. "It's me!" Buck said.

"We are in the kitchen," Willy replied.

As Buck walked in, Olivia was pouring him a cup of coffee.

"Oh, you don't know how much I need that," he said referring to the coffee.

"Take a seat," Olivia said. She took the bag from Buck's arm. She looked inside. She placed the steaks in the freezer and the rest of the contents in the fridge.

Buck saw she was making sandwiches like she said she would. When she was done, she placed them in the fridge, also. She went to the stove and brought back scramble eggs and sausage links. She then poured herself a cup of coffee and made a new pot for Louie and his friends. At a quarter of eight, the Wendell's appliance truck pulled up. They were supposed to be there at nine. Buck walked out to greet them.

"Are we too early?" one man asked.

"Not at all," Buck said, "One set goes to the first floor and the other to the second floor. I'll get everything unlocked for you."

Buck called over one of the men, he pointed at the stair lift, "That won't be in your way, will it?"

"No, not at all," was the workers' answer.

Buck unlocked upstairs and downstairs. When he returned to the first floor, the men were rolling in the refrigerator.

"We are going to do the second floor first if you don't mind."

"Whatever's good for you," Buck said. Buck then went and got Olivia.

"They're bringing the fridge upstairs in your house."

Olivia went up to make sure they put it where she wanted it. She then told the men where the gas pipe was for the stove. By the time she got back downstairs, they were coming with the stove. They put it in place and hooked it up. They lit the pilots and were done with the second floor. When Olivia went back up, she thought they forgot to plug in the refrigerator. They did have it plugged in, it was just very quiet.

Buck watched as they brought his fridge in and placed it where he wanted. The stove was quicker and hooked up in no time. Buck really didn't know if he should tip the men. When he went back outside, they were gone.

Louie and three friends pulled up. Louie got out and said, "Are we ready to go?"

"Yes, start anywhere you would like."

Louie introduced his friends to Buck and then brought them inside to meet his aunt and uncle.

"This is going to be a lot easier than you thought," Willy said.

"What do you mean?"

"You won't be moving any refrigerators or stoves."

"Why not?"

"We bought new ones, the ones here go with these apartments. Which I didn't think about until yesterday."

"Then, what is the heaviest items we need to move?"

"I guess the dressers," Willy said.

"We will start with them."

Louie had two friends load up the one from Willy's bedroom and he and another friend headed over to Buck's house.

Buck went to sit with Olivia and Willy while the young men went to work. Olivia poured Buck a cup of coffee. Before he could finish it, the young men were there to move the kitchen table.

Louie walked in and said, "Buck, your all done." It wasn't even ten o'clock. Buck first went to his old apartment to check it out. Everything was gone, except for the refrigerator and stove. It looked as if they even swept the floor. He then left to see his new place with the furniture in it. He walked to the kitchen first and the table looked very small in this large room. "Need a new table," he said to himself, hoping to make a mental note. He walked in knowing the dining room would be empty. He opened the door to his bedroom and saw his dresser and bed, he also noticed his nineteen-inch T.V. was placed on his dresser. He would move it to the living room later. He saw his sofa and chair and cocktail table against the left side wall. When he walked all the way in, he saw a sixty-inch T.V. mounted on the wall across from the sofa.

Buck started to head over to Willy's old place. Louie met him in the hall. "They are upstairs," he said.

When he reached the top of the stairs, he heard Olivia, "This is a whole lot bigger than the other place," Buck knocked, even though the door was opened.

"We're in the kitchen, Buck," he heard Willy say.

As he walked in, he said, "You didn't have to get that T.V. for me."

"It is a house warming gift," Willy said.

"But I didn't get you anything," Buck said.

"No, you didn't; except for a refrigerator, a stove, and a house of our own."

Buck just smiled.

"Buck, you have changed our lives for the better. Not just recently, but from the time you moved here," Olivia said.

"I really want to thank you, too, for helping me deal with a lot of turmoil in my life."

"If you experienced turmoil, we never saw it," Olivia added and then asked, "Do you remember what tonight is?"

Buck thought for a second, "Yes, it's church night."

"Service starts at seven, we will leave here at six-thirty," she added.

Louie walked in with his friends.

"I have sandwiches in the cooler by the wall," Olivia offered. Olivia heard Louie whisper to his friends, "We better have a sandwich before we leave or my aunt will think we forgot to eat."

"Everything is done. Can you think of anything else you may need?" Louie asked with a mouthful of sandwich.

"Don't talk with your mouthful," Olivia said.

Buck pulled out his wallet and took out the money for Louie and his friends. Louie didn't look at the money.

"Only half would be good, we all agree on that."

His friends nodded in agreement.

"It wasn't nearly as bad as we thought it would be."

"That's very nice," Olivia said.

Buck forced the money into Louie's hand, "It so nice to see friends that agree on something. Look at the other half as a tip."

"But…"

Buck stopped Louie there, "You have helped us out a great deal. Helping me get to Newburgh. I know you will take me back when I need to go."

"Anything for you, Buck," Louie said.

Buck turned to Willy, "You know what we forgot?"

"What?"

"Getting our phones switched over."

"I'll handle that," Louie said. Two of his friends left and Louie took out his cell phone and walked near the window for better reception. When his friends returned, they were holding Willy and Olivia's phone. Louie hung up and took the phone and plugged it in, "Buck, yours is all set downstairs."

"What did you do?" Buck asked.

"I called and gave them a change of address for both of you."

"Well, thank you Louie," Olivia said.

"Oh, Buck, I forgot to tell you. I called the utility company and had the lights and gas turned on in our names," Willy said.

Buck gave a little laugh, "I guess we are good to go."

Willy and Olivia laughed also.

Louie gave his aunt a kiss on the cheek and said, "You need me, you know where to find me."

Then he and his friends left.

Chapter Eleven

Buck went back downstairs after dinner and turned on his giant T.V. He felt as if he was in the movies. He only had an hour before they would be leaving for church. Buck tried to remember the last time he was in church. He thought it was probably fourteen years ago, before Rose passed, "Sorry, God."

Buck talked to God a lot. He now prayed at night before he slept. But he still had that big question, "Why did You give me the ability to talk and hear statues?" This was a puzzle that Buck thought he would never solve.

Buck heard the stair lift coming down the stairs. It wasn't noisy, but it wasn't completely silent. He waited for the knock, he clicked off the T.V. and walked to the door. When he opened the door, Olivia and Willy were talking. "Let me grab a sweater," Buck said.

"Don't rush, we still have time," Olivia replied.

When he returned, Olivia and Willy were outside on the step.

"It's been a long time since I have been in a church," Buck said.

"Us, too, about a year and a half," Olivia said. Buck said nothing. The church was only two blocks away; Capital City Baptist Church. Buck remembered the Baptist church back home when he was a child. There were only two cars parked outside of it. There were many buckboards drawn by two horses, small carriages pulled by a horse or a mule, or horses tied up to the post.

As they entered the church, the preacher was greeting members at the door.

When he saw Buck, he stopped, and walked over to him, "Welcome to our humbled church, may I ask you your name."

Olivia spoke up first. "I am Olivia and this is my husband, William," she hesitated for a second. "This is Buck Thompson," noticing that the preacher never took his eyes off of Buck.

"I don't know why but I am thrilled to meet you," the Preacher said as he shook hands with Buck. Then he looked at Olivia and said, "And you are?"

"I am Olivia and this is my husband, William," the preacher shook hands with Willy and gave Olivia a small hug, "Welcome to our church." He then moved on to other members. As Willy and Olivia and Buck entered a pew, "He is still looking at you, Buck," Olivia said.

"Maybe he thinks I'm somebody else."

Willy looked back, "He is still looking at you, Buck."

Buck took a bible out of a slot in front of him, Willy and Olivia followed his lead. The choir began to sing 'I'll Fly Away.' As the preacher walked up to the front of the church, he turned once and looked directly at Buck.

"This is getting a little scary," Buck said.

"I agree," Willy added.

Olivia said, "We are in God's house, nothing scary can happen here."

The preacher mentioned things that were happening at the church. After that they took up a collection, while the choir sang 'The Old Rugged Cross.'

The choir followed that song with 'As the Storm Passes By' and then the preaching started.

The preacher walked up to a podium that held his Bible; you could see different pieces of colored paper sticking out, the Bible laid open. The preacher stood there, he looked down at the Bible, and closed it.

"I worked since Sunday night on a sermon I chose for this night. I feel that God wants me to talk about something different, about righteous men. And how would we know who is righteous and who is not. It is no secret that only God knows those answers. We may think some people are righteous, because they are at church all the time or they help out at church all the time. They like helping people.

"God may thank these people, but he would only reward a righteous person.

"Now you may say God gives me what I ask for. God helps me when I need His help. He does this because He is our Father and he helps His children. Like we would help our children. God heals the sick, because the sick are his children. I have asked God many times to help with my sermons. He has helped many times, because he wants you to understand the Bible better. You all know what I do every day and I will tell all of you, I am not a righteous person. No one." He stopped and started again, "Not everyone in this church would meet Gods requirement of being righteous. I don't know what the requirements would be, but I could never reach them. Now we all know Jesus was righteous. You may think all the apostles were righteous. I wouldn't think that. To me, one in a billion might be righteous, or one in a trillion and there isn't a trillion people on this earth."

Buck knew he wasn't a righteous man, even though the preacher said no one knows the requirements. *I haven't gone to church in a long time, yes, I talks to God, so does a million people every day,* he thought.

"I think love has a lot to do with it," the preacher said and continued, "I don't know why, but I feel so blessed to be here tonight. I feel with all my heart that God is looking down upon us and he is smiling. I have never felt this way before. Let us bow our heads and pray. Thank You, God, for filling our church with such joy and love, I know You are here with us tonight. I thank You for letting me feel your presence. Please watch over all of us and help us. In Your name, I pray."

Members started leaving the church, some it seemed were in too much of a hurry. Willy, Olivia, and Buck took their time. The preacher was wishing members farewell, but every now and then, he looked at Buck. When they reached him, he took both of Buck's hands in his, "It was a great pleasure meeting you." Olivia stepped up and asked if she could talk with him sometime.

"I am here every morning to assist members, any morning would be fine."

"How about tomorrow about ten o'clock?" Olivia said.

"Like I said, I will be here," was the preachers reply.

Willy shook his hand and quickly moved towards the front door. Buck was waiting there for him and Olivia.

When they all got outside, Olivia said, "I am going to meet with him and talk to him about you talking to statues."

"He will think I'm a nut."

"No, there was something about you, only he could see it."

The following morning, Olivia headed to the church. The preacher lived in the house that was attached to the church. She didn't notice the sign last night that read 'Service on Wednesday evening at 7:00 p.m., Sunday School at 10:00 a.m., Morning Service at 11:00 a.m. also 5:00 p.m., Brother Jeff Jingles.'

Olivia rang the bell and Brother Jingles answered the door, "Good morning, how may I help you?"

"I would like to talk to you about Buck Thompson."

The preacher thought a minute, "Is he a member of our church?"

"Not yet, you met him last night."

The preacher guided Olivia to his office.

"I don't remember, but what was it that you wanted to share with me about Brother Thompson. That's his name, right?"

"In your sermon last night, you talked about righteousness."

"I did? My sermon was to be about David."

."You told us that God wanted you to not follow what you chose. He wanted you to talk about righteous people."

Brother Jingles looked puzzled. He called for Peggy, a middle-aged woman appeared in the doorway of the preacher's office, "Peggy, you heard my sermon last night, what was it about?"

"Brother Jeff, after the collection was taken. I went to your back office and counted it and wrote it up in the treasurer's ledger. When I finished, you were done."

"Can you get me the D.V.D. from the church? We record all of our sermons, that way I can cross reference with new sermons. It should only take her a minute."

"Buck has the ability to talk with statues and hear what they say," Olivia blurted out.

The preacher stared at Olivia, "We have a member with Parkinson's that talks to people that are not there."

"I'm not joking," Olivia said. At that moment, Peggy stepped in and handed Brother Jeff the D.V.D. from last night's sermon. The preacher placed it in the D.V.D. player on his desk and clicked on the T.V. As it came on, it showed Brother Jeff talking about things that were going on in the church, the choir began to sing.

The collection plate was passed around and the choir sang another song. Brother Jeff stopped the D.V.D. and said, "We don't take up a collection on Wednesday night. But at Sunday service, we were asked to. To help a family who needs to travel to visit their sick son." Brother Jeff clicked on the player again. They watched as he walked up to where his Bible was, to start his sermon "I have worked on this sermon since Sunday night." Then the tape went blank. Brother Jeff backed it up. He fast forwarded it, there was nothing on the tape, "The machine, next door, must have broken down. I will have it checked out."

"If you would like, I could have one of our deacon's talk with Brother Thompson and try to help him through this."

It dawned on Olivia that the preacher didn't remember anything that happened last night. "No let me check it out first. I could be wrong," Olivia said.

"If you need me, I'll be right here willing to help if I can. It was very nice to meet you."

He stood up and walked Olivia to the front door. "Have a blessed day," he added.

Olivia was very puzzled that the preacher didn't know what he talked about at last night's service. It came across to him that Buck may be a nut. Olivia hurried home. Buck and Willy were in Buck's apartment watching his sixty-inch T.V. Olivia knocked on the door and walked in. "You're not going to believe this," she looked at Buck, "What was the sermon about last night?"

"If I knew there was going to be a quiz, I would have taken notes."

Olivia gave Buck a stern look.

"It was about righteous people," Buck quickly said.

"Yeah, he said something about there may be one in a billion, or a trillion," Willy added.

"The preacher thinks he spoke about David and he may think that you're a nut. I'm sorry, Buck."

Buck smiled, "He's the one with a problem if he doesn't remember what he said last night."

"Another part that is puzzling is when he said, 'No One,' then he stopped. When he continued, he said, 'Not everyone in this church would meet the requirements of being a righteous person.'"

"Yeah! I remember that," Willy said.

"I know that I am not a righteous person, I haven't been to church since Rose passed."

"The preacher said no one knows the requirements of being a righteous person," Olivia stressed, "He said that God would reward a righteous person."

"I still don't believe I am a righteous person." Buck replied, "I don't know why he gave me the ability to talk with statues. I do believe He was the one who gave me this ability."

"Do you have plans for today, Buck?" Willy asked.

"After dinner, I might go and visit Jamie and see if George Washington is there."

"Can I go with you?" Willy asked.

"Yeah! I wouldn't mind the company."

"You will only hear one side of the conversation," Olivia said.

"I realize that," Willy replied.

"Dinner will be at five o'clock. Willy, I need you to go to the store later."

"Just tell me when," Willy answered.

Olivia headed to the stair lift and rode it up to the apartment.

"I need to go to the store, too, I have to put something in that refrigerator," Buck said.

"You should make a list of what you need," Willy said, then added, "Always remember to take the list with you. That's my big mistake. Olivia hands me the list and somehow, I leave it on the table."

"That sounds like an age thing to me," Buck said with a slight laugh.

"Let's do that now and get it out of the way," Willy said.

"Sounds good," Buck said as he and Willy headed upstairs to get Olivia's list.

Willy took Olivia's list and put it in his pocket. They headed back downstairs and headed north on Pearl Street to a mom and pop corner store. Willy took out the list and started gathering up everything Olivia had written down. Buck picked up a jar of coffee, bread, eggs, ketchup, mustard, and mayo. He placed his stuff on the counter. The clerk rang it up and quoted the price. Buck handed him a twenty and he received a fist full of change.

Willy recited things on the list while he placed them on the counter. After he was done, they headed home. Half way home, Buck said, "I should have gotten some soda."

"That's why you need a list," Willy answered. "You do realize, that we sound like a couple of old women," Willy added.

Buck just smiled. When they reached home, Buck went to his house and Willy went to his. Buck put his groceries away, he saw a pad of paper on the kitchen table and wrote down soda, then cold cuts. *My first grocery list*, he thought.

He looked at the monument book and remembered he had to renew it. He decided to do that now. He called a cab and then went to tell Willy and Olivia where he was going. As he came back down and went outside, the cab pulled up. Buck motioned to the cabbie to hold on a second. He went back inside and grabbed the book. He laughed to himself he almost forgot it.

Willy would have said, "It must be an age thing," And Buck would have deserved it. When they reached the Albany Public Library, Buck paid the cabbie and then went inside. The same woman he saw before was at the counter, he didn't remember her name.

"How can I help you today, Mr. Thompson?" She asked.

"You remembered my name, I am sad to say I forgot yours."

"I am Mrs. Burke."

"Mrs. Burke, I need to renew this book."

He handed the book to her. She went to the inside of the back cover, "It's due back tomorrow, good timing." She stamped the book and handed it back to Buck, "You're good for another two weeks."

This took all of a minute. Buck looked around the library and decided to spend a few minutes walking around to see what they had. There was a section for fiction, non-fiction, local writers, how-to books. Social studies, science. They carried everything and anything someone would want.

Buck walked outside and the sun was blinding, he shaded his eyes. He waved down a cab. When he got back home, he saw the light on his phone blinking. He walked over and picked it up and hit the flashing light. Then he heard,

"Mr. Thompson, this is Harley Davidson again, can you give me a call?"

Buck retrieved Harley's Business card from his wallet. He dialed the number and had to leave a voice message, "Harley, this is Buck, I am returning your call."

Harley never called back that day. After dinner, Buck and Willy decide to walk over to the Education Building to talk with Jamie.

"Are you here, Missy?" Buck asked.

"She should be here any time." Mr. Todd replied.

"And how are you today, Pete?"

"Very well and you?"

"I'm doing fine, let me introduce my cousin Willy."

"Can he talk to statues, too?"

"No, he does believe that I can."

"How do you know he does?"

"Willy, whisper something into Pete's ear. I'll move down to the street."

When Willy was done, he called Buck back up. "This really isn't going to convince me," Pete said.

"What did he say to you?" Buck asked.

"He said, 'I think Buck's a righteous person.'"

"I told you, Willy, I am not a righteous person."

"But I really think you might be," Willy said.

"You could have set that up before you got here," Pete said.

"Pete, I would never do that."

"I know you wouldn't," he heard Jamie say.

"Could you give me a moment with Peter, I need to tell him something," Jamie said.

Willy and Buck walked down to the street again. "What's up with this?" Willy asked.

"I don't know," was Buck's answer. Somehow, he knew Jamie wanted him to come back-up.

"Is everything all right?" Buck asked.

"Yes, and I am sorry I didn't believe you," Pete said.

"I don't know if I would have believed me, too."

"How is the statue of Rose going?" Jamie asked.

"That seems to be a puzzle."

"Whatever do you mean?" Jamie asked.

"Harley started sculpturing her head, he said it takes three months. He created a perfect likeness of Rose in six hours. He doesn't know how that happened, he said when he stopped that night, he knew he still had a way to go. But when he came in the following morning, there was the perfect likeness of Rose."

"That does sound puzzling," Jamie said.

"I don't know why, but I thought of you last night," Pete said.

"We went to church last night," Buck added.

"How was it?" Pete asked.

"It turned out to be a strange evening. Olivia talked with the preacher this morning and according to him, what we heard, wasn't what he was talking about."

Buck heard Jamie giggle.

"It really isn't funny."

"I'm sorry, I was giggling at something else."

"Do you have any questions for me, Pete?"

"Yes, it looked as if you got to talk with George Washington the last time you were here."

"Yes, I did, it was great. I'm going to see if he is there tonight. He said it was a pleasure to talk with me."

"That does sound very impressive, did you ask him about the cherry tree?"

"I decided that if I got to talk with him, I would not ask that question."

"Why?" was Pete's response.

"The cherry tree thing, *I must not tell a lie*, I think that was used to build him up to children."

"Why would you say that?" Pete asked.

"He pledged his allegiance to the British when he was young. That turned out to be a lie, wouldn't you say?"

"What college did you graduate from?" Pete asked.

"I only got to the fifth grade in school."

"Your intelligence is beyond reproach."

"Thank you, I think," Buck said.

"Buck, he and I agree you are very intelligent."

"Thank you, Missy."

Buck saw that Willy had no idea what was being said. *After all, he could only hear me.* Buck thought.

"I think I am going over to see if President Washington is there," Buck said.

"Hope to see you again," Pete said.

"Hopefully, next week?" Jamie added.

"Yes, I will be back next week."

With that said, Buck and Willy headed over to see President Washington.

As they approached President Washington's statue, Buck asked. "Are you here, Mr. President?"

"Buck, Welcome back," The President said.

"Is he here, Buck?" Willy asked.

"Yes, he is. Mr. President, this is my cousin, Willy,"

"Can he talk to statues or hear them talk.?"

"No, Mr. President. He does know that I can."

"Have you found out why you can."

"No, only God knows."

"I think you may get your answer in the near future."

"Why would you say that?" Buck asked.

"It's just a feeling."

"I hope so."

"Oh, I talked to Philip Schuyler and he is eager to talk with you."

"That's great!"

"And, he isn't afraid of the dark," the president added

"You served with all the founding fathers, how was Ben Franklin?"

"He was a notorious womanizer, other than that, he was a lot of fun. He was a great foreign diplomat. Sometimes, it took five messages to get him to come home."

"It there anything you would like to say about yourself to clear the record?"

"Yes!" the President said, then continued, "I never had wooden teeth. I never chopped down a cherry tree. And I never slept with any other woman other than my Martha."

"I will spread that around to anyone who would listen."

"Thank you, Buck, I appreciate it."

Buck noticed Willy was sitting on the bench, he seemed lost.

"I need to leave Mr. President but I will be back."

"When you come the next time, as you're getting ready to leave, I will have Philip wait for you."

"Thank you, Mr. President."

"Hope to see you soon, Buck."

"Good night, Mr. President."

Buck and Willy headed down the hill.

"It is hard, only hearing you, never hearing the answers," Willy said.

"I thought it would be. You are always welcome to come."

"Thanks, Buck, but it really is your thing."

When they reached the house, Willy headed upstairs and Buck went into his. Buck took a shower and put on his P.J's. He watched T.V. for about an hour and decided he needed to sleep. After he said his bedtime prayer, he fell off in to a deep sleep.

Chapter Twelve

The following morning, Buck woke up to the sound of the phone ringing. By the time he got to it, the message started, 'Hi! Mr. Thompson, this is Harley again.'

"I'm here," Buck said when he picked up the phone.

"Well, again, something very strange happened the night before last," Harley said.

"Like what?"

"You were here Tuesday. After you left, I decided to place the sculpture into the molding plaster, which I said will have to stand for a month. We were hit with high winds the night before last and one of my windows broke. When I came in yesterday morning, the sculpture mold somehow was pushed onto the floor."

"Is everything alright?" Buck asked.

"The mold was cracked around the entire shell. I knew I would have to start over from scratch. I loosened the mold to remove the sculpture and create a new mold. When I removed the mold, it was solid."

"What do you mean?"

"Believe me, I know what I am doing."

"I know you do."

"The mold is solid, I can pour the bronze today."

"I don't understand."

"The mold should have been soft, like I said, no air, it takes a month to dry. It turned out that the mold is solid. I will pour the bronze today and, in a month, you will have your statue."

"That sounds great."

"You don't understand what I am saying. This shouldn't be happening, there are some strange things going on here."

"I understand what you're saying. It seems kind of weird, the way things are happening. But I am truly happy about it."

"I will pour the bronze today, and keep you updated."

"Thanks, Harley. I will mail you off that second check."

"There's no rush," was Harley's reply.

They hung up and Buck went upstairs to tell Willy and Olivia.

"I got a call from Harley, he said some strange things are happening. He poured the mold Tuesday after I left. They were hit by a storm that night, somehow, the mold got pushed off the table onto the floor and broke; the shell cracked. He thought he would have to do it all over again. The mold should have been soft, see there is no air to dry it. When he opened it, it was solid. He will be pouring the bronze today."

"This is God," Olivia said.

"I agree," Buck said.

"It seems pretty scary to me," Willy added.

"To me, the quicker I get to talk with my Rose, the better."

"There is something going on with all of this," Willy added.

"Yes, it's God," Olivia reiterated again.

"After breakfast, I am going to the store, do you need anything?" Buck asked.

Olivia thought for a second, "No, I don't think so."

Buck ate and then he headed for the store. Anything he saw that would go in the refrigerator; cheese, cold cuts, lettuce, tomato, cucumber, and salad dressing he placed it in the cart, then he remembered soda. Apple pie was the last thing in the cart. The woman at the counter rang up everything and placed it neatly in a large paper bag. Buck paid the amount due and headed back home. The bag was a little heavier than he would have thought.

When he got home, he unloaded everything and placed it in the fridge. Still the refrigerator looked empty.

There was a light knock on the door. "Come in," Buck yelled.

It was Willy, "Olivia just went to the beauty parlor."

"Getting her hair done?" Buck asked.

"No, just to gossip with her friends."

"What are your plans today?" Buck asked Willy.

"We have had a lot going on these past couple of weeks. I think I'm just going to relax today. What about you?"

"I plan on going to the furniture store and pick out some stuff for the house."

"Like what?" Willy asked.

"Dining room set, another chair for the living room, and a new kitchen set. Anything else I see that I think I might need. I also want to get a phone for the bedroom."

"It looks like you have a full day ahead of you. Is there anything I can do to help?"

"No! Stick to your plan and rest."

Willy left to start his relaxing. Buck called a cab, about five minutes later, he heard the cab beep out front. When he got into the cab, he said, "Take me to that furniture store on Central Avenue."

"There's about three on Central Avenue," the cabbie replied.

"You pick one out and take me there."

Of course, the cabbie took him to the one that was the farthest out. Buck didn't mind, he was in no rush. When he walked into the furniture store, he saw three sales men and none of them came towards him. There was a young woman straightening out pillows on a bed that was on display. He walked toward her, "Mam, could you help me?"

She turned and saw the men talking over near the far wall, "Yes sir, what can I help you with?"

"Do you make a commission on whatever you sell?"

"Yes, besides I make minimum wage, also, why?"

"Today is your lucky day."

"I need a dining room set, a new kitchen set, end tables, and a chair for the living room."

"Let me show you the dining room tables and chairs."

Buck picked out a beautiful set.

"Let me show you the kitchen sets."

Buck picked out another beautiful set. The woman looked at Buck and said, "Is this a joke?"

"What do you mean?" Buck asked.

"I didn't know if those guys had you come to me, buy a bunch of stuff, and then walk out. They would get a big laugh at that."

"I promise you I will pay for everything I pick out."

"Thank you, sir," she said.

"I wanted a new chair for the living room, but after seeing some of these living room sets, I think I want to buy a set."

She pointed at a set and said, "You said something about end tables, this set comes with end tables and a cocktail table."

"I like the color of that, too, I'll take it." Buck looked around and said, "You deliver, right?"

"Free delivery on all orders over a hundred dollars."

"Let's look at the beds and dressers," Buck said.

She walked Buck to a room filled with all size beds and all size dressers.

He saw a full size that he liked, it came with a side table and a large dresser.

"I'll take two of them."

She went to the cash register and started ringing up everything that Buck wanted. Buck said, "I will be over there, you call me Buck and yell out how much everything comes to. The guys over there are going to have a fit."

Buck wandered off, she finished, and she yelled. "Buck, that all comes to seven thousand, eight hundred, and ninety-six dollars and seventy-five cents."

"Sounds good to me," he walked over and took out his check book and wrote a check, "How much commission are you going to make?"

"Seven hundred and eighty-nine dollars."

"That's great," Buck said.

"Thank you, sir."

"Glad to help."

Buck left his address and was told it would be delivered tomorrow in the morning. Buck almost made it to the door and turned back, "Mam, I need to buy a phone."

"Cell phone or a land line?"

"The kind you have in your house," he replied.

"Go next door and ask for the five-phone bundle. It cost seventy-nine dollars. You plug the main line into the wall where the phone jack is and the other four you can place in any room, just plug them into an outlet."

"Really! That's it," Buck said.

"Yes, sir," she replied.

Buck went next door and purchased the one she said. He asked the clerk if she could call him a cab. He went outside to wait, then saw a car pull up. The license plates had the name of the furniture store on them. Buck stopped the man, "If you're going in there, they have a great sales girl. She got me to spend over seven thousand dollars." The man's mouth dropped open. He nodded and walked in. He went right over to the young woman. Looked at the paperwork and he shook her hand. "I thought he was the owner," Buck said aloud.

Buck waited twenty minutes before the cab came. He gave him his address and just leaned back. Buck was thinking, in a month I will be talking to my Rose. When the cab pulled up, he paid him and saw Olivia walking down the street.

"Where were you?" she asked.

"I went and bought some new furniture."

"Where were you?" Buck asked.

"I was visiting some friends at the beauty parlor."

"What's in the bag?" Olivia asked.

"New phones."

"How many?"

"Five."

Then Buck walked away, he unlocked the door for both of them.

"What are you going to do with five phones?" Olivia asked.

"Use them," Buck said. He then headed for his place. He plugged the main line into the phone jack in the living room. He put one in the dining room, one in his bedroom, one in the kitchen, and the fifth went into the bathroom. *Harley might call when I'm in there*, he thought.

The phones all rang at once, "Hello!" Buck answered.

"We will be eating in one hour," he heard Olivia say.

"I'll be up in a couple of minutes."

When Buck got upstairs, he explained about the furniture he purchased. "If you or if you know anyone who could use my old furniture, take it or give it away."

Olivia called Betsey, "Sis, do you know of anyone who could use some old furniture?" Olivia asked, "There is a sofa and chair in good shape. A cocktail table and a kitchen table with four chairs. You could, that's great. When can they pick it up Buck?"

"Any time, the new stuff is coming tomorrow."

"Any time, sis," Olivia said, "Buck, how about now? Louie has a buddy over who has a truck."

"That would be great," Buck replied.

Olivia hung up the phone, "My sister said her kitchen table broke today and the chairs were in bad shape. The springs are shot in her sofa, too."

"Then that works out great for all of us," Buck said.

Willy looks at Olivia and said, "This is another God thing, I bet."

"Now you're starting to get it," Olivia said to Willy.

It was only fifteen minutes later they heard the doorbell ring. "That must be Louie and his friend," Olivia said.

"I'll get this," Buck said and headed downstairs. When he opened the door, Louie and a friend were standing there. "Hi, guys," was all Buck said. They followed him into his place.

"Mom said thanks a lot, this will come in handy," Louie said as he and his friend picked up two chairs each from the kitchen set. When they came back, Louie grabbed the kitchen table and directed his friend to grab the cocktail table. When Louie and his friend were lifting the sofa, Willy walked in. "I'll grab the chair," he said.

"No, you won't," was Louie's remark. "We will be right back for that," he added.

Willy looked at Buck and shrugged his shoulders. "They are young, we're old. That's how they look at it," Buck said.

Soon Buck's house was empty, except for some phones on the floor.

"Those are your new phones I take it?" Willy asked.

"Yeah! Only the phone in the living room had to be plugged into a phone jack. The rest just plugged into an outlet."

"That's cool," was Willy's reply.

Louie walked back in, "We're all set. Do you need anything done while we're here?"

"Nah!" Buck said. Louie thanked Buck again and he and his friend left.

"Dinner is ready," they both heard Olivia yell from upstairs.

At dinner, Olivia asked Buck, "What are your plans for Saturday?"

"Don't really have any."

"Willy and I are going over to Washington Park for Tulip Fest," she said.

"We are?" Willy asked.

"We always do."

"I'll go with you," Buck said. "I have never gone to the festival. Rose and I would go over and see the tulips in bloom, usually before the Tulip Festival. They are delivering my furniture in the morning," he added.

"We will leave after that is done," Olivia said.

After dinner, they had some small chit chat. Buck decided to go back downstairs. When he entered, it dawned on him that he had no place to sit to watch his big screen T.V. He went into his bedroom and turned on the nineteen-inch. He sat at the end of the bed, he then went back into the kitchen, and retrieved a soda from the fridge and went back into the bedroom. He stacked his pillows to sit at the head of the bed. *Tomorrow, Tulip Fest, Sunday, my Rose,* he thought. Buck was doing what the kids called 'channel surfing', to Buck, he was just trying to find something to watch.

"Are you a righteous person?" a preacher on a religious channel was asking. Buck stopped surfing for a moment to hear what the preacher was saying, "Only God knows that answer."

This is what I heard the other night, Buck thought. He began surfing again. Going from channel to channel, he heard the word 'Righteous' on almost every channel. *It must be this month's topic*, he also thought. He ended up on the history channel, 'Searching for God' was the title. He watched as he was led from country to country, from town to town in this search for God. It showed different religions around the world. It showed how they worshiped and praised God. Then the word 'Righteous' started popping up here and there. "I think you're righteous," Buck remembered Willy saying. Buck thought on that for a while. He knew he couldn't be righteous, he didn't go to church regularly. That must be one of the requirements.

Buck felt tired and started to fall asleep. He stayed awake, long enough to say a prayer. This night he dreamed he saw him and Rose walking together on what looked to be a cloud. He was in a hypnotic trance. Rose looked so beautiful, he could feel her in his arms.

When he woke up the next morning, he remembered every bit of his dream. He thanked God for letting him have such a beautiful dream.

He heard a tapping on his ceiling then he heard Olivia, "Buck, breakfast will be ready in fifteen-minutes." He didn't answer her call. He went straight to the shower. After his shower, he started to get dressed. All this time, he was thinking of his dream. He thanked God again, before he headed upstairs.

On his way upstairs, he caught the smell of bacon which caused his mouth to water. As he entered, Willy was at the table, Olivia was finishing at the stove.

"Perfect timing," Olivia said.

"Everything smells great," Buck added.

Chapter Thirteen

"Had a great dream last night, Rose and I were walking on a cloud, I could feel her in my arms."

"You must dream about that stuff a lot," Willy said.

"I wish I did, I very seldom dream at all."

Olivia was placing eggs and bacon on Buck's and Willy's dishes. She returned to the stove and brought back some fried toast and the greatest home fries Buck has ever eaten.

"Olivia, this was a great breakfast," Buck said as he finished the last morsel on his dish.

"Thank you," was Olivia's reply.

Buck heard a truck pull up outside, "That must be the furniture," Buck said. He headed downstairs. As he opened the door, the man there was ready to push the bell.

"Looking for Buck Thompson."

"That's me," Buck said.

"Can you show me where everything is going before we start?"

"Follow me," Buck said as they walked in, "This is the dining room, that is the living room, and there is the kitchen. The new beds are going in the two bedrooms off of the kitchen."

"Thank you, we will handle it from here." the man said. Two other men had the new sofa on a hand cart. Buck heard the man tell them where to put it. As they sat it down, they also carefully removed the plastic covering. Another man was carrying two of the dining room chairs in, "Over there," he directed. They were followed by the other chairs and the rest of the living room set, end tables, and all. In no time, the bedrooms had the beds, dressers, and end stands. The kitchen set looked great. The last item moved in was the dining room table.

"Can you sign here, sir?" the man asked Buck. Buck placed the papers on the kitchen counter and signed both pages. "Thank you, sir, it was our pleasure to help get everything in its place," he then picked up the papers, shook Buck's hand, then he and the crew left.

Buck heard Olivia and Willy coming down the stairs. "Come on in," Buck said.

As they entered the dining room. "Oh, my," Olivia said, "This is all beautiful and fits perfectly in here."

Willy peeked in the bedrooms off the kitchen.

"You have to see the bedrooms off the kitchen," Willy said. Olivia headed right to them, "Beautiful Buck, you should be a designer, everything is perfect."

Buck felt good at his accomplishments. Then Olivia said, "Lamps, you need lamps for the end tables and for the side stands in the bedrooms."

"I never thought of lamps, but you are right. I'll get them next week."

It was nearing ten o'clock. "When did you want to leave for the Tulip Fest?" Olivia asked.

"Any time is good for me," was Buck's answer.

"We will leave in a half hour," she replied.

"I'll be right here," Buck said.

Willy and Olivia went back upstairs. Buck put water on for a cup of coffee. When the kettle whistled, Buck looked at the clock, he still had twenty minutes. He brought his cup of coffee into the living room and sat on the sofa. He liked the new furniture and was pleased Olivia liked it, too. Buck knew someday it would belong to Olivia and Willy. The one thing Buck remembered to do was to bring the monument book into the living room. He read a little more about Philip Schuyler, then he heard Olivia and Willy heading downstairs. He was walking out his door as they reached the bottom stair.

"I called a cab, it should be here anytime," Willy said.

They all stepped outside to a beautiful sunny day. Buck felt so peaceful and calm and held the bits of last night's dream in his mind. The cab pulled up, Olivia told him, "Washington Park."

The cabbie brought them in the back way over Northern Boulevard. When they exited the cab, Olivia led the way. The park was full of people, and they all seemed to be having a good time. Buck could see they were approaching the Lake House where it looked like children were performing. There were all kinds of vendors and they all seemed to be making money. Buck sort of wished he and Rose came while everything here was going on. Buck looked down upon Washington Park Lake, which was a good size pond at best. Buck excused himself from Willy and Olivia, he wanted to walk around more and see all the stuff.

"We will meet back here in an hour," Olivia said.

Buck walked around looking at everything, some of the home-made candles were unbelievable. Painted dishes, so many nice things. Then he heard someone say his name, it came from behind him. When he turned around, he was looking at the statue of Moses.

"So, you are Buck," he heard Moses say.

With so many people around, he was afraid to say anything.

"You can talk. No one will see you or hear you."

"I am not worthy," he said with a low voice.

"What would you say if I said I am not worthy to you?"

Buck didn't know how to answer that question, "You are Moses, you wrote parts of the old testament in the Bible. You guided your people out of Egypt. You received the Ten Commandments from God."

"It was the First Testament. There were six hundred and thirty Commandments, but we will talk about that another time. I did what God wanted me to do. I did make mistakes, God did still help me."

"How did you know who I was?" Buck asked.

"It is not my place to reveal that."

"What do you mean?"

"Soon, you will know, the how's and whys. It is not up to me to reveal that."

"Your statue looks so powerful. You look the way I would have picture you to."

"Thank you, but I didn't pose for this statue. Like you, someone pictured me looking this way."

"I was afraid to come here and try to talk with you," Buck said.

"Why would you feel that way?"

"Because you're Moses. You have talked to God."

"You have talked to God, haven't you?" Moses said.

"But He never answered me."

"Why would you say that? Because you didn't hear a voice. He answers everyone."

Buck was feeling very confused. Was he really having this talk with Moses? He began to doubt himself.

"Buck, don't ever doubt yourself. I need to go. I am being called."

Buck felt Moses leave that area.

Buck looked around, no one paid him any attention. He saw Willy and Olivia standing near a food cart, he walked towards them.

"Where did you go?" Olivia asked.

"I was talking to Moses."

"We stood in front of that statue for the past twenty minutes. You were nowhere around."

"And if you did, a lot of people would have saw you," Willy said.

"I will tell you everything when we get home," Buck said.

As they were getting ready to leave, they saw a number of cabs parked on one side of the park. They walked over there and got a cab home. No one spoke until they were inside their house.

"If you were there talking to Moses, why didn't we see you?" Olivia asked.

"I was standing in front of the statue, not realizing I was. Then I heard a voice say, 'Buck.' I turned around and saw the statue. I didn't say a thing because of all of the people. Then Moses said, 'You can talk, they won't see you.' I said, 'I am not worthy'. Then he asked, 'What would you say if I said to you I am not worthy?' I didn't know how to answer him. I said you wrote some of the Old Testament, you guided your people out of Egypt, God gave you the Ten Commandments. He then said, 'There were six hundred and some, but we could discuss that at another time. I said, 'You have talked with God,', then he said, 'You have talked to God.' Then I said, 'He answered you'. He said, 'God answers every question.' He said, I only did what God asked me to do,' then he said he was being called away. I could feel it when he left. Then, when I looked around, I saw you two."

"Wow! You talked with Moses," Olivia said.

"I am very confused," Willy added.

"I'm pretty mixed up myself," Buck said, "I asked him how do you know who I am. He said something about it wasn't up to him to reveal. I am mixed up, this is getting to be more than I could handle."

"That does sound strange," Olivia said.

"I don't know if I am telling it to you the exact way he said it to me."

"You should rest, take it easy for the rest of the day," Willy suggested.

"I think you are right. Livy, I have cold cuts in the fridge and bread. I think I'm going downstairs and make a sandwich and take it easy for the rest of the night."

"Are you walking to see Rose tomorrow or taking a cab?" Olivia asked.

"I'll take a cab, because I know you would feel better."

"Thank you, Buck. That's sweet."

Buck headed down stairs; he made his sandwich and grabbed a soda, then flopped down on the sofa and watched some T.V.

He went to the kitchen and brought back his pad and pen. He wrote down things that happened this week, he would share them with Rose.

He watched T.V. until ten o'clock and went into the bedroom. When he said his prayer, he asked God to forgive him. He knew he must have messed up bad today. After his prayer, he closed his eyes and drifted off to sleep.

He had another dream of Rose, he and her were walking hand -in -hand on what looked like a cloud. All he could do was smile. He wondered why he didn't talk to Rose in the dream. All he did was smile.

The following morning when he got out of bed, he remembered the dream.

Rose was so beautiful. He started the water for coffee, then turned it off. He would get coffee at the Miss Albany Diner. He called a cab after he washed up and got dressed. He stuck his notes in his back pocket. He walked outside to another sunshiny morning.

When the cab pulled up, the driver said, "Hi! How are you today?"

"I am doing very well and you?" Buck replied.

"Making a living, thank God."

"That's good to hear," Buck said.

"You going to the Miss Albany Diner?"

"Yes! You must have taken me before on a Sunday morning?"

"Yes! Last Sunday. Sunday mornings really aren't that busy. Would you like me stop back in an hour to take you to the Albany Rural Cemetery?"

"That would be nice, thank you."

When they reached the diner, Buck handed the man a ten-dollar bill and said, "Keep the change."

"Thank you, sir," was the cabby's reply.

As Buck walked into the diner, the owner behind the counter asked, "Buck, you want your usual?"

"Yes, thank you, Sam," Buck said. Buck was thinking everybody is really getting to know my needs. The owner brought Buck a cup of coffee.

"Going to see Rose?" Sam asked?

"Yes, my Sunday excursion."

"I am glad to see your taking a cab. You always made me tired, thinking of you walking that distance every week."

"I never really thought about that walk. I always spent my time thinking about what I would tell Rose," Buck answered.

"I saw you one Sunday walk by, it was during a blizzard. You must have been freezing cold."

"There wasn't one time I can remember being cold," Buck said.

"Wow! Your love for your wife kept you warm all those times?"

"It did."

Sam brought Buck his usual and began wiping down the counter. It didn't need it, Buck thought he did it out of habit. Buck just finished his second cup of coffee when the cab pulled up. Buck stood up. "Have a blessed day, Sam," he said as he left the money on the bill that Sam placed in front of him. He headed back outside.

"Welcome back," The cabbie said.

"Thank you, glad to be back," Buck said with a smile on his face.

As the cab pulled up to the Albany Rural Cemetery, the cabbie asked, "Who is buried here?"

Buck looked around and said, "A lot of people."

"You know what I mean," the cabbie continued.

"My wife, Rose."

"How long has she been…?" the cabbie stopped and thought about rewording what he wanted to say.

"She passed fourteen years ago."

"In fourteen years, how many times have you missed?"

"Never missed a Sunday," Buck replied.

"I wish with all my heart that everyone could find someone to love, that they would be that devoted to."

"I hope everybody would."

Buck got out of the cab, he started to hand the money to the driver. The driver put up a hand as if he was stopping traffic, "This is on me, have a great visit."

"Can you stop back in three hours?"

"I'll see you then," the cabbie said.

Buck started up the hill to see his Rose. He saw the sun gleaming off of Elizabeth's bronze body.

As Buck stood in front of Rose's grave, he closed his eyes, "I hope to be talking with you in a month." He felt a kiss touch his lips. He sat on the ground, he took out his notes. He explained what had happened at the statue factory. He also mentioned how the owner Harley Davidson seemed a little scared. He touched on everything that happened in his notes. He ended up with the Moses' visit. That seemed a little scrambled in his mind. He explained what he could. He did leave out some of the things that had happened that weren't put in his notes.

He then started telling her about his dreams, Rose knew he never dreamed. He mentioned how he wished they went to the Tulip Fest while it was going on. He even told her about his cab driver. The three hours zoomed by. He looked at his watch. "The cab will be back in about twenty minutes," he told her. He felt another kiss, this time, on his cheek, "Oh, I love you so much, Rose. I can't wait to be with you." He folded up his notes and placed them back into his back pocket. He looked at Elizabeth, "Are you here, Missy?" There was no answer. When he looked back at Rose' grave, he felt the kiss on his lips again.

"Buck, she is being called away," Elizabeth said.

"Oh! You're here, Missy?"

"Yes, I'm here."

"Why was she called away?"

"I don't know, but be assured nothing is wrong."

"Talked with Moses," Buck said.

"I heard about that up here."

"He also got called away."

"We all do from time to time."

"I got to talk with President Washington. He is going to tell Philip Schuyler when I will meet with him."

"He is buried right over there," Elizabeth said.

"I will have to stop over there and check it out sometime."

"Buck, I have to tell you that I feel so honored to have been the first statue you talked with."

"I feel honored that you were the first statue that talked back."

He heard Elizabeth giggle.

"You will understand one day, Buck."

"What does that mean?"

"Your cab just pulled up," Elizabeth said.

"Oh, I have to go. We will talk again next week."

"Yes! I will see you next week," Elizabeth said.

As Buck left the spot, he saw the cab sitting by the entrance. He hurried to it and opened the door. "Sorry if I'm late," Buck said.

"No, I am early by a few minutes," the cabbie replied.

After Buck got situated in the cab, the cab sped away. Buck was deep in thought. He and the cabbie, never spoke. When he pulled up in front of Buck's house, Buck got out and began to take his wallet out of his pocket, before he could retrieve the cash, the cab pulled away.

When he entered the hall, Olivia yelled down, "Dinner is at five o'clock."

"See you guys then," Buck answered back.

He felt a whole lot better knowing he shared everything with Rose, he never realized some things he never mentioned. When he went to sit on the sofa, he felt the wad of paper in his back pocket. He took the papers out and walked to the bedroom. He had a box that he kept all his notes in; he flung the notes in there. He returned to the sofa and clicked on the T.V.

He heard a preacher say, "Who knows the requirements to be a righteous person?" To Buck, he heard this same sermon before. He turned the channel. This time, he heard, "Jesus was righteous. What requirements does it take to be righteous?"

He turned to a children's channel and settled on cartoons.

At a quarter to five, he headed upstairs. Willy was looking at the Times Union newspaper. Olivia was standing at the stove.

"How did it go today?" Olivia asked.

"It went very well, I felt her kiss me again."

"Can Willy and I go next week with you?" Olivia asked.

"Any time you want to go, you're invited. Willy will tell you that a one-sided conversation is kind of hard to understand."

"I think we should go," Willy added.

"Then we will all go," Buck said.

"When are you going over to visit you friends at the State Education Department?" Olivia asked.

"Who?" Buck answered.

"She means Jamie and Peter," Willy said.

"I don't know, maybe tomorrow night. Want to come?"

"No," Willy and Olivia said in unison.

For some reason, Buck felt tomorrow night would work out great.

After dinner, Buck went back downstairs; he watched some T.V. and hoped he would dream of Rose again. That night, when he went to say his prayer, he asked God to let him dream of Rose.

That night his dream of Rose was so vivid, he thought he could touch her arm and it felt solid. But, of course, to Buck, it was only a dream.

Chapter Fourteen

Monday morning was another beautiful morning. He remembered the way the sun gleamed off of the statue of Elizabeth. At eight o'clock, he went upstairs. Olivia's breakfast was so delicious. When Buck thought about it, everything thing seemed a little better.

"You hoping to talk with the president tonight?" Willy asked.

"Yes, and if I do, I will also be able to talk with Philip Schuyler, too."

"How so?" Olivia asked.

"The president told me he would alert Philip Schuyler that I was heading to his statue."

"You are writing all of this stuff down, aren't you?" Olivia asked.

"Yeah! I have a box in my bedroom with all my notes in it."

"Good to hear that, keep them safe," Olivia added.

When Buck was ready to go back downstairs, he started for the door. Olivia said, "Wait, I got you something and I have been forgetting to give it to you."

Olivia walked into the bedroom and returned with a large box, "Here you go, Buck."

Buck saw the picture on the outside, it was a vacuum cleaner. "Thanks so much. I would have never thought about getting one until the dust got about an inch high," he then laughed.

"I got a new one for us and knew you would need one."

"Let me pay you for it," Buck said.

"No, get out of here," Olivia replied.

"Willy, she's kicking me out," Olivia stepped up and gave Buck a kiss on the cheek, "We love you Buck."

"I love you guys, too."

He brought the box downstairs and opened it. He placed the vacuum in the tiny closet in the kitchen. He noticed there was an old broom and mop in there. He placed the box on the back porch, it would go out with the trash Friday.

He started to look at the monument book, he wanted to read more about Schuyler. When he opened the book, he saw the statue of Moses again. *I talked with Moses*, he thought. The thought was overwhelming.

He found the information on Philip Schuyler and re-read it all. *It would be good to talk with Jamie and Pete again*, he thought. In his mind, they were becoming old buddies. He laughed to himself at the thought. He thumbed through the book wondering who he would meet next. There were many statues, but none caught his eye.

He watched some T.V. and had a sandwich and soda for lunch. He heard someone walking down the stairs. He yelled, "Come in," before they reached the door. Olivia opened the door and said, "How did you know I was coming to see you, I could have been going out."

"I didn't know. I don't know why I yelled come in."

"I just wanted you to know we are eating at four instead of five today."

"No problem, you going out after dinner?"

"Yeah! I'm going over to visit my sister."

"Tell Betsey and Louie I said hi!"

"I will. What time you heading over to see Jamie and the others?"

"I'll leave about six-thirty. I am going to walk, I need the exercise."

"Don't expect an argument from me. See you later," Olivia said. She headed back upstairs.

Buck thought the next time he had to go to Newburgh, he would have Louie take him to Washington's Headquarters; if there was time, maybe to his last encampment. He learned that it was located in New Windsor or something like that. He laid the book down and clicked on the T.V. again. He turned the channel as soon as he saw a preacher walking up to a podium. He wondered how come, when he turns the T.V. on, it's always on a religious channel? He knew it wasn't when he turned it off. The thought floated from his mind faster than it entered it.

He settled for 'Gun Smoke' again, he could watch them over and over and always enjoyed it. His favorite old western was Sugar Foot. It was about a young man who traveled all over the country. He carried a law book. No matter where he ended up, he always solved whatever problem there was with the law book.

He leaned back on the sofa to watch Festus solve a problem he also created. He fell asleep, when he woke up, it was ten minutes to four. He went into the bathroom and washed up really quick, then headed upstairs.

"Come in," he heard Olivia say before he knocked on the door. This caused him to smile.

"Something really smells great," Buck said.

"It's my new body wash," Willy said.

"It's my stuff peppers with bacon wrapped around it."

Buck walked over next to Willy, "That body wash isn't working."

Olivia laughed at that.

After dinner, Olivia placed everything in the sink. "I'll be back in a couple of hours," she said and left for her sister's house.

Buck walked over to the sink and washed all the dishes and pans. Willy tried to talk him out of it, Buck insisted. Buck still had over an hour to wait before he would leave for the Education Department to visit Jamie and the others.

The hour seemed like it took two hours to go by; at least, that is how it felt.

Buck started his walk over at a leisurely pace. He looked forward to hearing Jamie's voice. When he reached Washington Avenue, he glanced over at Schuyler. *See you later, I hope*, he thought.

He looked at the Tri-County Vietnam Veterans monument in the center of Lafayette Park. The statues of the soldiers there looked tired. He now considered it as a possible endeavor.

As he reached the Education Department steps, he walked up to Jamie and Pete. "Are you here?" he asked. He heard no reply. He was a little earlier than usual. He sat for a moment. He decided to stay seated for ten minutes. After five minutes, he heard, "Hi! Buck."

"Hi! Jamie. How are you on this beautiful day?" Buck heard her giggle.

"I'm in Heaven," she said and giggled again.

"I should have reworded that. How is everything in Heaven?"

"It's getting pretty exciting."

"Really, why?" Buck asked.

"Don't really know, something's happening."

"And you don't know what it is?"

"I have no idea."

"Hi! Buck."

"Hi! Pete. Jamie says something's happening in Heaven, but she doesn't know what."

"Something very exciting, I don't know what it is either."

"How do you know something's happening?" Buck asked.

"There is a lot of singing. Everyone is wearing a beautiful smile."

"I would picture everyone in Heaven singing and smiling all the time, they're in Heaven."

"I know what you're saying and in a sense, you are right. But lately, everything has been kicked up a notch."

"When you find out, let me know."

"I will," Pete said.

"Me, too," Jamie added.

"You going to check on George Washington tonight?"

"Yeah! If he is there, I will be able to talk with Philip Schuyler. The President said the next time I see him, he will alert Philip to go to the statue in front of City Hall."

"I hope that works out the way you want it to," Jamie said.

"I should have Rose' statue done within a month."

"I thought you said it would take three months?" Pete said.

"I did, but some strange things have been happening at the Bronze Works."

"Like what?" Pete asked.

Buck told them all he knew. They both thought it sounded strange, too.

"I think it is great that you will be able to talk to Rose that soon," Jamie said.

"That goes for me, too," Pete added.

"Something's happening, we are being called away," Jamie said.

"We will see you the beginning of next week, Buck," Pete said.

Buck, somehow, could feel them leave the sight. He wondered why everyone he has been talking to was being called away.

He walked over to George Washington's statue, "Mr. President, are you here?"

"Yes, Buck and how are you today?"

"I feel great, but something strange is happening."

"What do you mean?"

"Lately some of the statues I talked to were being called away,"

"That does happen up here from time to time."

"Have you ever been called away?" Buck asked.

"Yes, once I had a cousin who died and I was called away to escort him."

"I was hoping I didn't do something wrong that was forcing them to be called away."

"That would never happen to you, some people maybe, not you."

"Thank you, Mr. President, that makes me feel better."

"Did you want to talk with Philip today?" President Washington asked.

"That would be great if he is available."

"He wants to meet you. I think it would be his pleasure."

Buck couldn't understand why meeting him would be a historic figures pleasure. The thought drifted from his mind instantly.

"If you would like to leave now, I will tell him you are coming."

"Thank you, Mr. President, that is very nice of you."

"I will see you at the beginning of next week."

"I will come back, I don't know exactly what day," Buck felt the President leave this site.

As Buck walked down to speak with Philip Schuyler, he was thinking of all that he had read. Buck thought he would call him Senator Schuyler, he hoped this would be proper. As he walked in that direction only, two cars passed him. *It's good that there is not a lot of traffic*, he thought. After all, his statue was in the middle of the road.

He walked up to the front of the statue, "Senator Schuyler, are you here?"

"Yes, I am Buck. I have heard a great deal about you."

"I have read a great deal about you."

"You have, like what?"

"You served in the N.Y.S. Assembly and Senate in the Continental Congress in the U.S. Senate. Your daughter married Alexander Hamilton. You were a great leader and soldier."

"History has been very kind to me, I see," Philip Schuyler said.

"My wife is buried in the same cemetery as you. The Albany Rural Cemetery. Your mansion is a historical sight and also your home in Schuylerville. You are one of Albany's most famous sons. You served with and as a Founding Father of the United States of America. You have a great deal to be proud of."

"Thank you, Buck, for all of your kind words. But you left out that I met Buck Thompson."

"Thank you for your kind words, Senator Schuyler."

"I will see you at the beginning of next week?" Senator Schuyler said.

"Yes, but I don't know what day," Buck answered.

He felt Philip Schuyler leave this sight. He felt that with everyone he talked with today. It started with Moses. All these thoughts left his mind immediately.

As he walked home, he thought of what he would tell Rose about his meetings today. The dream of Rose came back into his thoughts. What joyful thoughts they were. On the walk home, he felt inspired, he would be talking to Rose sooner then he thought. So far, he has talked with everyone he wanted to. Moses was the only surprise. It was truly a great surprise.

Buck looked up and thanked God again for letting him talk and hear statues. He didn't ask God, but he hoped he would still have this ability, so he would be able to talk with Rose.

He thought about Wednesday night, he wanted to ask Olivia if they were going back to the same church or was she thinking about going to a new one. As he approached his new house, he decided to ask Olivia tomorrow. He wanted to go to sleep in hopes of dreaming of his Rose.

He took a shower and then headed to bed, he said his prayer and thanked God for the day. What a great day it was. This was his last thought before he fell asleep.

God granted him his request, he dreamt of Rose.

In his dream, he saw Rose walking towards him with the most beautiful smile. He walked towards her, when they met, they embraced. Buck felt her body, it was solid. When they kissed, Buck felt her lips touch his. Buck gazed at their surroundings; in the sky above them was the brightest of lights. It covered them with warmth and kindness. Buck looked into Rose' eyes and saw a never-ending eternity filled with love. Buck had never felt this way before. A calmness centered around them. Lighting the love they had for one another.

When Buck woke up, he laid still with his eyes closed and the picture of Rose still in his mind. He threw her a kiss and opened his eyes.

He put the kettle on to heat up the water for coffee. According to the clock, it was seven-eleven. A smile came over his face thinking of the dream God provided. He only had one question in his mind. We never talked, he wondered why, but this thought like so many others lately was erased from his mind. It was Tuesday morning and Buck thought about what he may do today.

He had no plans, he didn't need to go to the store. He would check with Willy and Olivia to see if they had something, they wanted him to do. When he thought about last night and the discussions he had with Jamie, Pete, and President Washington and to finally talk with Philip Schuyler, all his thoughts were pleasant. He hadn't thought about the feeling he had when they left their spot. He didn't remember the entire conversation with any of them. These, too, were memories that vanished from his mind. He showered and got dressed. He sipped his coffee and thanked God again for the dream he had. He noticed that it was seven fifty-five. He headed upstairs so Olivia wouldn't have to call him for breakfast. As he reached the top of the stairs, he heard Willy say, "It's open."

When he entered, Willy was reading the Times Union Newspaper and Olivia was at the stove.

"Good morning, Buck," Olivia said with a joyful sound in her voice.

Willy folded up the newspaper and asked, "How did it go last night?"

"It went perfectly, I talked with Jamie and Pete. I then went over to see if the President was there."

"Was he?" Willy asked.

"Yes, and we discussed," somehow Buck couldn't remember what he and President Washington talked about, "Doesn't matter. I got to talk with Philip Schuyler and that was very interesting."

"Like how?" Olivia asked as she placed breakfast on the table. Buck grabbed three buttermilk pancakes and two pieces of bacon.

"We talked about all the offices he held, about the Schuyler mansion, and his historical house in Schuylerville. I think he was impressed with what I had read about him. He said he would see me the beginning of the week. I told all of them that I didn't know what day I would be there. I should have thought about that before I visited."

"It seems to me that they're there almost any night you go," Willy said.

"You're right, I guess, I really didn't have to mention a certain day. I have no plans for today, do you guys have anything you need me to do?"

"Yes!" Olivia said.

"What?"

"Take it easy today, this is probably the first day you haven't had plans."

"I will," was all he said.

Chapter Fifteen

When Buck was finished with breakfast, he said his 'see you later,' and headed back downstairs. When he entered his apartment, he felt a warmth that he had never felt before. This was because he had a place to call his home. The new furniture brought a soft glow to everything. *Life was good,* he thought and it can only get better with his statue of Rose.

He picked up the Monument Book and for no reason he could think of, he had the urge to bring it back to the library. It was near noon when he called a cab to do just that. The cab appeared within minutes and when they reached the Albany Public Library, Buck asked the driver to wait. He went in and walked up to the desk.

"Mrs. Burke, I am returning this book."

"So, did you find what you wanted to find?" she asked.

Buck felt puzzled. "I must have," was his reply. He left the library and took the cab back home. When he reached his house, he paid the cabbie. As he walked towards the front door, all memory of the library left his mind. He looked around and wondered why he was outside. He went into his place and sat down on the sofa. He turned on the T.V., ready to hear a preacher, but was delighted that a cartoon came on.

A short time later, he heard someone coming down the stairs. He heard them coming to his door.

"Come in," he said, it was Willy.

"Did I hear you go out before?"

"Yeah! But I couldn't think of what I wanted to do. I hope I'm not losing my memory."

"You were gone over a half hour."

"No, I wasn't, I walked out and then came back in."

At this point, Buck looked at the clock, it was one-thirty.

Willy heard Olivia calling him. "See you in a little bit," he said, then he went back upstairs.

Buck looked at the clock. *Where did that hour go?* he thought. *He must have fallen asleep for a little while*, he also thought.

He watched T.V. for the next couple of hours. He started to doze off when the doorbell rang. Buck sat up, wiped his eyes, and headed for the front door.

He was a little startled to see the cabbie from last Sunday standing there. Then he remembered. "You pulled away before I could pay you Sunday," he said.

"I'm not here for that, I wanted to know what time did you want me to pick you up this Sunday?"

Without hesitation, Buck said, "Ten o'clock would be fine."

"See you then," the cabbie said with a smile.

Buck walked back into his apartment and thought, *Why did I say that.* He knew he always left at eight o'clock. He then remembered that Olivia and Willy wanted to go. He knew for sure that Olivia would be making breakfast. Ten o'clock would work out fine.

At four-thirty, he headed upstairs for dinner. Willy was in the living room watching T.V. Olivia was at the stove cooking something that smelled great. "What's on the menu tonight?" Buck asked.

"Pasta and meatballs," Olivia answered. Buck watched as Olivia poured the Rigatoni in the boiling water.

"Is there anything I can do?" Buck asked.

"Will you slice the Italian bread, it's on the table."

Buck saw the bread knife alongside of it; as he picked up the knife, Olivia handed him a cutting board. "I guess I would need that," he added with a smile.

"How is your day of rest going so far?" she asked.

"Fine, everything is fine. Oh, the cabbie that usually takes me to the cemetery, well, at least, the last couple of times, stopped by to ask what time did we want to leave."

Olivia spoke up and said, "I hope you said ten o'clock, not eight o'clock, I plan on giving you a special breakfast Sunday."

"I said ten o'clock without any hesitation. It wasn't until I came back in that I thought I usually leave at eight o'clock. But, somehow, I was sure you were making breakfast."

"It's a God thing," Willy said as he walked into the kitchen.

"It's not nice to joke about God that way," Olivia stated.

"I am not joking. I have saw or heard so many things for the past few weeks, you convinced me it has to be God."

"I'm glad to hear you say that," Olivia said and then threw him a kiss.

As a joke, Buck ducked.

"Why, did you do that?" Olivia asked.

"I didn't know if it would be one of those really wet kisses."

Olivia and Willy laughed.

"You're a great cook," Buck said and added, "No matter what you cook, I can count on it being great."

Olivia smiled and said, "That's really sweet." Then added, "Why don't I hear that from you."

"Honey bunch, you are the greatest cook in the world," Willy said.

"It sounds like you're trying to make up for lost time," Buck added.

Willy put his arm around Olivia's waist as she set the meatballs on the table, "You know I love everything about you, always have and always will. That includes your smile, your kind heart, and you great cooking. If you want, I will write up a list."

"Thank you, honey. I appreciate you and all that you do."

"Can we start saying a prayer before we eat from now on?" Buck asked.

"Yes, from now on, we will. Every night, someone different will say the prayer. Tonight, we will start with you, Buck."

"It would be my pleasure," Buck said.

Olivia finished up and sat down. Willy started to reach for the meatballs; Olivia slapped his hand with hers.

"Dear God, thank you for the day and for everything you do for us. For this bounty you have provided. Please watch over us and protect us from evil. Thank you, once again, God for letting me dream of Rose. Thank you for giving me Willy and Olivia, who has guided me back to You. In Your name, we pray."

"That was very touching," Olivia said.

As they began eating Willy asked, "Do you have plans for tomorrow?"

Buck thought for a second and said, "Maybe, tomorrow night, I might go and visit Jamie and the rest."

"That would surprise them, seeing you were only there yesterday," Willy said.

"They have no concept of time. Every day is Sunday in Heaven," Buck added.

"Yes, you mentioned that before," Olivia said.

"Where did you get the Italian bread?" Buck asked.

"At Prinzio's Bakery on Delaware Avenue. They only sell rolls and bread."

"They have the best hard rolls in town," Willy added.

"The bread is really good."

After dinner, they all helped with the clean-up. "I'll do the dishes," Buck said.

"Oh, I forgot to thank you for doing the dishes the other night, Buck."

"How did you know it was me?"

"Willy hasn't washed a dish in all the years we have been married."

"You guys clean off the table, I got the dishes," Olivia said.

After everything was done, Buck headed back downstairs and put water on for coffee. The house seemed to become a home every time he walked in lately. He loved the feeling it gave him.

When the kettle began to whistle, Buck had his cup ready and poured his coffee. He walked into the living room and sat on the sofa. He clicked on the T.V. and remembered he forgot to ask Olivia about church. He would be sure to ask her tomorrow morning at breakfast. Then he thought he wouldn't be able to visit Jamie and the rest until Thursday. At this thought, he saw his week expanding.

He watched Highway to Heaven, it was followed by Touched by an Angel. He enjoyed both of these shows.

About ten o'clock, he felt tired and went to bed. He decided that from now on, he would kneel at his bed side and say his nightly prayer.

When he woke up Wednesday morning, he didn't remember dreaming. He looked up and thanked God for another day.

At seven-fifty, he headed upstairs. Olivia was reading the paper this time, "Willy's in the bathroom," she said without taking her eyes off of what she was reading.

"What about church tonight, we going back to the same one?"

"I haven't thought about it, I really don't want to go back there. That preacher couldn't remember what he said in his sermon and didn't remember you at all."

"What other church is there?"

"Over at the Cathedral, they have a catholic mass every evening at five o'clock, I think. I'll check it out, would you mind going to a Catholic Church?"

"Will God be there?"

Olivia looked at Buck, "God is everywhere."

"Then let's go," Buck said.

"We will eat at four and take a cab over after dinner."

"Would you mind if I don't come back with you. I would like to stop and see Jamie and the rest of my new friends."

"Not at all."

After breakfast, Buck headed back down stairs. He felt like just taking a walk. When he walked outside, the warmth of the sun made him feel very good. He headed north on Pearl Street, he would walk a few blocks down and cut over to Broadway and walk back.

As he walked, he saw children playing and laughing. *That's a blessed sight*, he thought. He heard a girl singing on the steps in front of her house. "Very good, Missy," he told her; she smiled and thanked him. *What a wonderful day,* was another thought that came into his mind. Everything seemed so perfect, even the air smelled sweet.

As he was approaching his house, Rose appeared in his mind. They held hands to the door. He gave a sigh, if felt so real. "Thank You, God," he said again.

When Buck went inside, he looked for the monument book. He must have misplaced it. He knew he would come across it eventually. He looked forward to talking with Jamie, Pete, and the President and Philip Schuyler. Somehow, tonight would be special. Buck didn't know why, he just had that feeling.

At three-thirty, he went up-stairs. Willy yelled, "Come in," before he got to the door. He walked in and saw Willy sitting at the kitchen table.

"Where is Livy?" Buck asked.

"She brought the trash downstairs," Willy answered.

Buck heard her coming back up. By the time she walked in the back door, she was completely out of breath. Buck went to the sink and got her a glass of water. "Little sips," Buck said; in a few moments, she was fine. Willy got worried, "Are you okay?" Willy asked, then said, "I'll take the trash down from now on."

Olivia stood up and walked towards the stove. "Are you okay, Livy?" Buck asked again. Olivia took a deep breath and smiled and said, "I am a whole lot better."

She uncovered a dish that was on the stove, "We're having hamburgers, Willy get the potato salad out of the fridge." Willy retrieved the salad and placed it on the table. Buck heard the hamburgers sizzling in the fry pan. He watched as Olivia flipped the burgers. Dinner will be ready in a minute.

She brought the pan over to the table and unloaded a large burger on each plate. Willy scooped up a spoonful of potato salad, he placed it on Olivia's plate. He scooped another and put it on Buck's plate, the final scoop went on his plate. Olivia reminded them about their prayer before meals. After the prayer, they ate.

After dinner, they cleaned up and then headed to the Cathedral Church on Madison Avenue. Buck noticed no one was there to greet them at the door. They walked in and the size of the church was the biggest he had ever been in. They sat in a pew that was in the middle of the church. Buck saw a priest walking up the aisle. He stopped at their pew and walked in and shook hands with Willy and Olivia and when he turned to Buck, he froze. "Do I know you, sir?"

"I don't think so," Buck said as he shook hands with the priest.

"Tonight, the service will be held by our bishop."

None of them knew what a bishop was; none of them have ever attended a mass before. Buck did feel like God was there, that made him feel better.

As the Bishop walked out with two younger priests on either side, all the people there stood up. "Do what they do," Olivia said in a whisper.

When the congregation knelt down, they knelt down, whatever the congregation did, they followed. Buck spent the time talking to God. At one point, everyone stood up; Olivia had to nudge Buck, he had his face down.

The Bishop climbed some stairs and appeared above the congregation. He talked about some things happening with the church, then he began a sermon. Buck sort of laughed to himself when he heard the word 'Righteous.' He listened and heard the bishop say that he felt God was with them here tonight. The bishop went on to say that something was happening, he didn't know what it was, but he felt a change occurring. Buck kept talking to God. He felt as if God was listening.

After the sermon, the bishop went back to the altar; he reached for something that was behind a Gold door. Olivia whispered again, "This must be their last supper." She heard him say as he held up the round piece of bread, "This is my body." Then he held up the cup of wine and said, "This is my blood." Then she watched some of the congregation walk to the front of the church. "Should we go?" Willy asked.

"I don't think so," Olivia said. At the end, she heard the bishop say, "Go, the mass has ended." She didn't understand the response. Her, Willy, and Buck began to leave.

"This is a very beautiful church," Buck said.

"They must have a lot of money," Willy said, only to feel Olivia jab him in the ribs again.

"Sorry," he said, "I think it would cost at least a thousand dollars a month just to heat this place."

"I can't believe you always associate money with everything," Olivia said.

When they got outside, Buck said, "I am going to head over and see my friends."

Olivia and Willy knew what he meant. Willy and Olivia walked up Madison Avenue to hail a cab. Buck headed north on Eagle Street, which would take him right over to the statue of Philip Schuyler. It was still daylight, but that part of the city was deserted. When he reached Philip Schuyler, he asked,

"Senator Schuyler, are you here?" There was no response. He asked again, "Senator Schuyler, are you here?" There still was no response. He decided to walk up Washington Avenue to visit Jamie and Pete. After he climbed the steps, he asked, "Jamie, Pete are you here?" There was no answer. He decided to wait twenty minutes, he was early.

He waited the twenty minutes and tried again, there still was no answer. He sat there and waited another twenty minutes and tried again. Still no answer.

He walked over to George Washington's statue, "Mr. President, are you here?" He received no answer. He waited a little while more and tried one last time, again no answer. He sat on the bench that was close by.

"God, did you take away my ability to talk with statues?" He didn't expect an answer. Then he remembered what Moses said, "God answers every question." As that went through his mind, he felt a calm wash over him. As if God was telling him everything is alright. "Thank You, God," he said, then headed back to his house.

He felt as if his ability to talk with statues was still with him. Every day got him closer to be able to talk with his Rose.

When he got home, he settled in for the night. When he was ready to go to bed, he knelt down and prayed, "God, if it's Your will, let me see my Rose tonight."

God granted him his prayer, he saw his Rose running towards him. When she reached him, she placed her arms around him, she whispered in his ear, "I am so proud of you." He didn't understand, but he felt her in his arms. No other words were spoken. Again, Buck saw a bright light above them. It looked like clouds below them. He held her the entire time.

When he woke up Thursday morning, the dream seemed to fade fast. He could always picture her face in front of him, but the dream was gone.

He went upstairs for breakfast. Olivia was at the stove humming a tune, Buck couldn't actually remember the title of it. Willy walked out of the bathroom fixing his shirt.

"How did it go last night?" Willy asked. Olivia stopped humming to hear what Buck had to say.

"No one was around last night, Jamie and Pete weren't there, President Washington wasn't there and neither was Philip Schuyler. I thought that I might have lost my ability to talk with statues."

"Did you?" Olivia asked.

"I asked God, I didn't expect an answer, but then I remembered what Moses said, 'God answers every one.' Then when I looked up, I felt a calm come over me that assured me I still have the ability."

"This is truly amazing," Olivia said.

"Of course, it's amazing, it's a *God* thing," Willy added.

"You going to try again tonight?" Olivia asked.

"No! I don't have to," Buck said, then added, "Somehow, I feel that God will tell me why I have this ability. I feel it will be in the near future."

After breakfast, Buck headed downstairs; he wanted to look for the monument book.

He searched every room, he couldn't find it. He didn't panic like most people would have done. *It will turn up*, he thought.

He turned on the T.V. and cartoons were on again. He watched for about an hour, then the phone rang. "Hello!" he said, then he heard some static. He again said, "Hello!"

"Mr. Thompson, this is Harley Davidson from the Bronze Works. Your statue is missing. I have called the police, they are on the way over now."

"What do you mean its missing?"

"It was here last night when I left. When I came in this morning, it was gone. I don't know how this could have happened. It was just too heavy to be carried off. The building doesn't have any sign that someone broke in. I checked the video tape, which scans the room twice every hour. There it was, then it was gone."

Buck didn't know what to say, "Keep me posted, let me know whatever you hear, I will be here all day."

They hung up and Buck wondered how could this have happened. He was so close to being able to talk with his Rose. Buck was afraid to go up and tell Olivia and Willy, he was afraid to even call them. He couldn't miss any call from Harley. He sat by the phone for three hours, it rang. He picked it up so fast, he almost dropped it, "Hello!"

"Buck, this is Willy,"

"Come down," was all Buck said. He heard Willy almost running down the stairs. He opened the door and entered. It looked as if he was ready to fight.

"What's a matter?" he said half-way out of breath.

"I got a call from Newburgh, someone stole Rose' statue."

"What!"

"Harley said it was there last night, now it's gone. The police are there, as soon as he finds out anything, he will give me a call. I was afraid to call you, I didn't want to miss his call."

"This is terrible."

"I know I was so close to being able to talk with Rose."

The phone rang.

"Hello!"

"Buck, this is Harley, outside in the back, the police found the mold. I will pour another one when the bronze is delivered Monday. This will only set us back a week. I am truly sorry. The police took all the videos with them. I was going to have you come in next week to approve your statue. But the bronze I ordered for you, I will use for Rose."

"If there is anything you need from me, just give me a call."

"I will do that, this will only set us back a week," Harley said.

After their conversation, Buck felt a little better. It would only delay Rose' statue for a week.

"Is there anything we can do?" Willy asked.

"I feel better, they found the mold and he will pour a new one Monday when the bronze comes in."

"I have to go and tell Olivia, this will upset her, too," Willy said.

"Tell her it will only delay the process a week."

"I will, you coming up for dinner later?"

"Yeah, I'll be there," Buck said. He felt very calm, he had no animosity towards those who stole it, he felt no rage. *Maybe they needed the bronze to sell, to feed their kids*, this thought floated through his mind.

I guess a week is better than a month, he thought. *I will have to tell all of this to Rose this Sunday*, he also thought.

Buck heard the stair lift coming down the stairs, he knew it was Olivia. She walked in and went straight to Buck, she took his hands in hers.

"I am so very sorry. If you want, I will bring your dinner down later."

"No, that's okay, I would prefer to come up," Buck answered.

Olivia left to go back upstairs. Buck sat there in the silence for a while and then clicked on the T.V. for some noise. He heard a song playing during a commercial 'Everything's Going to be Alright.' He felt this could be a message from God, at least he hoped.

Most of the rest of the day, he felt fine, he thought he should feel numb. That didn't happen, he kept reassuring himself. *This will only delay the process by a week,* these thoughts filled his head for the entire day.

At four-thirty, he headed upstairs, again, something smelled great. He was nearing the top step when Olivia opened the door and walked back to the stove.

"How you doing?" Olivia asked as he walked through the door.

"I feel fine, I could even say I feel good, very good."

"We're glad to hear that," Willy said.

"I thought you would be very upset with everything that had happened," Olivia said.

"I don't know why but I never did get upset. Disappointed, yes, upset, no."

"Do you have plans for Friday?" Willy asked.

"No, not really. How about I treat you both for dinner? It will give you a night off," he said to Olivia.

"I would like a night off," she replied with a smile.

"Where do you want to go?" Willy asked.

"What would you suggest?" he asked Willy.

"How about The Old Steer Steak House on Central Avenue?"

"That sounds good to me, how about you, Livy?"

"A night off, I don't care where we go, McDonald's would be fine," she replied, again, wearing her beautiful smile.

After dinner, Willy got up and began to fill the sink to do the dishes.

"What are you doing?" Olivia asked.

"You sit down. I will handle the dishes," he replied.

"Buck, thank you for rubbing off on Willy," Olivia added.

Buck smiled as he watched Olivia walked up behind Willy and kissed him on the cheek. "Love you," was all she said.

"Thank you, Buck, for helping us fall in love again," Willy said.

After everything was done and dishes were put away, they all sat at the kitchen table and had their cup of coffee.

After his cup of coffee, Buck excused himself and headed back downstairs. He turned on the T.V. and watched Bonanza. This was another one of his favorite T.V. shows.

When he got ready for bed, he knelt down and prayed. He thanked God for the day, for the guidance he had provided Buck. Then he said, "I know lately I have asked for a lot, please let me dream of my Rosebud."

Chapter Sixteen

His dream was so vivid, he heard singing all around them. When he looked at Rose, he thought his heart would burst. He looked up and said, "Thank You, God." He knew God would know why he said that.

There was a point when they were holding hands, he felt Rose squeeze his and he squeezed hers back. They still never talked. Buck would never think about that until he woke up.

When he woke up, the dream was still in his mind, it did not fade away. Again, he looked up and thanked God. He went in to the bathroom and took a shower and shaved. He felt something, but couldn't describe it. Then bubbly came to mind. He did feel bubbly.

He went upstairs for breakfast, Olivia made pancakes again. She also fried up some breakfast sausage.

"How were you last night?" Olivia asked.

"I had a beautiful dream of Rose, we walked together. We stared into each other's eyes. I felt her squeeze my hand and I squeezed hers. It was so vivid, everything I saw is still in my mind."

They all decided to go out for dinner at four-thirty. Buck spent some of the day looking for the monument book. He assured himself it would turn up. He started to write up some notes to take Sunday and share with Rose. It wasn't a very busy week, so he decided he could remember everything that happened. Willy and Livy would be with him. They would be able to help him out if he needed help.

They gathered at Buck's place, Willy called a cab. Olivia was looking at the furniture, "Buck, I think I would have picked out everything you did, it goes perfect."

Buck smiled at his achievement.

The cab beeped and all left for the Steer Steak House.

"I got this, I am going to use my debit card," Buck said.

"I have some cash on me if you need it," Willy added.

"I got this!" Buck said again.

The waitress brought over the menus and asked, "What would you like to drink?"

"I'll take a beer," Buck said.

"Me, too," Willy added.

"I'll have a glass of white wine," Olivia said.

The menu was gigantic, it had to be two-foot-tall and a foot and a half wide.

"Prime rib looks good, but it might be more then I can eat," Buck said.

Without looking away from her menu, Olivia said, "Get a doggy bag, put the rest in the fridge."

"This is why we need women," Buck said aloud.

"The prime rib looks good for me, too," Willy said.

"Let's make that three," Olivia said as the waitress brought their drinks over.

Buck gave her the order. Olivia held up her drink and said, "I want to make a toast," the men raised their glass of beer, "To Buck, for blessing us in so many ways."

"Cheers," Willy added.

"To me, it has been both of you who have blessed my life," Buck said.

It took thirty minutes before the meal came. Buck and Willy were on their second glass of beer while Olivia almost had a full glass of wine. The waitress came over holding a huge tray. Another waitress helped her set the plates out with all the sides done family style.

"This is way too much for me," Olivia said, Buck and Willy agreed. The prime rib was three inches high and covered the entire plate.

"We will all be taking home leftovers," Willy said.

Buck told Willy and Olivia to wait; he grabbed an empty plate and cut his prime rib in three pieces. He stacked Olivia and Willy's prime rib on another plate and shared what he cut up with them both.

"Maybe you could give the rest to Betsey, for her, and Louie," Buck said.

"That's sweet Buck, we'll do that."

After they all ate as much as they could, they still had some prime rib on their plates. Buck asked the waitress to wrap up the rest to be taken home. When she returned, she had two large bags.

Buck handed the waitress his debit card, "This is for the meal," then he handed her some cash, "This is for you."

The waitress left and returned with a slip, for Buck to sign.

"Thank you so very much," the waitress said to Buck.

"Could you call us a cab?" he asked the waitress.

"Consider it done," she replied.

The cab came soon, they were home a few minutes after seven. "You want to stop up for some coffee?" Olivia asked.

"I think I'm going to go inside and relax," Buck answered.

Willy was adjusting his belt for the third time.

Buck walked into his place and went into the living room. He looked around and was pleased everything did go together like Olivia said.

He turned on the T.V. and sat on the sofa, he watched a movie. He decided to turn on a country music channel. He laid back and listened to a lot of his favorite hits. He began to fall asleep while Randy Travis was 'Digging Up Bones.' He woke up at one in the morning. He went into the bedroom and remembered to say a prayer. As soon as he got in bed, he fell asleep.

He got up at six-thirty, showered and shaved. He got dressed and went upstairs at seven-forty. He tapped on the door, Olivia opened it, "Sorry, Buck," she said.

Buck saw that the table was set; dishes next to the stove had eggs, bacon, and toast sitting on them.

"Where's Willy?"

"He'll be back in a second, he had to run over to the store and get milk and butter."

Olivia hadn't finished what she was saying and Buck could hear Willy coming up the stairs. Willy put the milk and butter on the table and took a seat. "What you doing today?" he asked Buck. Before Buck could answer, Olivia said, "I'm going over to Betsey's and bring over that prime rib, if anyone would like to go, you're welcome to."

"I think I am going for a walk," Buck said.

"I'm going to stay home and relax, maybe watch some T.V.," Willy added.

After breakfast, the three went their separate ways. Buck headed downstairs to get his umbrella in case it did rain. As he was leaving, Olivia was coming down on the stair lift. She had the two bags from last night's dinner on her lap.

"You need a hand with that?" Buck asked.

"No, they're not that heavy."

Buck walked out of the house and crossed the street, he headed for Broadway. He traveled north on Broadway for a block when he heard music coming from a first-floor window of a two-story brick house. As he got closer, he saw movement inside the window. A daddy was singing and dancing with his little girl. *This would melt the coldest heart*, he thought.

Farther down the street, he saw two young boys trying to play one video game. This sparked them yelling at each other while never taking their eyes off the game. Then he spotted an elderly woman sitting on her porch, "Good morning," Buck said. The woman turned her eyes away from Buck. She looked scared, so Buck moved on. As he turned a corner, a little girl almost ran into him. "Whoa, Missy!" he said. She looked up at him and asked, "Are you God?"

"No, God's a lot more beautiful than I am."

"You look beautiful to me," she said.

"Where is your momma?"

"She is sleeping."

"Does she know your outside playing?"

The little girl lowered her eyes to the ground and softly said, "No."

"I want you to go back into your house and wait until your momma wakes up, then ask her if you can go out. Will you do that for me?"

She looked up at Buck and said, "Yes," she ran into the house.

Buck moved down a few houses farther and waited to see if she came back out. He asked God to watch over the little girl and to help her mother. Buck felt as if God told him her mother worked a double shift, they will be fine. A calm came over Buck. "Thank you, God," Buck said.

He walked a few houses farther and saw an elderly gentleman sitting on the bottom step of a porch. "Good morning!" Buck said.

The man looked up from the step and said, "How are you doing?"

"I'm doing fine, what's your name?" Buck asked.

"Grady," was all he said.

"What's your last name?"

The man raised his head and looked at Buck in the eyes and said, "I don't know."

"Do you live here?"

"I don't know," was the man's reply.

Buck walked up the steps and rang the bell. A woman came to the door, "Does this man live here?"

"No, he is my friend's father, he has Alzheimer's. I'll call her."

It was only a minute before Buck saw a woman, seven houses down, come out and call for her father. Buck helped the man to his feet and guided him to his daughter.

"Thank you very much, we try to lock him in, but he manages to get out."

She guided him up the few steps to the house, before she closed the door, she said, "Thanks again." Buck watched as she closed the door, then he heard her set the lock.

Across the street, he saw a man yelling at the sky, he wasn't talking to God, he was cussing too much for that. At first, Buck was afraid to cross the street. He did it anyway, he walked up behind the man and placed his hand on the man's shoulder. The man froze, he turned slowly towards Buck, "You saved me, you saved me. You sent the demons away. They said the only way to get rid of them would be to kill myself." The man fell to his knees, "You sent them away, you sent them away. Thank you, thank you. Are you a preacher?"

"No, I am just a friend."

"No, you're an angel of God, you, drove the demons away."

"Do you have money for food?" Buck asked.

"Yes, I do. Thank you, you saved me."

"Where do you live?"

"I live on Bleeker Street."

"Do you want me to hail you a cab?" Buck asked.

"Yes, please. You saved me. How can I pay you back?"

Buck saw a cab coming towards them, he waved it down, "Now give this man your address and he will take you home."

"How can I repay you?" the man asked a second time.

"Go to church," Buck said.

"I will every Sunday, I promise. I'll go to church every Sunday."

Buck helped the man into the cab, he looked at the cabbie, it was the same young man who didn't except his money last week. "We still on for Sunday, ten o'clock?" the cabbie asked.

"Yes, we are," Buck replied.

"I'll handle this, take care," the cabbie said and then drove off.

A real nice guy, Buck thought about the cabbie.

A lot happened in a two-block area, he thought. The rest of the walk was uneventful. Except for one incident that Buck didn't notice. A block away from his house, it started to rain. By the time Buck got his umbrella out of his back pocket, it was an official down pour. He opened his umbrella, he never noticed the pouring rain never fell on him. He never noticed he didn't hear the rain hitting his umbrella. When he reached his front door, he automatically opened and closed the umbrella a few times to get the excess water off of it. He didn't notice there was none. He laid the umbrella on the floor in the hallway and went into his house. When he walked into the living room, he looked out of the window, the rain stopped and the sun came out.

Buck went into the kitchen and put the water on for a cup of coffee. He thought that he would spend most of Friday doing nothing. He heard Olivia come in the front door. She was returning from Betsey's house. He heard the stair lift take her upstairs. He remembered the elderly gentleman with Alzheimer's, he thanked God for giving him a healthy life. He asked God to watch over that man. He thought of the man who thought he saw demons. He asked God to help him, also. All of this made him feel very lucky. He and Rose had some challenges in life, there was nothing that came close to what he saw these men experience today.

He heard the kettle whistle, he fixed a cup of coffee and brought it into the living room. He turned on the T.V., it was on the Country Music Channel, someone was singing 'Love Lifted Me.' *It certainly did*, Buck thought.

He closed his eyes just to see his Rose' smile. She didn't just smile with her mouth, her entire face lit up a room with that smile. He saw her eyes twinkle as she smiled. "I will be talking to you soon," he whispered.

When he looked at the clock, it was four-thirty. *Where did the day go?* he thought. He went upstairs for dinner. Olivia yelled, "Come in," before Buck got to the door. *That seems to happen a lot*, he thought. He walked in and saw Willy working on a small device no bigger than a Rubik's Cube.

"What you got there?" Buck asked.

"It's a music box I got Olivia on our first anniversary."

"It stopped working a month later," Olivia said.

"Can I take a look at it?" Buck asked.

Willy was tapping it on the back with a screw driver. He went to hand it to Buck, as soon as Bucks fingers touched the box, it started playing.

"I fixed it," Willy exclaimed. He sat it on the table and they all listen to the beautiful melody it played. It sounded familiar.

"What's the name of that song?" Buck asked.

Olivia spoke up, "Love Me Tender."

"It was our favorite song when we got married," Willy said.

"It still is our favorite song, that's why Willy was trying to fix it."

"Rose and I had a favorite song when we got married."

"What was it?" Olivia asked.

"You might not think it was romantic, we had a special meaning about it."

"What was it?" Olivia pried.

"He's got the Whole World in His hands."

"What was the meaning?" Willy asked.

"We would be together forever, as long as God holds us in his hands. I realize it isn't great to dance to."

"No, that's beautiful," Willy said. Olivia gave Willy a loving smile.

Olivia went to the stove and brought back a plate of pork chops, a bowl of mashed potatoes, and a small bowl of black eye peas. She grabbed the bread and butter and a gravy boat filled with pork gravy. No one moved, Olivia and Buck looked at Willy. He lowered his head and said a beautiful prayer with such meaning it brought tears to Olivia's eyes. She stood up and walked over to Willy, she hugged and kissed him, she dried her eyes, and returned to her seat.

"Again, Olivia you make the tastiest meals, these pork chops melt in your mouth," Buck said.

"Betsey wanted me to thank you for the prime rib I brought over this morning."

"No thanks required, she's family," Buck said.

"How was your walk?" Willy asked Buck.

"It was heartwarming, scary, puzzling, and beautiful."

"Don't leave us hanging; explain," Willy prompted.

"I saw a daddy who was dancing with and singing to his little girl, I saw two boys trying to play one video game that caused a lot of yelling between them. I saw an elderly woman that was afraid of everything. I met a little girl who told me I looked like God. Her momma was asleep in the house. I convinced the little girl to stay in the house until her momma woke up."

"She should be turned in to Social Services," Olivia said.

"God sort of told me she worked a double shift and they would be fine."

"Then what happened?" Willy asked.

"I saw a man with Alzheimer's who left his daughters house and didn't know his name or where he lived. I got him to his daughter's house. What I saw next was a man cussing at the sky. At first, I was afraid to approach him, but I did. When I placed my hand on his shoulder, he stopped all movement and turned slowly towards me. He started yelling, 'You saved me. You scared away the demons.' After he calmed down, I waved down a cab, I knew the cabbie, he would take him home, then I headed home."

"Your day was pretty active, I watched some T.V. and took a nap," Willy said.

"I forgot to tell you, Betsey might have to move."

"Why?" Buck asked.

"Her landlord is selling her house."

Buck took a deep breath and said, "It will work out fine for Betsey and Louie."

"I hope you are right," Olivia said.

"What's your plans for Saturday?" Willy asked.

"I don't have anything planned, do you?"

"Nah!" Willy said.

"Me neither," Olivia interjected.

"I know it will be sad to tell Rose about her statue. It only adds on a week, it's a week longer then it was last week."

"Rose will understand," Olivia said.

After dinner, they had their coffee, had a little more chit chat, and then Buck left. He noticed his umbrella at the foot of the stairs. It looked dry so

Buck closed it and brought it into his house. He listened to more music on the C.M.A. channel. He forgot all about the monument book. He looked forward to going to sleep tonight in hopes of dreaming of Rose again. He decided to watch T.V., Gone with the Wind had just started. It would be on for four hours, Buck has watched it a few times. The slavery shown in the movie had Buck thank God for helping end such a terrible thing. Buck's favorite movie about slavery was 'Roots' by Alex Haley. He thought of the first night it came on, he and Rose sat together on the sofa. The president's wife, Roslyn Carter, had to explain that the movie was true to facts and would show the real way life was back then. When it came on, all the African women were, as it would have been, bare breasted. As harsh as the movie was, Buck felt proud to be a black man.

He fell asleep after the first two hours. He woke up at two-fifteen in the morning. He turned off the T.V. and went into the bedroom, he disrobed, knelt down, and said his prayer. He ended the prayer with, "if You feel it to be Your choice, let me dream of my Rose."

God granted Buck his prayer.

Chapter Seventeen

He saw his Rose standing in front of him, he took her hands in his and brought her closer. They kissed, Buck heard the singing getting louder and louder. Not deafening, but louder. Buck tried to speak, Rose placed her finger over his mouth, and led him away. The singing was the best Buck ever heard, he could not understand a single word, but this thought was erased from his mind.

He again saw the brightest of lights above them and the softest of clouds below them. They walked and just smiled at each other. Buck felt totally content with that.

When he woke up Saturday morning, there was a power of delight that engulfed him. Everything seemed to climb a notch higher. He didn't understand those thoughts, but loved the feelings they brought. He got ready to go upstairs for breakfast. He felt his heart singing, but he had no clue of why.

At seven forty-five, the phone rang. Buck picked it up and said, "Hello!"

"Hi! Buck, this is Harley Davidson. I was wondering if I could stop by tomorrow and show you pictures of your sculpture?"

"I spend my Sunday visiting with my wife, Rose."

"Would you mind if I stop by at the cemetery? That would also allow me to see where the statues will be placed."

"I guess that would be fine," Buck answered.

"When will you get there? I can get this done before your visit."

"We should be there about ten-fifteen or ten-twenty."

"Do you have others going with you? I can come some other time if you would like?"

"No! The sooner, the better."

"I will see you there," Harley said. Both men hung up.

Buck started to head upstairs and the phone rang again. Buck thought that Harley forgot something, "Hello, Harley!"

There was a pause.

"Mr. Thompson, this is Simon Templar from the credit union. It's important that I have you sign your beneficiary contract. We forgot to include your investments."

"Are you in your office? I can stop over today."

"I am in Chicago, I won't be back until late tonight. The investment firm wants you to sign this as soon as possible."

"Tomorrow is my day with Rose, I will be at the cemetery. I won't be home until four or five o'clock."

"What time will you be leaving in the morning?"

"At ten o'clock."

"Can I stop by before you leave?"

"Yes! It has to be before ten."

"I will see you before ten."

Buck hung up and the phone rang again, "Hello!"

"You coming up to eat?" Olivia asked.

"I'm on my way," Buck said and headed up. When he reached the door, Willy opened it. "Come in. I was afraid you might be sick," he said.

"I received two phone calls, one from Harley Davidson; he will meet us at the cemetery. He wants to show me the pictures of the sculpture of me, and he can also see where the two statues would go. Then Mr. Templar called, he's from the credit union, he will stop by before we leave. He needs me to sign another beneficiary contract, so you will inherit my investments. The investment firm wants these papers signed as soon as possible."

"Can't he stop by today?" Olivia asked.

"He's in Chicago, won't get in until late tonight."

"When it rains, it pours," Willy said.

Olivia made French toast for breakfast, with bacon on the side. Buck liked the way she would sprinkle cinnamon and powder sugar over the top.

After breakfast, Buck headed back down stairs. He thought about going for a walk, that thought was erased from his mind. He thought about taking Olivia and Willy out for dinner, again that thought was erased from his mind.

He walked in his bedroom to get some other clothes out of his closet. He grabbed a white shirt and hung it on the door of his bedroom. He saw a pair of white pants Rose bought him when she bought him a red blazer. They reminded him of his dreams of Rose. *They were both in white*, he thought. This thought was erased from his mind. He took out a pair of brown pants and hung them on the door next to the shirt.

He walked back into the living room and turned on the T.V. again. Randy Travis was singing a song he and his wife and another person wrote called 'I'm

Free,' the song made Buck feel that he was proud to be a Baptist. The lyric's blended into his way of thinking.

He changed the channel when the song was finished. He heard a preacher judging people that drank, not drunkard's like the Bible says. Anyone who even took a sip of any kind of alcohol was going to hell. He heard him judge people because of their assumed life style. Everyone in California was a drug addict. Before he changed the channel, he said aloud "Only God can Judge us," the channel changed by itself. This startled Buck for a moment and he thought, *God is in -charge.*

He started channel surfing until he came across a show about his life. It was about a share cropper in North Carolina who had a son and a beautiful wife. It was a white family. Buck knew many poor white families, some were share croppers. Others were, in a sense, white slaves. The Dugan family owned one of the largest farms in North Carolina. When the depression hit, they had to sell a piece here and a piece there in order to survive. Not before long, they had to sell everything. They became share croppers of the land they owned for generations. Buck became a little depressed watching the movie, he changed the channel again. He ended on a children's spy movie that he enjoyed. It seemed that the day flew by. Buck looked at the clock, it was almost five o'clock. He turned off the T.V. and headed upstairs. In the hallway, he stopped to see if he could figure out what Olivia was cooking. It smelled great, *Roast Beef.*

The door was partly opened.

"Hi, Buck!" Olivia said before he walked in.

"Is that roast beef I smell?"

"Yes, it is," Olivia answered.

Willy was at the table reading the Times Union Newspaper.

"So, what's new?" Buck asked Willy.

Willy closed up the newspaper and said, "I decided from now on I would not read about politics and street gangs. So, nothing's new according to what I read."

Buck laughed at that, "I don't ever watch the news. Once in a while, I would look through my neighbor's newspaper. I never liked what I read."

"Willy, cut the roast beef," Olivia said.

Buck watched the juices flow with every cut. His mouth watered as he anticipated eating it. Buck noticed there were no steak knives out, "You want me to take some steak knives out?"

"For what?" Olivia asked.

"To cut up our pieces of roast beef."

"My momma, always said, 'If you can't cut up roast beef with a butter knife, it's not worth eating,'" Olivia explained.

Buck said the prayer, then it was time to eat.

Buck took a piece of roast beef, he grabbed his butter knife and started cutting. The butter knife cut each piece without hesitation, "This is unbelievable," Buck said, "So tender, cooked perfectly."

"Thank you," Olivia said, then added, "Breakfast will be served at eight-twenty on the dot, tomorrow morning."

Buck nodded in agreement, mainly because his mouth was full. Tonight, Buck had to adjust his belt a few times. After dinner, before Buck left, Olivia made him promise he would be up here by eight-fifteen the latest in the morning.

When Buck got downstairs and after adjusting his belt one more time, he put water on for coffee. He walked into the living room and turned on the T.V. He thought of going to see Rose. The dreams God gave him were so perfect. He wanted to ask God for a dream again tonight. But he thought that would be pushing his luck. If God gave him one of those dreams a week, he would be satisfied.

He watched T.V. until ten o'clock and decided to go to bed. Instead he went in and took a shower, he would shave in the morning; this way, he would look good for Rose. When he got to the bedroom, he knelt down and said a prayer.

He didn't ask, but he hoped all would be well with Rose's statue. He remembered that Harley would meet them at the cemetery and Mr. Templar would stop by before they left for the cemetery. He also remembered the cab would be there at ten o'clock. He didn't feel really tired, so he clicked on the T.V. and started to watch another episode of Bonanza. Little Joe and Hoss started to fight, it was quickly ended by their father. After a while, his eyes began to feel heavy, he started to doze off.

He felt someone touch his hand, he opened his eyes, it was Rose. she helped him up and they walked again on the road of clouds. In Buck's mind, he thanked God for another dream. They walked holding hands and smiling, he heard the singing once again and spotted the bright lights above them. He felt so carefree.

They walked awhile, then Buck noticed they were no longer walking on a cloud, but a street of gold. "I'm in Heaven with you?" he asked. Rose motioned with her head *no*. She pointed up. Buck could see a golden door.

"Is that Heaven?" Rose nodded her head *yes*. It just dawned on Buck that he talked to Rose. He went to ask another question, but nothing came out. They both stopped and held each other, Buck thought, *Holding Rose, this is Heaven to me.*

Buck tried to listen to the singing, but he still could not make out any of the words. The song was divine, the singing was always on key. He just could not understand what they were singing. Rose brought him to a golden bench where they sat. Rose had her head nestled in to Buck's neck. Buck's eyes were closed, he felt truly blessed. He held her for what seemed like hours. When he opened his eyes, he was lying in bed. The T.V. was off and he still felt that carefree feeling he experienced with Rose. He got out of bed and went to the bathroom to shave.

After he shaved, he looked at the clock, it was eight-ten. He promised Olivia he would be there by eight-fifteen. He put on his white shirt and brown pants, his shoes looked like they were shined. After getting completely dressed, he headed upstairs. The door was opened and Olivia was sitting at the table. She stood up as Buck walked in. "Willy, Buck's here," Olivia said.

Willy walked in from their bedroom with a tiny box, he handed this to Buck. "What is this for?" Buck asked.

"It's for you because we love you," Olivia said.

Buck opened the tiny box, there was a heart shape golden locket attached to a fine thin golden necklace.

"Open it up," Olivia said.

When he opened the locket, there were a picture of him on one side and a picture of Rose on the other, "This is very beautiful, but I don't think I would ever wear it in public."

"It's for you to put around Rose's neck when her statue is ready."

"That is very thoughtful," he hugged Olivia and then Willy.

"Did you dream of Rose last night?" Willy asked.

Buck thought for a second, "I don't remember. Mr. Templar is supposed to come by this morning."

"Let's eat before he comes," Olivia suggested. Olivia made all of Buck's favorites; eggs over easy, home fries with onions and peppers mixed in, crispy bacon, grits with melted butter and sugar on top and fried toast.

It was Olivia's turn to say the prayer, "God, thank You for all that You do for us. We thank You for Buck who has changed our lives forever. We ask You to lead us, guide us, protect us, and please forgive us where we fail You. In Your name, I pray." They all said Amen in unison.

To Buck, this was the perfect breakfast. Willy and Olivia enjoyed it, too. After they all ate, Willy poured Buck, Olivia, and himself a cup of coffee. As he began to walk away, his foot hit the leg of the table, causing Buck's coffee to pour into his lap. It wasn't very hot. That was the good point. Olivia had

Buck go into the bathroom and sent Willy down to get him another pair of pants. The white shirt was in good shape. He didn't need a shirt, just pants.

When Willy entered Buck's house, the phone began to ring. He answered it in case it was important. "Hello!" Willy said.

"Mr. Thompson?"

"No, this is his cousin Willy, he's upstairs, can I take a message?"

"This is Simon Templar from the credit union. I was supposed to meet him before he left for the cemetery. I am running late. Can I meet him at the cemetery?"

"I guess so, It's the Albany Rural Cemetery in Menands. We are leaving here at ten o'clock."

"I'll meet you all there, it will only take a minute for him to sign the papers."

"I will let him know."

"Thank you, very much," Mr. Templar said.

Willy went into Buck's closet, he only saw a white pair of pants and brought them upstairs. He handed them to Buck and said they were the only ones he saw.

"I am glad I didn't have these pants on when the coffee got spilled," Buck said.

"I'm sorry about that Buck," Willy said.

Buck came out a few minutes later. Willy explained about the phone call from Mr. Templar and how he would meet us at the cemetery, too.

Olivia had everything cleaned up and most of the leftovers put away. "We have about twenty minutes before the cab will be here," she said.

Willy looked at Buck and said, "There is something about a black man dressed in white, you look really sharp."

"We now have Harley and Mr. Templar meeting us at the cemetery. I hope they are there when we get there. I want this time with Rose to be special. I need to explain about the statue."

"Would you like us to stay here, we can go next week," Olivia suggested.

"No, I need for you to come. I need you to be there when I tell Rose about her statue."

"Then we will go, let's sit in the living room and wait for the cab," Olivia said. Willy grabbed his cup of coffee and started for the living room. Then stopped and brought the cup to the sink. *I don't want that to happen again*, he thought.

Buck looked at his watch, still five minutes to wait.

"Let's wait out front," Willy said.

What a beautiful morning, no humidity, seventy-two degrees. *A perfect day*, Buck thought.

At ten o'clock, the cab pulled up. "You look good Buck," the driver said.

When they got in the cab, Buck looked for the driver's name, it seemed smudged. "What's your name, pal?" Buck asked.

"Everybody calls me Jay."

"Thank you for being on time, I do appreciate it."

"Thank you for letting me take you," the cabbie replied, "Will you need to be picked up in a few hours?"

"Yes, that would be great," Buck answered.

"That was really nice of you to tell that man to go to church," the cabbie said.

"He had some problem beyond my scope and knowledge. When he asked, how can I repay you? I felt church would do him good."

"I drove him to church at seven o'clock this morning. He looked a lot better today than he did the day you flagged me down."

"I am glad to hear that," Buck said.

"You didn't notice me, I drove by while you were helping that elderly gentleman down the street. What was his story?"

"That man had Alzheimer's, he couldn't remember his last name or where he lived."

"I guess he, like the other guy, was pretty lucky you were there."

"Thank you, that is nice to hear."

As they reached Menands, the cabbie said, "Oh! It looks like they have a funeral going on today. I can see about six cars parked along the road." Buck looked and saw four men talking to each other, then he thought he saw Mr. Templar. Behind him looked like Harley, but Buck wasn't sure.

The cabbie pulled in and stayed to one side, opposite of where the cars were parked. He pulled in farther than the rest.

"What do you thinks going on?" Olivia asked.

"I have no idea," Buck replied.

As they got out of the cab, Buck saw Harley, they waved to each other. Buck looked around for Mr. Templar, he didn't see him.

One of the four men talking approached Buck, Buck could see he was a catholic priest, "Excuse me, I was sent here to meet with a Mr. Buck Thompson."

"That's me, but I didn't call you. Are you sure you have the name, right?"

"My secretary got the call from our cardinal in New York City."

"I really don't know why he would call you about a meeting with me. I truly have no idea. I'm a Baptist, not a Catholic."

"My orders were to come here and talk with you, also, I was ordered to stay until eleven o'clock."

"I wish I knew what was going on but I don't," Buck said.

The priest walked back to the other men, another one of the men approached Buck, "I am Rabbi Lutz, I was asked to come here to talk with a Mr. Buck Thompson."

"That is me, but I don't know why you were asked to come here to talk with me."

"I came from Israel. I received my orders from our temple. I was to talk with you and was ordered to stay until eleven o'clock."

"I am not Jewish, I am a Baptist."

"These were the orders I received."

"I don't know what to say," Buck said.

The rabbi went back towards the others, another member of the group came to Buck, "I was sent here from Mecca, I was at a morning prayer. I was given a plane ticket and given orders to come here on this day. I was told to talk with a Mr. Buck Thompson."

"I am Buck Thompson, but I have no idea why you were told to come and talk with me. I am not Muslim. I am a Baptist. If I knew what was happening, I would be the first to admit it. But I have no clue."

"You don't understand, Mr. Buck Thompson, we have all talked, we have all received the same orders. It is not a mistake."

Olivia and Willy walked up to Buck. "What's this about?" Willy asked.

"I really don't know. One came from Israel, another from Mecca, the priest was sent by a Cardinal. Here comes the last one now," Olivia and Willy moved away.

"Mr. Buck Thompson, I am just a Christian preacher. I received no orders from anyone. I woke up this morning and drove here. I don't know why. I did see the written orders that those representatives have. I told them just what I said to you. I feel God wanted me here."

"I wish I knew why God wanted you here. I come here every Sunday, my wife is buried over there. I come to talk with my Rose, that's all."

"I believe that, for some reason, God wanted all of us here."

Buck saw the cabbie talking to Harley, he didn't see Mr. Templar.

Chapter Eighteen

Willy saw it first, "Hey, Buck, look." He pointed towards Rose' site. The sun was shining but a strange light started to appear above Rose's grave. Everyone walked over.

"What is it?" Buck heard some say, Buck thought he might know what it is.

He walked over and stared up. It looked like the light Buck saw in his dreams of Rose. They walked on clouds and a bright light appeared above them. This light wasn't as bright as the one in his dream. He noticed the Catholic priest with his hands in the praying position.

He watched as the Muslim knelt down to pray. The Rabbi fell to his knees. The Christian preacher seemed to be praying.

As Buck looked up, the light did get brighter. He noticed that Willy and Olivia held each other tight. Harley had his mouth open, he didn't know what was happening. Buck then saw Mr. Templar walking over and stunned at the sight of the light. He kept walking right up to Buck.

"I don't know why, but you must sign this."

Buck took the paper and a pen appeared in his hand, he knew God wanted him to sign this paper, he did. Mr. Templar took the paper and stepped back.

Buck looked around, everyone was smiling as they looked at the light. As the light got brighter, the color started to turn from white to gold.

The religious men started praying out loud, each speaking a different language. Olivia and Willy were also praying. Buck couldn't see Mr. Templar or Harley or the cabbie, they stood behind him.

The light became so bright Buck had to shield his eyes, so did everyone who was there. Buck felt the light dim a slight bit. When he looked up, he saw the statue of Rose. Everyone let out a gasp.

The statue was so beautiful, it gleamed of a golden tint. She stood on a Marble base with room next to her for Buck. It started to glow brighter and brighter, they all had to shield their eyes again.

When the light dimmed again, Buck looked up, he lost his breath. He saw Rose outside of the statue. He watched as she floated down to his open arms. She hugged him and said, "I am so proud of you!"

Buck heard the priest say to the Rabbi,

"I can't move."

The rabbi replied, "I can't move either."

Buck heard a voice, "You have a blessed day." In front of Buck and Rose, Elizabeth appeared. She walked over to Buck and Rose and hugged both of them.

"I was asked to be here for both of you." Elizabeth said, then she stepped back.

"I was asked to be here for you and Rose."

Buck looked around. In front of them, Jamie appeared.

She was as her twelve-year old self. She stepped forward and hugged them both and took a step back.

"I was also asked to be here for both of you," the thirteen- years old Peter Todd appeared. He stepped forward and hugged them both, then he stepped back.

Buck, couldn't take his eyes off of them, "What a thrill to see you, how you looked when you were alive."

Then a strong hardy voice said aloud, "I asked to be here, for you and Rose."

Every one froze when President George Washington appeared.

"Buck, I knew there had to be something very special about you when I first spoke with you."

He hugged Rose first and then saluted Buck; he took Buck's hand and nearly shook it off, "I am so proud to be able to say. I know Buck Thompson." Then the President stepped back behind the others.

Buck had no idea why this was happening. He pulled Rose closer and whispered, "What is this all about?"

Rose replied, "Wait for it!"

Buck had no idea what he would be waiting for.

Then another voice spoke, "I asked to be here for this monumental occasion. I might be Buck's newest friend," Senator Philip Schuyler appeared.

"This is the greatest event I have ever attended and that includes my daughter's wedding to Alexander Hamilton," Philip Schuyler stepped forward and hugged Rose. When he stepped in front of Buck, he snapped to attention and saluted, he then shook Buck's hand and said, "You have given me this great honor to be here today."

"What is this all about?" he asked Rose again.

She replied, "Wait for it!"

The Light returned over all of them this time. They all looked up, they all had to shield their eyes, it got brighter and brighter.

"What is this about?" he asked Rose again.

"Wait for it!" was her reply.

When the light started to fade, everyone looked to see what it was.

A white light beam came down from the sky. It disappeared instantly.

Everyone was looking at Moses.

Moses turned to Buck and said, "I am not worthy."

"What is going on?" Buck asked Moses.

Rose whispered in his ear, "Wait for it!"

Buck settled back and decided to take Rose' advice. Buck noticed his parents and Rose' parents standing together behind the religious leaders, beaming with pride. He then noticed many others standing with them. *These are all of our relatives that have passed*, he thought. He tried to move towards them. "You will be able to talk with them soon," Rose said, then added, "Wait for it!"

Moses turned to the religious leaders. To the rabbi, he spoke in Hebrew. Everyone except the Rabbi heard him speak in English.

"Who is Enoch?" The Rabbi answered in Hebrew, everyone heard him answer in English, "Enoch was so loved by God, God brought him to heaven."

"He was not dead?"

"No!" the rabbi replied.

"God brought him to Heaven and he was not dead."

"Yes!" the rabbi answered.

"Why did God Love Enoch so?"

The Rabbi said, "The Bible doesn't tell us."

"What are the qualifications to be righteous?"

None of the religious leaders answered.

He looked at the priest, "Name one man who walked this earth that was righteous."

The priest answered, "Jesus."

"I wrote some of the first testaments. I wrote why God Loved Enoch so. I wrote the qualifications to be a righteous person. The so-called religious leaders removed the qualifications to be righteous. They thought no man could meet the qualifications, they didn't want to give man a chance to try. Enoch and a few others became righteous people. Not since Jesus walked this earth, has there been a righteous person.

"Not until a few weeks ago, Buck, the day you spoke with Elizabeth, was one year completed with *no sin*. Not a bad thought, nothing but love in your heart. I am not a righteous person. That is why I say to you, 'I am not worthy, Buck.' This being the first righteous person in over two thousand years. There is a great celebration in Heaven today.

"God does reward Righteousness. He gave you the ability to talk and hear statues, but He did this to keep you busy while the celebration was being planned."

Then Moses turned to the religious leader and asked, "So, what happens now?"

They stood there, not knowing how to answer.

"*God*!" Moses' voice was amplified.

"Only a righteous person is escorted to Heaven by *God Himself*."

Moses turned to Buck and Rose, he held his arms outstretch. "Almighty God, do Your Will." From behind Buck, the cabbie stepped forward and placed a hand on Buck's shoulder and His other hand on Rose's shoulder and in a flash, they ascended to Heaven.

FOR GOD SO LOVED BUCK, HE BROUGHT HIM TO HEAVEN

Epilogue

All of the visitors from heaven disappeared in a blink.

Willy looked at the cab, it disappeared also.

Mr. Templar looked at Willy and Olivia, "May I have the honor to take you home?"

"That would be sweet," Olivia answered.

The religious leaders approached Willy and Olivia. One spoke, "We are so honored to be chosen to witness such a blessed event."

Another asked, "Did Buck write down the things that were happening to him during this process?"

"Yes, he kept notes," Olivia said.

"May we see the notes to bear witness to his great achievement?"

"Yes, I think he wouldn't mind sharing them."

Willy walked over to Mr. Davidson, "Let us know what Buck owes you and we will get the money to you."

"I am not a religious man, I know God did this work."

A Bright light flashed once more. The statue of Buck appeared next to Rose.

"You owe me nothing, I will send back the pictures. May I keep one of Rose and one of Buck?"

Willy nodded yes.

"If you can stop by and see me, I will transfer all of Buck's estate over to you two. Now I know why Buck had to sign those papers today. I thought it was odd that I was ordered to get those pages signed today. It was all of God's Work," Mr. Templar said.

"May we follow you home to pick up the notes?" the priest asked.

"Yes, that would be alright," Olivia answered.

Mr. Templar escorted them to his car. He held the door opened to let Olivia and Willy get in.

Willy took Olivia's hand and said, "I always thought Buck was a righteous man since we attended our Baptist church."

"I do remember you saying that a few times."

"I will miss him," Willy said.

"We always miss those we love when they leave us. Buck will always be right here," Olivia said as she touched Willy's heart.

Willy and Olivia squeezed each other's hand.

When they arrived at their home, Mr. Templar bid his farewell and drove away.

Willy held the door for the religious leaders to enter. They all walked into the dining room.

"I will get his notes," Olivia said and went into Buck's bedroom. She saw a box on the floor filled with pieces of paper. She saw nothing else that could be his notes. She brought it out and placed it on the dining room table. The four men looked through the box. Each piece of paper was blank. When Olivia noticed, she said, "Buck told me he kept all his notes."

"Don't worry," the Rabbi said.

"God did not want us to see them," another said.

They lined up to shake Willy's hand and to give Olivia a small hug.

"It, again, has been our honor to witness such a blessed event," they all spoke in unison, then they left.

"How do we share this story?" Willy asked.

"God will do that," Olivia responded.

FOR GOD SO LOVED BUCK, HE BROUGHT HIM TO HEAVEN

Part Two
The Celebration

Prologue

This book is entirely fiction, some of my hopes and dreams become a part of this story. The celebration is of the blessed event that occurred with Buck Thompson and God. This story is the continuance of Statues in the Dark.

There are many people who believe Allah is not God. Your dictionary will tell you Allah is the Islamic word for God. There is a movie called the 'Messenger,' the American Muslim Association, indorse this movie, it stars Anthony Quinn; it was made in 1976. It would answer a lot of questions you may have. Abraham and his son, Ishmael, built the Kaaba, which is the center of the Muslim religion. Abraham built it for those in Mecca to worship God. After Ishmael's death, people placed their pagan gods in there. It was Muhammad who destroyed the pagan gods and rededicated it to (The One and Only God) Allah. Muhammad once said, "The Jews have their Bible, the Christians have their Testament, we should never question them, for we all believe in *one God*."

Buck and God will work together for harmony among the people of the World. God will give Buck the knowledge to know the answer to any question. Buck also learns some heavenly secrets along the way.

Most of the unbelievers are the religious leaders who think they know everything. But we know only God knows everything. This story takes you to Heaven and back.

This is the symbol that appears when you're leaving one place and going to another.

***

Buck has some major missions to take on behalf of God. The only roadblocks are those set-in places by people that say they represent God, but they really represent themselves. (God bless you and send your donation to…) was never on God's agenda. Rose and Buck continue spreading their love and showing the love of God to everyone. They beam with delight knowing they are helping God.

Chapter One

In a blink, Buck found himself and Rose standing next to God in Heaven. God had His arms around both of them and squeezed.

"You are now both home," they heard God say.

Buck saw what he knew to be Jesus sitting on the throne to the right. God stepped away and headed to the throne in the center. He no longer looked like the cabbie. He was a majestic figure beyond description. Buck was overwhelmed, Moses walked over to him, "Buck, you will be honored as we all rejoice in heaven knowing righteousness lives on." Buck felt Rose squeeze his arm, he looked at her and her beauty filled Buck's heart.

"I know what you want to do first," they heard God say.

At this point, Buck's and Rose' parents walked toward them. Buck let go of Rose and hugged his mother and then his father.

"We have to be the proudest parents," his father said. His mother beamed at the sight of her son.

His parents hugged Rose as he stepped over to her parents. As he hugged Rose' mother, she whispered, "We are so proud of your great accomplishment." As he hugged Rose' father, her father whispered, "I am not worthy."

Buck saw all of his and Rose' relatives standing behind their parents. His father introduced Buck to his parents. Buck never met them, they passed of the flu ten years before Buck was born. His mother introduced her parents which again Buck never met them. Her mother died giving birth to his mother. His mother's father looked a lot like Buck. The introduction went on, but time did not exist.

Buck looked back at God and said, "Thank you." God looked at Buck with a big smile and replied.

"No, thank you, you have proven that righteousness will prevail and grow among all My children."

Jesus stood up and walked over to Buck and Rose, "Today, you brought the brightest of lights to heaven." Jesus introduced the elderly gentlemen that stood near our God. Buck and Rose met Abraham, Isaac, Jacob, Enoch, Noah, and all the great and mighty. Then Buck looked to his left, there stood Mary and Joseph, his heart was about to burst.

"Let the Celebration begin," God said, as he stood and blessed the feast that appeared. Jesus was still standing next to Buck and Rose.

"If you have a question, you need to only ask," Jesus said.

Buck looked at the other throne on the left of God. "Will I get to meet the Holy Spirit?" he asked.

Jesus smiled and said, "That seat is for you. You have made My Father and all of us very happy."

Buck didn't know how to answer, then he said, "I really am not worthy to sit on a throne next to God."

"Why not, you sat on His lap when you were a baby."

Again, Buck didn't know how to answer.

"Your love for Rose and your Love of God has set you on this course and guided you throughout your life. Early when you were a child, you would work the fields talking to My Father. When your father passed, your heart was broken, it was mended when you looked at your mother. When your mother passed, you lost your will to live. That was when My Father stepped in and guided you away for your new life."

As Jesus was talking, Buck not only heard the words, he felt them. Buck heard the singing get a little louder. He also understood all the words. They were singing about him and the joy he brought to God.

Jesus started to walk away and turned back to Buck, "The Holy Spirit is every man, woman, and child in heaven and this also includes you. There is no greater power; together, we supply the grace that is needed in the world."

Buck's heart felt such joy that he had never felt before. He really couldn't comprehend what was going on completely.

"Rose, I really don't know what to say about all this."

"Buck, you have accomplished a great deed, especially in the eyes of God. That is why he allowed me to be with you in your dreams."

"Now I know why they felt so real."

"He knew that certain things would remind you of what was happening, so He would erase those happenings from your mind. When you heard the singing, I heard the praising of you. But I knew you couldn't understand the words."

"I can't believe this is all being done for me."

"To God, you deserve this and more. He is so proud of you. You have proven that man can be righteous."

As Rose said this, the catholic priest is talking to the cardinal in New York City about what he witnessed. He e-mailed him a copy of the paper they all signed. The cardinal will go to the Vatican and report to the Pope.

The Rabbi is calling Israel, he is talking to the head of his temple. He explained what he witnessed and was told to fly back as soon as possible.

The Muslim is ready to board a flight back to Mecca to make his report in person.

The Christian preacher had called all those T.V. preachers about getting the word out. They all thought he was a wacko.

But then Brother Blair received a call from a wealthy businessman, who stated he didn't know why he called, but he thought the preacher could use his help.

Olivia and Willy are sitting in their apartment, wondering what they should do. Olivia turns to Willy and says, "God's got this."

Buck hugs Rose after her beautiful comments, he then sees Elizabeth. He and Rose walked over and sat on a bench with her. "It is so lovely to see you, Elizabeth," Buck said.

"I have grown to like the title 'Missy'," she replied.

"Okay. Missy,, it is, where are your parents?" Buck asked.

"My mother is with her mother and sister."

"Where is your dad?"

"He didn't make it up here. He thought that if he killed himself that he would see me sooner. It is one of the worst sins you can commit, taking your own life."

"That is terrible to hear, I know he loved you with all his heart."

"God whispered in his ear that it doesn't work this way. He decided to ignore God. I wish he had more faith then he did," Elizabeth said, then added, "You have made my heart grow. You have restored all of our faith in mankind. I really am so glad that I was the first statue you talked with. I will always be around you, it will be my honor to stand in your grace."

Buck placed his arm around Elizabeth and squeezed, "I love you, Missy."

"I know you do, Buck," she replied, "and I, you."

With that said, Elizabeth was being called by her mother, before she left, she kissed Rose and Buck on the cheek. "Have a blessed time," she said as she left.

"You too, Missy."

Rose was the first to stand, she took Buck's hand and guided him to a special spot. "Look down," was all she said. Buck looked down and saw Olivia and Willy, they were saying their prayer before dinner, "This is where I would come to watch you kneel down at night and say your prayer."

"I know that I will never miss them as long as I can see them."

"We all think that same thing up here. But many of them suffer through their loss like Elizabeth's dad," Rose guided Buck back to the waiting crowd, they just wanted to see him. "They have all been waiting for this celebration to see the man who made God smile," Rose said.

Buck said hello to everyone as they walked through the crowd. His loving eyes showed all they needed to see. Buck saw food on many tables and canters of wine.

"I didn't know you would need to eat in heaven."

Rose laughed a little and said, "We don't, but this is a celebration, have you ever gone to a celebration where there was no food. You can think of your most favorite meal and it will appear on the table closest to you. It will also taste like it is the best you have ever eaten."

"After this celebration, you will no longer think about eating. It will never appear in your mind."

"Where do you stay?" Buck asked.

"God has promised us a Mansion. Our family all lives there."

"Do you sleep?"

Again, Rose laughed a little, "No, you are never tired, we can spend as much time as we want looking at God's wonders. We can sit on a bench and look at the most beautiful waterfalls you have ever seen. Anything of beauty that you can think of will appear."

Buck was staring at Rose, "Little Rosebud, you are the only beauty I want to see."

"Hi, Buck, it is again so nice to see you."

Buck turned but didn't recognize the man standing there. Then his name appeared in Buck's mind. "Peter, how are you?" Buck said and then introduced Rose to Peter Todd.

"Remember, it's Pete. Buck, I am so proud to be a part of all of this. Jamie and I had no idea of your true blessing. Sometime, I would like to take you trout fishing."

"You can trout fish in heaven?"

"This is heaven, you can enjoy everything you have ever enjoyed."

"Where is Jamie?"

"She is right behind you."

Buck turned and saw the ninety-nine-year old Jamie. Without hesitation, he put his arms around her and gave her a loving hug. When he looked in her eyes, he saw the beauty of a woman with a great big heart.

"Buck, you have made us so proud," she then looked at Rose, "You are as beautiful as I thought you would be. It is my honor to finally meet you."

"Thank you so much," Rose said and she hugged Jamie and then Peter, "Buck always talked about you both every Sunday. I knew you both loved him the way he loved you."

"That is so sweet, we really do love you, Buck, and now we love both of you."

"I hope we will meet from time to time, just to see each other," Buck said.

"Here in heaven, you just need to think it and it happens," Peter stated then added, "We will go fishing and talk."

"That sounds good to me," Buck said as he took Peter's hand and shook it. He turned once again to Jamie and gave her another loving hug. Jamie and Peter then moved away.

"We should go to our God," Rose said.

Buck and Rose walked in that direction. As Buck looked at God on his throne, he heard the voice of God call him. Rose released his hand and Buck approached our God.

"Please sit here on your throne," God requested.

Buck was overwhelmed again as he sat. "What is that beautiful smell?" he asked God. God placed a finger on Buck's forehead. They appeared in front of the most beautiful tree Buck had ever seen. The leaves were full and smooth to the touch, the fruit looked to be like a fig, but Buck wasn't sure, he never saw a fig tree. The smell again was the sweetest he had ever smelled, God picked a piece of fruit and handed it to Buck.

"Taste it, for you are worthy," God said.

As Buck took a bite, he knew this was the Tree of Knowledge. They reappeared back on their thrones.

"We all appreciate this day dedicated to you. You have revived My heart and brought the meaning of humanity back to Me. There are many good people down there. But there are many bad people, also. In this time, it doesn't take a lot to turn good people bad. I was about to lose a little bit more trust in humanity.

"Then you proved that humanity can become righteous. I have a great feeling that humanity may understand the ability they have to become righteous. You will see what is happening on earth, right away. The news of you will spread throughout all religions and that makes Me very happy. If you had one wish, what would you wish for? I have to say up-front world peace cannot be a choice, but you may have set the path for world peace."

Buck had everything he could have ever wanted, "I have no wish for me."

"Continue," God said.

"I know it is against the rules," Buck said and before he could continue, God said, "You would like to see Elizabeth reunited with her father."

"I know he committed the most terrible sin of all."

"He did, and he didn't listen to Me when I warned him."

"I know, but the devil must have convinced him this would work. You remember the man I touched who said he was told by the demons to killed himself and they would go away."

"I understand what you are saying, that man was being possessed by demons. Elizabeth's father wasn't being guided by the devil, it was his grief that convinced him to do what he had done."

"I am very sorry that I brought this up. You know what is right," Buck stated.

God pointed to his left and Buck looked. He saw Elizabeth sitting on a bench holding her father very tight, "It is your love of your fellow man that I do this for you. Your soul is one of the whitest here in heaven. I grant your wish."

Buck saw the love in Elizabeth and her father's eyes. Buck looked at God and said,

"You knew what I would have asked for."

"Yes, of course, I did. But you had to ask and I had to answer. I watched as Elizabeth's father cried at her burial site, I felt his pain and his sorrow. I hear the prayers of many who deal with such sorrow. I could wave my hand and do away with all sorrow. I have given humanity ways to learn from mistakes and have provided methods to right all wrongs. Some don't learn and some do and some over -learn which doesn't work in dealing with everyday life.

"Many times, I will place a roadblock to stop someone going in the wrong direction. But humanity looks at it as something they have to overcome. They should first examine why the roadblock is there. With you, you always walked the right path."

"You also are aware of how overwhelmed I am. In all my life, I thought I would be good enough to go to heaven, now I am sitting here talking to *God*."

"You have talked to Me throughout your entire life, and I heard every word. I listen to everyone and help when I feel it is needed. No one realizes how my Son travels continuously bringing children and babies from earth to heaven. This could end if the world worked together, that was My plan. But freewill ended my dream. I witness more sin in the world today than ever before. It hurts me when I see Christians support sexual predators and those who lie and are believed.

"There should never be bigotry, racism, hate towards others that are not like you. My heart aches for the victims and those who commit these actions have no place here. Those who kill in My name will never see heaven. You are the beacon of hope that I see changing the way things are today."

"I, like everyone here, would be willing to do anything to make this come true," Buck said.

"I know you would. Rose is picturing you in her mind, you should go to her. I will look forward to having more talks with you."

Buck felt as if he should bow before he left. But then God turned to Jesus. Buck saw Rose smiling at the sky. "What are you smiling at?"

"Nothing, I am just so happy. This smile will be on my face forever."

"I am glad, I love your smile."

They held hands and began to walk, Rose would squeeze his hand and he would return the movement. Buck again saw Elizabeth holding her father and he saw her mother standing behind them smiling. Buck saw Elizabeth stand up and he watched her guide her mother to the seat next to her father. Elizabeth ran towards Buck, her eyes beaming with a heartwarming joy. Buck opened his arms and Elizabeth stepped in, as Buck closed his arms around her, he saw something that Elizabeth needed to see. Buck turned Elizabeth around and she saw her parents kiss for the first time ever in her memory.

"You did this for me. I never thought I would see him again," she squeezed Buck harder this time.

"I didn't do it, God did it."

"It was your wish and actions that brought this about. We all heard your wish. Thank you, Buck, I love you so much."

"We love you also, Missy," Buck said as he saw the love for him in Rose' eyes. She hugged them both.

Chapter Two

The Vatican ordered the cardinal to take the next flight to Rome. As he sat on the plane waiting for it to take off, he thought of what the priest relayed to him about God escorting this man name Buck to heaven. The other puzzling part was that his office never called this priest to attend this blessed event. Somehow, he knew it did happen. He looked at his notes as the plane took off.

He read of all those who appeared, some children, George Washington. Philip Schuyler and Moses. There was the Priest, a Rabbi, a Muslim, and a Christian preacher. They all signed the affidavit he was carrying to present to the Pope. They all talked as one. Thinking of what the priest saw, he fell into a deep sleep.

"Cardinal Burke," he heard the person sitting next to him say. He opened his eyes and saw a young man looking at him. "What can I do for you?" the cardinal asked.

"I am here to reassure you that this really did happen."

"What do you mean?"

"God did escort Buck to heaven, because he was the first righteous man on this earth since Jesus. Buck Thompson is the Hope that God sees for all of humanity."

Cardinal Burke couldn't believe what this man was saying, how did he know about the mission he was on, "How do you know about this?"

"God felt a slight doubt in your mind. You need to have *no* doubt, whatsoever."

"Do you now understand the word of God?"

At this point, a warm feeling filled the cardinal's heart and he replied, "I am your loyal follower." His eyes felt heavy and they closed, when he opened them a few seconds later, the man was gone. The cardinal knew he was visited by someone from heaven. Now only joy and faith filled his heart from this day forward.

The Muslim was in a cab riding to his mosque. He looked at the paper that they all signed, he knew Allah was going to guide him. His body felt a tingling since he witnessed this sacred scene. He soon arrived at his mosque. As he was getting ready to pay the cab driver, the cab driver turned and said, "Allah needs you to believe with all your heart. You are to relay your message with a beam of joy and faith."

"I will do what Allah wants of me. I will do it with all my heart," was what he said in reply to the driver. When he went to hand the driver his money, it was not the man who just said these glorious words of praise. He left and entered his mosque. Standing just inside the door was the leaders of Allah's house. No one spoke, the men led this man of Allah to a room which had a table and twelve chairs, they all sat. The Muslim who went on this journey was Mohammad Elsah.

He placed the paper he had in his hand on the table. A copy of the page appeared in front of each man. They all stood and fell to their knees reciting, "Praise Allah, Praise Allah." Mohammad stated, "Allah wants us to tell all of our brothers and sisters about what He did, about this man called Buck Thompson. How we can rejoice in Allah's company and receive from Allah the love we seek. I feel honored to be the messenger from Allah. I know what Muhammad must have felt being a messenger."

"What if this is a trick of the infidels?"

Everyone looked at this man and asked Allah to forgive him for the lack of faith he exhibited.

The man replied, "It isn't faith, it is our war with the infidels. We can never associate with Jews."

The men witnessed this man disappearing before their eyes. They fell to their knees again, "Praise Allah, Praise Allah," was the sound that filled the entire mosque.

As the Rabbi entered his synagogue in Israel, those who waited for his return fell to their knees as they saw this man glowing as he entered the synagogue.

"We can see that you have looked upon our God as Abraham once did. We will receive your words as if they are the words of God."

The rabbi followed the leaders to an office below the Synagogue, no one spoke as they walked. The men circled a table that sat in the center of the room. The head rabbi recited a prayer of praise to Almighty God above, then they all took a seat. As Rabbi Lutz placed the paper he was holding on the table, it appeared in front of each rabbi there. Most, not all, said a prayer to God for this sacred moment. Those who did not pray sat there stunned at what they just saw happen.

As Rabbi Lutz started to talk, everyone listened, "I did see God and I also saw Moses. I felt that we all were on trial for what religious leaders have done before us. I know, without a shadow of doubt, that God wants us to work with other religions to tell the story of what we witnessed. I feel truly blessed that God had chosen me to represent the Jewish religion. Not as a leader, but as a witness. This man named Buck Thompson has brought Hope to all of humanity on behalf of God Himself. We need to get God's message out to all the world. We will stand next to Muslims and Christians and tell this story to all."

The Christian preacher, whose name was Thomas Blair, sat next to his phone in a small office in his home. He stared at the paper in front of him and began to pray, "God, thank you for everything you do for us. Help me get this word out to the true believers. Thank you for letting me represent Christians. I now feel worthy and blessed. We need to silence those who say they believe, but don't truly believe that you are with us daily. You know who they are and I feel there are too many out there that will question the word of God. Even though they say they are men of God, you know the truth. I am so honored to have stood in Your presence. Please, guide us, direct us, and please keep on loving us."

He remembered all who he called for help to get God's word out and how they laughed at him. They called him names such as a nut, crazy, wacky. None had the faith of God in them to believe that God did all this for humanity.

At this point, the phone rang, "Brother Blair here, how may I help you."

"Hi, I am Blake Edward's, I have a feeling that I am supposed to work with you to get some sort of message out."

"You were sent to me from God, I would like to meet with you to inform you of all that has happened and why God sent you to me."

"I don't know why I had your phone number in my phone made of gold numbers. I would like to meet and find out what is happening."

Brother Blair set a time for them to meet the following day.

Chapter Three

Rose and Buck walked and talked to many people. They wanted to know if he worked at being righteous or did it just happen. Everyone Buck saw had a wonderful smile on their face. Buck heard someone call him, he turned and there were a few men, Buck didn't recognize at first. Buck walked towards them, "May I help you?"

"I am Trent Marlin, I served with General Washington during the Revolution. I am so happy to meet you. He didn't know about your righteousness when he started telling me all about you. But he knew that there was something about you that was very special."

Another man spoke up, "I am Len Griffey…"

"You were my teacher in first grade in North Carolina," Buck interjected.

"I remember you ran to school and ran home every day. I know why you did that now. You needed to be there to help your father. I am so proud that I had something to do with your young life."

"Mr. Griffey, you taught me to read, to sound out words. What I also remember you never got upset with any of the children in your class. You are a very fine man."

"Thank you, Mr. Thompson, for your kind words."

"Please call me Buck, thank you for all you have done for me."

The third man spoke up, "You shouldn't remember me, but I…"

"You stopped at our house when your car broke down. You needed to make a call, but we didn't have a phone. You asked me where the nearest phone would be. I really had no idea. I walked out with you. You lifted the hood of your car and I saw that there was a wire that came undone. I reattached it and your car started. You reached in your pocket and handed me a ten-dollar bill. I wouldn't except it, it was way too much money."

"But then I told you to buy your momma something special. You then said, 'God Bless you, sir.' That day was your momma's birthday and you thought God brought me to you. I loved telling people that story."

"My momma said it was the best birthday she ever had. I bought her candy, a new house dress, and placed the change in a card I made for her. When she asked about the money…"

"I know you said that God provided it to you for her birthday."

"Yes, I did, how did you know?"

"God told me when I arrived up here."

"Thank you all for everything you have done and said. It was a pleasure to meet and see you again," Buck said, then Rose led him away. Buck noticed a man waving and then he realized it was someone he grew up with. He saw someone else and recognized her from when he was a child at his church.

He is beginning to understand what happens in heaven and how you recognize people that you wouldn't recognize if you saw them on earth. It's a supreme knowledge which is bestowed on every one in heaven. *How cool*, Buck thought.

Rose guided Buck back to God. God smiled and Buck knew He wanted him to sit again. Buck stepped up to the throne and sat down. God was still smiling and everyone started to approach the area.

"Today, we celebrate a righteous man who may change the world. I know you would all like to speak to him. You will have plenty of occasions when you will be able to do that. Today, we celebrate. I will keep you informed about everything happening on earth. My thoughts will be carried to each and every one of you."

Buck knew God was finished talking to the crowd when they began to walk away. God placed His Hand on Buck's arm. Buck felt an energy flow within his body that he never felt before.

"Buck, I may need you to appear in different areas on earth."

"Anything I can do, I will do gladly."

Buck felt it was time to join Rose again and it was. Rose guided Buck to a group of children.

***

Meanwhile, back on earth, the cardinal showed up at the Vatican, the guards escorted him to the office of the Holy Father. They asked him to wait there. What Cardinal Burke didn't realize was that the Vatican contacted the priest that witnessed the event and informed him to fly to the Vatican immediately. He was one hour behind the cardinal.

The priest was Father Chaffee; he was from Albany, New York. He was an assistant to the bishop. He didn't have time to inform the bishop of what was going on. But somehow, he knew that the bishop was aware. He arrived at the Vatican one hour after the cardinal arrived. He was also escorted to the office of the Holy Father. He walked in at the same moment that the Pope entered from across the room.

Both men approached the Pope, they knelt and kissed his ring. The Pope guided the two men to a small conference table.

"I felt something happen in my heart the day you said this occurred," he looked at Cardinal Burke and explained, "I wanted the eye witness here. We couldn't contact you to let you know we ordered Father Chaffee to come here also."

"On my way here, I had the same thought that I should have brought Father Chaffee myself."

He handed the paper he was holding to the Pope.

"What made you go to this blessed event?" the Pope asked Father Chaffee.

"I received these orders from the cardinal's office."

He handed the papers to the Pope.

"You didn't send a message to Father Chaffee, did you?"

"No, your Holiness, my office did not send any communications to Father Chaffee," Cardinal Burke answered.

"The secretary at the Albany Diocese handed that to me the morning of the event. She stated that she received the call herself and it seemed very important that I attend," Father Chaffee stated.

"I can feel you are both telling the truth," the Pope said as he began to read the message Father Chaffee received, "The others present received similar directions?"

"Yes, your Holiness, I read the communications they all received. We were all told to go there and stay until eleven o'clock. The Christian preacher woke up that morning and drove there without receiving any orders, he stated that he knew God wanted him there."

"The affidavit you all signed was proposed by whom?" the Pope asked.

"It was me, your Holiness, I was the only one who had an office in that area. After we visited Buck Thompson's apartment, we decided to write that up."

"Why did you go to Buck Thompson's apartment?"

"A member of the family said that he wrote down everything that was happening during this time. We went to see his notes."

"You only found blank pages," the Pope stated.

"Yes, we did, your Holiness, how did you know?"

The Pope just smiled, "We must contact these other religions so we can formulate a release together. I would like both of you to dine with me tonight if you have no plans."

Both agreed to the invitation. The Pope stood to leave, they both stood, "I will see you both later." He looked at Father Chaffee, "God sent you that message," he said, then headed for the door he entered through.

"I should have asked you to come with me," Cardinal Burke said to Father Chaffee.

"When I received the call, I tried to contact you, but I couldn't get through."

"We need to get a hotel room. We don't know how long we will be here," the Cardinal said.

The guard standing behind them stated, "Will you follow me? You are staying here at the Vatican. I will show you to your rooms."

***

Rose guided Buck to a crowd of children sitting on the golden floor.

"Who do we have here?"

"These are children that wanted to meet you," Rose answered.

"What is your name?" he asked a boy who sat in the front row.

"I am Nathan Scott, it is a pleasure to meet you, sir."

Buck looked at all the children and said, "I want you all to call me, Buck." The children smiled at Buck. As Buck looked around, he asked the crowd if he may be excused for a minute to talk with his wife Rose. Buck and Rose stepped off to the side, "Rose, it just dawned on me that all these children died as children."

"Yes, many were babies when they arrived. God lets them grow so they may enjoy the life of a child. Some died from the lack of medication, others by guns, others in accidents, most by starvation. They don't remember how they died. They remember their loved one, which they will meet again up here. Now before you ask me how do I know, God gave me the answers to any of your questions. I didn't know that before you asked."

"Let's go back to the children," Buck said as he smiled at his beautiful wife.

"What is your name?" he asked a girl about ten.

"I am Gloria, it is also my pleasure to meet you, Buck."

Buck looked at all the children and said, "It is my pleasure to meet all of you. Now that I know all your names." A girl in the back raised her hand, "Yes, Maggy," Buck said.

"How can you know all of our names without you asking us?"

"It can only be God, he gave me this ability."

Maggy gave Buck a great big smile and sat back down.

"I will be around from now on, if you want to ask me a question or just talk, I will always be here for you."

Rose again guided Buck away. Buck noticed there were a lot of animals in heaven. Then, in his mind, he heard God say, "I love all my creations."

"Can we see Willy and Olivia again?" Buck asked.

Rose guided him to an empty space. As Buck looked down, he saw Olivia and Willy eating in the kitchen.

"I have never been so glad to be old," Willy said.

"What do you mean by that?"

"We won't have to wait a bunch of years before we see Buck again."

"I miss him, too, but of course, I can finally say, he is in a better place."

"Yes, and he was brought there by God Himself."

Buck looked at Rose and said, "I am so glad I have you to guide me."

"Everything you would like to know is already stored in your mind. God answered every question you may have when He gave you the fruit from the Tree of Knowledge."

Buck thought for a second, a big smile appeared on his face, "You're right. I wonder why it snows sometimes a lot in a certain year and other times a little. It's a method that God uses to prune his bushes and trees and to fertilize the ground, this is beautiful."

Rose said, "When I was a child, I remembered a preacher saying that in heaven, you will know the answers to any question."

"I remember somebody telling me that when I was a child also," Buck replied.

"What would you like to do now?"

"I would like to sit down and hold you for a while, is that okay up here?"

"God knows that love is the supreme energy in heaven. He enjoys seeing people that are in love, especially those that have been together for many years."

Buck looked behind him and there was a bench that God provided. Buck and Rose sat down and Rose nestled her head into Bucks neck. Buck remembered he and Rose doing this exact thing in a dream.

Chapter Four

Rabbi Lutz having ended his message, looked at the other rabbis.

"We must gather the religions together and send out this message of unity," one of the rabbis said. A man entered the room and whispered into the rabbis leader's ear. He nodded to the man.

"We have just received a call from the Pope in Rome, who would like us to all get together to work on a plan to get the word of God out. He is trying to contact the Muslim who attended. The Christian Brother Blair will be notified by the Vatican, also."

"Mohammad Elsah, gave me his phone number," Rabbi Lutz stated.

"Give it to me and I will forward it to the Vatican," the rabbi leader stated.

Rabbi Lutz gave him the phone number and he left immediately to make the call to Rome. When the Vatican received the number, they had Father Chaffee make the call.

Father Chaffee dialed the number and waited for it to be answered.

"Hello."

"Is this Mohammad Elsah?"

"Yes, and who is this?"

"This is Father Chaffee, the Catholic Priest that witnessed what you witnessed."

"Yes. Father Chaffee, I was expecting a call from Rabbi Lutz."

"He shared your number with the rest of us, I hope that is okay."

"Yes, it is. I didn't know how to contact you. I just got out of a meeting with the leaders of my mosque; they wanted me to call somebody to set up a meeting. They believe we should act as one voice."

"We have all agreed about that. The Vatican is contacting the Christian preacher as we speak. We need to decide where we should meet."

"I will ask the leaders of my Mosque, but I would suggest America. This is where it happened."

"I will bring that up at the Vatican. Will you call me after you speak with your leaders?"

"Yes, I will, your number is in my phone now."

"I will be waiting for your call Mohammad, thank you for everything."

Both men hung up.

Father Chaffee contacted Cardinal Burke, "I just got off the phone with Mohammad Elsah about where we would meet. He said he will talk to his leaders, but he is going to suggest America, because this is where it happened."

"We will also suggest it to the Pope."

"Do you think the Holy Father will attend this meeting?"

"I don't believe anything could keep him away," the cardinal stated.

"Rabbi Lutz where do you think the meeting should be held?" the head rabbi asked.

"I think America would be the right place, Mr. Thompson is an American and it did happen there."

All of the rabbis in the room agreed.

Brother Blair was meeting with Blake Edwards at a diner on Central Avenue in Albany. After a friendly greeting to each other, they sat in a booth.

"So, what is this all about?" Blake asked.

Brother Blair looked into Blake's eyes, "You will have to have faith to believe what I'm about to tell you."

"Go ahead."

"I attended an event where God himself brought a righteous man to Heaven, Moses was there, some children, Philip Schuyler. and George Washington. I was there with a Catholic priest and a rabbi and a Muslim. We all witnessed this event. I tried to call some T.V. Preachers, but they all called me names and hung up. Here is the affidavit we all signed," he handed the paper to Blake.

Blake read the paper, "Where did this happen?"

"Albany Rural Cemetery."

At this point, Brother Blair's phone rang.

"Hello, Brother Blair?" he heard a man ask who spoke broken English.

"Yes, I am Brother Blair," he replied.

"Yes, I will be available any time you choose. Would you like me to come there?" he asked, then hung up.

"That was the Pope, all the representatives on that list will be coming here to Albany for a meeting."

"Then we will host them, we will set a meeting place and provide lodging for all that will come."

"That will cost a great deal of money," Brother Blair said.

"I will handle all the cost. This is why God had me contact you, I think."

"They will call me back when they have a date."

"Through my many contacts, I will let them know that we will host this blessed meeting and find out what provisions they may need," Blake added.

"I didn't think you would have believed me," Brother Blair said.

"I was determined to help any way that I could. When you said on the phone that God sent me to you, I felt an inner energy that had me believe that."

Blake gave Brother Blair his private phone number and asked him to call when he heard anything.

At dinner, the Pope explained that all involved agreed to meet in the United States. He suggested that this unity could bring world peace. This meeting coming up will bring the four major religions together to speak as one, "God has set this in motion and depends on us to do our part. I talked with Rabbi Pearlman and he said that Rabbi Lutz felt that all involved were being judged on what other religious leaders did before us."

"Moses seemed to judge us, he explained what we have been teaching was wrong, because of what some so-called religious leaders took out of the Bible. Moses said that he did write in the Bible why God Loved Enoch and the requirements to be a righteous person," Father Chaffee said.

"The Bible states to be righteous you must obey the commandments," the Pope said.

"According to Moses, you must be free of sin for an entire year. He said that it was removed from the Bible because those so-called leaders felt no man could accomplish that," Father Chaffee added.

The Pope smiled. "Mr. Buck Thompson proved them wrong," he said.

"Pontiff, do you really believe no religious man can go for a year without sin?" the cardinal asked.

"I, for one, can't go a year without thinking bad things about certain people. We see a battered woman and hate the person who did it. We ask God to forgive them, but we hate what was done. Free will makes us think if we were unable to think, we would be like a baby. We ask God to forgive us daily. When I heard what some priest were charged with doing unspeakable things to children. I hate those people of God and have to pray to ask God to forgive me."

"I can understand what you are saying and now I agree wholeheartedly. Going an entire year does seem impossible," the Cardinal replied.

"I find it ironic that no news agencies have reported any of this," Father Chaffee stated.

"It's all part of God's plan, we will know when to release it," the Pope said, then added, "We will not announce our meeting in New York. I have received word that arrangements will be made for all of us."

"Was it the bishop?" Father Chaffee asked.

"No, it is a private person who is working with the Christian preacher."

"But I know the bishop would want us to stay there."

"You are right, but we have four religious leaders representing themselves. We can't force them to stay at a Catholic facility. It is better to have a private person set this up," the Pope replied.

That night everyone got a great and beautiful rest. The following morning at breakfast, the Pope told Cardinal Burke and Father Chaffee that they would be meeting in New York in four days, "I am asking both of you to dress in civilian clothes, I will do the same." At this point, another priest entered the room and handed the Pope a phone. "Thank you very much," was the Pope's response. He handed the phone back to the priest, who left immediately.

"The private person handling everything is also supplying the plane. We will be picked up first, then to Israel, and then onto Mecca. We will need to supply the names of those traveling. We are allowed to take twenty people. There will only be four of us," he added.

In Israel, the rabbi's met for breakfast. Rabbi Pearlman stated, "We will be meeting in New York in four days. One person is handling all the cost, his plane will land in Rome and then to Israel, then to Mecca. We can have twenty people all together, but we will send four."

In Mecca, Mohammad Elsah entered the room where they planned to meet after yesterday's meeting. The leader, Misha Ali, began to inform the others that the meeting would be held in four days in New York, he mentioned that a private person is handling the cost and they could bring as many as twenty people.

"I think we should only have four in our party," Misha Ali said.

"I agree," stated Mohammad Elsah.

The rest of those present agreed to send four.

Back in America, Brother Blair was sitting with Blake Edward's.

"Who should we have with us.?" Blake asked Brother Blair.

"I don't know, those who are famous rejected my plea. I do know a few good preachers that we may ask."

"Like who?" Blake asked.

"Two Baptists and a Methodist, Brother Nick Brady, Brother Marty Garcia, and Brother Ken Davis. They are the best that I know and true believers in their faith."

"Can you call them and we can all meet at your house if that is alright with your wife?"

"My wife passed a year ago. But she would have approved, 'Anything for God,' was her motto."

"Then call me when we will be meeting, I need to check on other arrangements."

"Will do!" Brother Blair responded.

****

Buck gave Rose a loving squeeze; they stood up and began to walk back into the crowd. Buck saw Moses wave him over. He and Rose headed that way.

"We will have a lot to do in a little while. The four religions that witnessed the event will be gathering in Albany, New York. They will be discussing how to work together to release in unity the requirements to be righteous. They will be releasing the entire story to the world," Moses said.

"I am so glad to be a part of this, I will do anything needed of me."

"You are the reason this is happening. Without your love and faith, none of this would be possible."

Buck felt that Jesus wanted to see him. He excused himself and let go of Rose' hand. He walked into the crowd and soon was standing in front of our Lord. They walked to a bench, Jesus asked him to sit down next to him.

"You have the support of all those people on earth. They really need you, you will restore the faith in all those who have been wondering what direction to go in. You will be yourself and Our Father will support you completely. I have found that all people need something to believe in. There will always be those who will try to fight you. They can also be turned around. I was up against the religion my Father adopted. Those men couldn't see beyond their own self. There were those who were afraid to come to me. If they did come, they may have been crucified also."

"You won't have that kind of problem. You are blessed and will bless those that will see you. They will gain the feeling of being blessed. If you are asked a question, the answer will be in your mind, just open your mouth and the words will come out. No matter what you say, those that will hear you, will hear you in their own language. I am so proud that all of this is finally happening."

Buck felt every word. He absorbed the glow from Jesus. He knew he was on a mission and was very proud to do whatever God wanted. He watched as Jesus moved away and he saw Rose.

"Walk with me, we must hear what our family is saying," Rose stated.

Buck saw his family standing by a large mansion. As he got closer, his mother and father approached him. "Son, again, we are so proud that you have proven yourself to God. You are being asked to guide the world into a direction that has been needed forever," his dad said.

"We are not here to support you, we are here to honor you. You will do what is needed to be done," his mom said.

Buck wasn't sure of what that was, but he knew God would see him through whatever he had to do. He and Rose stayed a while with all the family members. Buck felt a very pleasant joy of being with all the members of his and Rose' family. Every family member felt so proud of Buck. No one could have ever realized that this meek family would be so honored and blessed.

It took a while, but Buck hugged every family member that was present. He and Rose started to walk away, as they turned, they were standing in the presence of God.

"It is starting to happen," God stated.

Chapter Five

As the plane landed in Rome, the Pope and Father Chaffee and Cardinal Burke watched from inside the airport. They, with the other priest, stood in civilian clothes, which drew no attention. They were brought to a door which led them out to the plane. When they entered the plane, a gentleman brought them to a beautiful room, which had overstuffed chairs with seat belts. They were informed that they would be taking off in five minutes.

Rabbi Pearlman and Rabbi Lutz stood side by side with the other two rabbis, they were also dressed in civilian clothes. When the plane landed in Israel, they were boarded within minutes. They were led to the same room as the Pope and they all introduced themselves to one another.

Mecca would be the final stop before heading to New York. Mohammad Elsah stood with the Muslim leaders of his mosque. They all knelt down and prayed for Allah's guidance. They, too, were dressed in civilian clothes. When the plane arrived, they were escorted to the entrance. The same gentleman brought them to meet the others.

After they all introduced themselves, the gentleman asked them to enter another room. This was a large conference room with twenty chairs. They all took a seat and a woman walked in and handed everyone a menu. The menus were printed in Arabic, Hebrew, and English. They were asked to pick out what they would like to eat and were also informed that they would be departing in thirty minutes.

God smiled as he watched them converse with each other. He placed this vision into Buck's mind. Buck felt a warm feeling at what he saw. He recognized those who attended the blessed event.

Just before take-off, the woman walked back in and gathered up the menus.

The Pope turned to the Muslim leader, Misha Ali, "This is such a blessed event we are involved in."

"I feel that I am not worthy to represent Allah."

"We all represent one God and He will direct us," the Pope answered.

"But I know there are greater leaders then myself," replied Misha Ali.

"God has picked his people to do this work, and He picked everyone here."

At this point, every one stood up and started to move around the table and took another seat. Rabbi Pearlman saw that God had them moved around so one of each religion was sitting together. Everyone saw the same thing.

Rabbi Lutz and Mohammad Elsah and Father Chaffee formed one group. "This is something else, isn't it?" Father Chaffee said.

"I am so proud to be a part of this, and to think our leaders excepted it without question," Mohammad replied.

"I had a feeling that God wanted us to work together," Rabbi Lutz added.

"I would have liked to meet this Buck Thompson," Rabbi Pearlman said.

"Me, too," replied the Pope.

"We will, if it is Allah's will," replied Misha Ali.

"We need to think about what we want to tell the people, also, when we will do it?" the Pope said.

"I agree and we must not act independently, but to be united in our efforts," Rabbi Pearlman added.

"I agree wholeheartedly, we are one voice."

The meals were brought out and everyone said a prayer before they ate. They were informed by the pilot that they would be landing in New York in eleven hours; they would re-fuel and then head to Albany. They were told that the forecast was very pleasant and the pilot saw no rough weather at all. The men aboard knew it was God's work.

God also intervened after dinner and had the men all feel tired and sleepy. They all awoke at the announcement that they were landing in New York's Kennedy Airport to refuel. They landed in Albany, New York ninety minutes later. The plane didn't pull up to the Albany Airport, it was directed to Million Dollar Air, which was a small facility which catered to privately owned planes.

Blake Edwards had men on hand to load all the luggage into a large bus. The religious leaders were transported to the Americana Hotel, they arrive at a back entrance.

A woman greeted them and asked them to follow her, she informed them that their luggage would be delivered to their rooms. She guided the men to an elevator which brought them to the top floor. On this floor, there were fifteen rooms on one side and a large conference room on the other. Each suite was elegant and large. They were informed to dial eight, which went directly to her. She was there to help them in any way. Meals would be served in the conference room and they could order any other food through her. Even though everyone had a great nap on the plane, they still felt tired. They decided to head to their rooms and take it easy until tomorrow morning.

Meanwhile, Brother Blair was meeting with some friends, Brother Ken Davis and Marty Garcia from local Baptist churches and Brother Nick Brady of the Methodist church. Mr. Edwards would be arriving after their meeting.

"I have asked you to meet me this evening to discuss what will be happening very soon, I will need assistance. I, along with a Catholic Priest, a Rabbi, and a Muslim, we witnessed a blessed event. We watched as God escorted a man to heaven who met the requirements to be a righteous person. I saw Moses, George Washington, and others from heaven. I received a call from the Pope, we are all meeting tomorrow morning to work together to get Gods message out. I would like you to work with me as representatives of the Christian faith."

"If the Pope is here in Albany, there would have been a great deal of commotion. I saw nothing on the news," Brother Davis said.

"God is in -charge, we need to go with our faith on that," Replied Brother Blair.

"When did this happen?" Brother Marty Garcia asked.

"Two weeks ago."

"How come we haven't heard anything about it if it happened two-weeks ago?" Brother Ken Davis asked.

"We decided or should I say God decided to have us act as one voice."

"But you said a Muslim was present, they don't believe in God. They believe in Allah."

"Allah is God," Brother Blair replied.

"I am not forcing anyone to help. You are the only preachers that I know. That are faithful in your faith. We would have to stand together throughout this entire saga."

"Why not some of the T.V. preachers, they have the recognition needed for this type of thing."

"They all laughed at me when I called them. Their faith has to be wrapped around money for them to get involved. I think God chose us."

"I'm in," said Marty Garcia.

"Me, too," replied Ken Davis. Brother Brady followed in suit.

"What time will we be meeting tomorrow?" Brother Garcia asked.

"We will be meeting at the Americana Hotel up by the airport. Someone will meet you at the entrance and will escort you to the conference room. Don't eat, breakfast will be provided," Brother Blair stated.

"What time?" Brother Garcia asked once again.

"God will let you know. When you get up, take your shower or whatever you need to do, when you are finished, get in your car and drive to the Americana."

He then stood up and excused himself, he had a meeting with Blake Edwards within the hour; the other preachers said nothing and left.

Within the hour, Blake Edwards arrived. "They are all checked in," Blake said.

"That is great to hear, would you like a coffee or tea?" Brother Blair asked.

"A tea would be fine, thank you."

Brother Blair walked into the kitchen and put on the water. Blake took a seat in the living room. "I'll be right there," he stated as he got the cups ready for the tea. It seemed the water came to a boil instantly. With a cup of tea in each hand, Brother Blair entered the living room.

"How many are there?"

"Four from each group," Blake said.

"Is the Pope there?"

"No one saw him, they were all dressed in civilian clothes, even the Catholic priest," Blake stated.

"I will have four also, those I mentioned before will all be there."

"I will be close by if you need anything," Blake said.

"I would like to introduce you to all the attendees, to see who is helping all of us."

"No, that is not why I am doing this. I really don't want any credit for this meeting," Blake added.

"I am wondering if we should have invited Buck Thompson's cousin and his wife."

"I could stop by the house and tell them what's going on," Blake said.

"I don't think they drive."

"I could find out if they want to go and if they do, I could send a car," Blake added.

"No, I will drive down after our tea, they would remember me. I will explain what is going on."

"You're right, they would remember you. If I need to send a car, let me know."

"God did send you, I'm sure of that," Brother Blair said.

After tea, the men parted ways, they would meet sometime tomorrow.

It was Willy who answered the door. Willy looked at Brother Blair a little strange.

"I am Brother Blair. I was at the blessed event."

"Oh yeah, you looked familiar, come on in."

Willy had the preacher follow him upstairs to the apartment.

"Livy, its Brother Blair," Willy said as they entered the apartment. Olivia was sitting in the living room, watching television. She stood up to greet Brother Blair.

"Let me tell you why I am here. The four religions that witnessed Buck's blessed event will be holding a meeting tomorrow about how to get this message out. I would like to invite you both to attend."

"I knew God was going to handle this," Olivia said.

"Do you want to go, Olivia?" Willy asked.

"I think we are supposed to be there."

"What time?" Willy asked.

"God will let you know. When you get up and dressed, don't eat, we will all have breakfast together. There will be a car out front that will take you to the meeting," Brother Blair said, then he excused himself, and headed back home. He called Blake and told him that Willy and Olivia will be there and they would need a ride.

Blake asked, "What time should I send the car?"

"God will let you know," was all that Brother Blair said.

Willy and Olivia were planning to visit Buck's and Rose' grave site this Sunday.

"The meeting will be held on Saturday morning. We should invite them all to come to the grave site."

"I believe we should," replied Willy.

Chapter Six

"The witnesses and their leaders will meet tomorrow to start to form their agreements on how to release all this information. On Sunday, they will go to your gravesite at the request of your cousin William and his wife, Olivia. I know we should do something at this gathering," God stated.

"That was really quick." Buck said.

God smiled at Buck again, "Time does not exist in heaven. How long do you think you have been here?"

"About three hours," was Buck's reply.

God smiled and said, "You have been here two earth weeks. Time does not exist in heaven."

At this point, Buck remembered Jamie and Peter, also, George Washington telling him that time did not exist in Heaven.

"Who do you think should go with you?" God asked.

Buck thought for a moment and replied, "Abraham."

"Why Abraham?"

"You are our one God, besides being part of the Trinity. Abraham is the father of the Hebrew, Muslim, Catholic, and Christian religions," Buck replied.

"That is very good, you are using your power of knowledge."

Buck felt a hand placed on his shoulder, as he turned, he saw Abraham standing beside him.

"I am not worthy," Abraham said.

Buck stood there before God and Abraham, "I feel that I am not worthy to stand here before both of You."

"I never went a year without sin, I never became righteous," Abraham said.

"Abraham fought many battles, he had some corrupt thoughts. He is my most reliable soldier," God added. "I feel you will work fine together." At that point, God disappeared.

Abraham pointed at a bench off to their left, they both sat and looked down upon where the meeting would take place. Then Abraham asked, "You have never seen your grave site since you came to heaven, have you?"

"No, I would like to see the statue of my Rose."

Abraham waved his hand and he and Buck were above the site, this was the first time Buck saw his statue standing next to Rose.

"You both emit love and kindness," Abraham said.

"Thank you, we don't even have to try. God has blessed us many times."

"You have blessed us all and made our God very happy. I am proud to be here with you."

"My life has changed since I came to Heaven. I am honored to be here and to be able to communicate with all of you. Will I have a moment with my Rose before we witness the meeting?"

Abraham smiled and stood up, Rose appeared behind the bench. Buck looked towards Abraham, but he was gone. Rose sat down next to Buck and they kissed, "I will be attending the meeting that will take place very soon with those religious leaders that attended the event. I will go with Abraham to our grave site and stand witness to those in attendance."

"I know, I am so proud of you, Say hi to Willy and Olivia for me."

"I will and I will report back to you as soon as we are finished," Buck added.

"That is not necessary, we will all witness it from here," Rose said with a beautiful smile.

"I love you, Rose," Buck said.

"I know you do. And I know you feel the same love from me."

***

Brother Blair parked his car and headed for the front door of the Americana Hotel. Brother Brady, Garcia, and Davis all approached at the same time. They exchanged greetings as a woman stepped out and asked them to follow her. As they began to follow, Brother Blair asked them to wait a second.

A car pulled up and Willy and Olivia stepped out. Brother Blair held the door as they also entered. "This woman will escort us to the meeting room," Brother Blair told Willy and Olivia. They took the elevator to the top floor, as the doors opened, they saw the conference room straight ahead. As they entered, they saw name plates stationed around the table.

The only two sitting together was Willy and Olivia. As they took their seats, the conference room doors closed.

Brother Blair thanked Willy and Olivia for attending, they nodded in unison. He introduced them to Brother Brady, Garcia, and Davis. The doors opened, the first to enter was a man who looked familiar, as he stepped in, the street clothes he was wearing changed to all white, it was the Pope, those in the room all stood. "No formalities, please," he asked. Then the next to enter, his clothes turned Red, was Cardinal Burke. The next two their clothes turned black with the white collar, they were Catholic priests.

The next four that entered were all rabbis whose street clothes changed to represent their religion. This also happened to the Muslim who wore street clothes and had them change before everyone's eyes as if they were holding prayer at a mosque. They all sat at their assigned seats. The Cardinal asked,

"Why don't we all introduce ourselves and then eat. Will you start Brother Blair?" At this point, they stood up one at a time and introduced themselves. Willy and Olivia were the last to speak. The doors opened and breakfast was delivered.

There was one individual from each group sitting together. Brother Blair, Rabbi Lutz, Father Chaffee, and Mohammad Elsah formed one group. They were the witnesses along with Willy and Olivia. Willy and Olivia sat next to the Pope and Rabbi Pearlman; on the other side of them were Misha Ali and Brother Marty Garcia.

The four all told Willy and Olivia how proud they were to be at this meeting. When there was a quiet time, Willy stood and informed everyone, he and Olivia were going to Buck's and Rose' grave site tomorrow and invited all to attend. They all wanted to go to the site of this blessed event. After everyone finished their meal, a small army of workers came in and cleared the table and placed water and a glass in front of everyone.

Someone heard a worker say to another worker, "Was that the Pope?"

The answer he heard was, "It can't be the Pope or we would have heard it on the news."

Brother Blair stood up and asked, "Does anyone have any ideas about how we should handle this?"

Misha Ali stood and said, "We need to act altogether on our statement."

"We all agree this is a message from God," the Pope said, everyone shook their heads in agreement. "Then we tell the world that God has sent us all a message and together we need to deliver it," the Pope added.

"What message do we want to state?" Rabbi Pearlman asked.

"I don't want to interfere with your meeting. I feel you would have a better understanding after you go to the grave site tomorrow," Willy said. "I don't know why I think that, it just came to me this very moment," he added.

Each group started to talk among themselves, one group said, "We agree," this was followed by each group. All agreed to wait until after they meet at the grave site.

"Miss Olivia, being the only woman in the room, do you have something you would like to say?" asked Brother Davis. All eyes turned to Olivia.

Olivia stood up and began to speak, "God has done so many things lately, he brought you all together to act as one. I don't know why, but I feel he will have a message for you all tomorrow. Buck was always a very kind and considerate person. He loved everyone and knew God was with him all the time. He changed our lives and now we can see he will change the lives of millions of people around this world. I feel God will provide a message tomorrow that will guide you in your actions." Olivia sat back down.

The Pope took her hand and said, "You are a messenger from God."

"I wouldn't say that."

"You were glowing as you spoke, that is a sign that you have been in God presence and He is with you."

Olivia didn't know how to respond, she just smiled. Willy looked at his watch, "It's four o'clock in the afternoon. Where did the time go? I feel we have been here about two hours?"

Everyone looked at their watches, the door opened and dinner was being served. Everyone didn't know how that could have happened.

"Maybe we are on Heaven's time," Willy said, everyone looked at him, "Buck told me that there is no such thing as time in heaven, the statues he talked with told him that."

Rabbi Pearlman stood up, "We are doing God's work, He has set the time for us to act." The rest all agreed. After dinner, everyone seemed tired. The Christian preachers left and drove home. Willy and Olivia left. There was a car waiting outside to take them home. The rest returned to their rooms and fell off to sleep.

The next morning, Willy woke up to the phone ringing, he reached for it, "Hello!"

"Uncle Willy, this is Louie, my car won't start, I won't be able to drive you to the cemetery."

"Don't worry about it, we have someone else that can take us. Tell your mom we send our love. You stay safe, love you."

"Love you, too, Uncle Willy, bye." They both hung up.

"Honey," Willy said as he gently shook Olivia, "Time to get up."

Olivia opened her eyes, "What time is it?"

Willy looked at the clock on his night stand, "It's seven in the morning."

Olivia sat up and looked at the clock herself, "It's eight o'clock."

Willy looked again, "I swear I saw seven o'clock." They both started for the bathroom. "I am going to take a shower," Olivia said. She turned on the water and set it to a warm temperature, Willy started to shave.

When Olivia finished, Willy stepped in and took his shower. Olivia had the water on for coffee, when Willy walked in from the bathroom, he heard the toast pop up. Olivia had the eggs done and began to butter the toast. After their breakfast, they cleaned up and headed outside. They expected to see a car, what they saw was a small bus. Everyone from the meeting were inside. Willy and Olivia had the front seat.

No one spoke on the drive to Albany Rural Cemetery. The bus driver pulled about one hundred feet inside the front gate and opened the door. Olivia and Willy were the first to get off, that was when Olivia noticed everyone else was dressed in regular clothes. As the rest got off the bus, they felt blessed to be at this site. They commented to each other about the feelings they were experiencing. Willy and Olivia led the way, everyone could see the statues of Buck and Rose. This was the first time most of them got to see Buck.

The Pope spoke up and said, "I think we should all say a prayer to our God." They all bowed their heads to pray, the Muslims and the Hebrews knelt down. Willy and Olivia closed their eyes and prayed. They all finished at the same time, at first, no one noticed anything different. Then Willy grabbed Olivia's arm and everyone looked behind them and saw Buck standing there.

"I am very happy to see everyone on this beautiful Sunday."

No one moved, Buck walked up next to Willy and Olivia, he hugged Willy and then hugged Olivia and whispered in her ear, "Rose said to say hi."

Olivia gave him another squeeze.

"God has sent me down to help you with your endeavor. I brought a friend," beside Buck appeared another man, "Now I know you don't know who this is. He is the head of all your faith."

Before Buck could say anything else, everyone fell to their knees, except for Willy and Olivia. Willy whispered in Buck's ear, "Who is it?"

Buck replied in a whisper, "Abraham." Buck then heard murmurs of 'I am not worthy.' When Abraham heard the murmurs he said, "Please. Stand," the Muslims heard him say it in Arabic. The Hebrew heard him speak Hebrew. The Catholics and Christians heard him in English.

"I said the same thing to Buck when I meant him also," Abraham knew they were speaking to him. "Buck is the only righteous person here," he turned to the different religions and said, "This is my favorite religion." They all heard him but didn't understand the meaning of what he was saying. "Who believes in the one and only God?" Abraham asked. They all raised their hand, "That is my favorite religion, all of us believing in the same God."

Buck stepped forward, "What would you like to know?" no one said a word.

"What do you plan on saying?" Abraham asked. No one said a word.

"I have an idea," Buck said, "When you go to make your announcement, do it on top of the Empire State Building."

Rabbi Pearlman asked, "Why the Empire State Building?"

"God will amplify your voice so the world will hear it."

All of the religious groups stood there in awe at what they are seeing and hearing. The Pope spoke up and asked, "What one of us should make the announcement?"

"You will all make the announcement," Abraham said, "The world will hear one voice from a united front."

Buck asked, "Do you know what to say?"

They all stood there and no one said a word.

"Oh, I forgot to tell you the announcement is in your hand."

They all looked at their hands and they were all holding the same two pages of paper.

"Don't read it yet, we have more to talk about," Abraham said, "I have to tell you I've been in Heaven a long time. Buck Thompson has placed a smile on our God's face. He has brought a harmony to the world that has been missing forever. God knows the world needs to unite and live as one. Your job will be not to convince all the people. But to convince your religions that this is what God wants."

"This should be easy for the Pope, he is the head of the Catholic religion. No other religion has a true leader that all your brothers and sisters can relate to. There will be some Muslims that won't agree and some Jews and Christians. You will have our support and guidance," Buck said.

Buck looked at Abraham and said, "We are being called away."

With that, the two men disappeared.

Chapter Seven

Rose stood there as Buck appeared, Abraham was reporting to God. Buck and Rose walked that way. "How did it go?" Rose asked.

"I hope we got it started, but we will have to wait and see. I'll be right back," Buck said as he approached God.

"You did well, Abraham and I like the way this is going. The Empire State Building was a great thought. These men are all devoted to their cause. Let's see what their reaction will be as they talk with other leaders."

***

All the men stood there not saying a word. They began reading the papers they held in their hand. It stated,

'We have all witnessed a message from God. You can become righteous, the true requirements were removed from our Bible many, many years ago. You only need to go an entire year without sin. It has happened recently with a man named Buck Thompson.

We have never known what the requirements were before. If you work at being righteous and attain your goal, you will be escorted to Heaven by God Himself. Buck Thompson was the first righteous man since Jesus walked this earth. There were a few before Jesus, but none for over two thousand years, let us rejoice and set our goal. You do not need to be righteous to get to Heaven. There are many good people on this earth that will be accepted.

We need to work together and show God that we have a goal to work for. He is smiling down on us right now. Many of you have gotten close, but you didn't have any idea that you were close. Working together, we can help each other attain what is needed in the eyes of God.

We were assured by God that every person in this world will hear these words and understand everything that is being said. We reassure everyone that God loves each and every one of you. He will be watching

"I feel we should spend tomorrow contacting out fellow leaders and setting this in motion," stated the Pope. They all agreed to contact the others and then make it public. As they began to walk back to the bus, they saw hundreds of people standing outside the cemetery gate. At this point, they also saw that they no longer wore civilian clothes. People were taking pictures and yelling questions. None of the group responded.

They all boarded the bus, as it began to pull out of the cemetery, people were still yelling questions. Reporters got in their vans and cars and followed the group first to Willy's and Olivia's house, they managed to get in the house before the press could get out of their vans and cars, then up to the Americana Hotel.

While on the bus ride, they discussed talking to the press. "God must have had them there for a reason," one stated. "God will guide us," another said. As they pulled up to the hotel, the men left the bus. They all walked into a crowd of reporters. They answered every question with the guidance of God. Now the press knew that these religions are working together to get a message from God to the entire world. Because of the press, no one had to contact anyone.

All the others were calling them. The Preacher, Brother Blair, and the other preachers were taking calls; the Pope's group was taking calls, also. The Muslims and Hebrew's received so many calls the Hotel phone system went down. It was Blake Edwards who set up the phone system not knowing why he did it. He made a call and was assured the system would be back up within the hour.

When the phone lines got back up, Brother Marty Garcia answered a call, it was from a T.V. evangelist.

"Hello!"

"Hi. I received a call from a Brother Blair a few days ago. I thought it was a joke."

"Now, you know it wasn't. You had no faith that God did what you were told. When you know God wants you to have this information, call back," with that, Brother Garcia hung up and took another call.

What no one was aware of was that all the calls that came through were from religious leaders, reporters tried to call, but their calls went to a pizza joint on Delaware Avenue. It turned out that over half of them ordered pizza, not knowing why they did it. ·

The Vatican set up a system that let the Pope talk to all the Cardinals that were present. He informed them that he witnessed a miracle, that he stood in the presence of Abraham and a truly righteous man named Buck Thompson that was escorted to Heaven by God himself. He told them of the requirements to be a righteous man. He also explained that a united message would be sent out to the world very soon. The Cardinals relayed the message to all the Bishops under them. They relayed the message to all the priests.

As each synagogue called, they were told basically the same message as the Pope relayed to his people.

For no reason, Mecca was flooded with twice as many Muslims than ever before. When the morning prayer was sung. Everyone heard the message about righteousness and Allah's message that needed to be delivered by a united religious front. Every one that heard the message believed it, except for many Muslim leaders. There were also many Jewish leaders that could not except the message as reality.

Outside of the Americana Hotel were all kinds of media networks, it got so bad that the hotel had to ask them to get off of their property, because their customers could not get through. The entire world was intercepting all of God's words. The message was getting out and this made God very pleased.

The Christians and Catholics along with the Jews and Muslims all agreed to adopt the name (The United Religious Front), knowing that God wanted this to happen. What amazed all of these men was when the newspapers came out and the nightly news was reported. All newspapers said the same exact thing, this also happened with the nightly news. No matter what the religious leaders said to reporters, it all came across as the same statement.

All the men agreed to meet the following morning to set a date for the message from atop of the Empire State Building. As evening approached, they all became very tired, they needed to sleep. God set the sleep to help these men calm down, He witnessed them all becoming very hyper. They were truly filled with the message they were meant to send.

***

Buck and Rose sat together on a bench, hearing all the detailed description of what was going on back on earth. "You made this all happen," Rose said to Buck.

"I wish it was something I worked on, like setting a goal."

"You proved God right, you didn't know there was a goal. You just lived your life the way you wanted, you became a righteous man. Now there are people out there that can try and change their lives and set a goal for themselves."

"I hope all that happens, I would love to see that."

185

"God would love that, too."

Rose and Buck stood up and began to walk. Everyone who saw them gave a great big smile. Buck found himself standing in front of God, Jesus was sitting on His right. Buck felt that God wanted to talk to him, he let go of Rose' hand and sat on the left of God.

"This is going very well, I have a great feeling of triumph. You and Abraham convinced those leaders to believe in something that they could see. I want to show you something."

God waved his hand. Buck saw a clock shaped wheel. To the upper left, he saw Muslims fighting over the truth, he heard what they were saying they didn't believe the leaders of the Mosque in Mecca. They complained that these men must have been drugged. "If it did happen, Muhammad would have been Allah's messenger," one said.

"I don't believe that Abraham would have ever taken a part in this, it doesn't add up," said another. The sound faded and a group of rabbis at a temple in Israel appeared to the right side of the circle.

"We need to get this message out to all the people, not just Jews," one rabbi said.

"How do we really know that this happened the way they said it did. We know the Bible states you need to obey the commandments to be righteous. I feel we should request to see the sacred scrolls. This would tell us if the requirements for being righteous were changed," another rabbi said.

"I think we would be going down the wrong road to question God. Rabbi Pearlman is a true believer, more so than many of us. I know he witnessed what he said, we need to believe. God is waiting for our reaction, I would think he is watching us now," Rabbi Mohr said. The sound began to fade, then the group of Christians appeared.

"I know Brother Blair and I believe him and the others," Brother Baker said.

"You don't think that God would have told Billy Graham before Brother Blair or any popular evangelist," Brother Adams stated.

"No, I don't. I believe God had the people picked out that he wanted to witness this event. We are Christians and we need to keep our faith and believe in one another," Brother Baker replied.

The sound began to fade, then Buck saw the Catholics, they all seemed to believe the Pope, no matter what he said, but that was a good thing, Buck thought. The circle vanished.

"The people believe because they want to believe, there are some leaders that won't believe because they did not see it themselves."

"Maybe, we should send Muhammad down to talk to the Muslims, he was Your messenger," Buck said.

"We really can't do that."

"May I ask why?" Buck asked.

God smiled at Buck and touched his head with one finger. What Buck saw was Jesus on Mount Olives talking to thousands of people. Then he saw Muhammad, it was six hundred years later, he was talking to people about Allah.

Buck knew what God meant.

Buck felt that God was finished with him at this moment. He walked over to Rose, "Did you know?"

Rose placed a finger over Buck's mouth, "There is so much you will learn, we were educated when we arrived in Heaven. You came with God, but He will fill your mind with all the answers you may need." Buck took Rose' hand and walked to a place that Buck would go when he wanted to check on Willy and Olivia. As they looked down, they saw Willy and Olivia sitting on the sofa and talking to each other.

"What should we do now?" Willy asked.

"God will guide us, He will get us to where ever we should be," Olivia replied and then gave Willy a loving hug. Willy returned the movement.

"They seem to be right on top of everything," Buck said as he and Rose moved away.

***

The phone rang and Olivia picked it up, "Hello."

"Is this Olivia?"

"Yes, who is this?"

"This is Brother Blair, we have set a date to announce the requirements to be righteous, and also to tell the world about Brother Buck and God. We will announce it on top of the Empire State Building in New York City. We will make the announcement in three days. Would you be able to attend?"

"Of course, we would love to be there."

"Would you like to fly or be driven? We have a benefactor who is covering all the expenses."

"How are you getting there, Brother Blair?" Olivia asked.

"I'm going to drive, I don't like flying." Brother Blair responded.

Willy and Olivia never even got on an airplane before.

"Willy, would you like to fly or be driven to New York City? They are going to make the announcement in three days."

"How much do you think it will cost to fly?" Willy asked.

"There is a benefactor who is covering all the cost."

"Then let's fly, it will be a new experience for both of us," Willy added.

"Brother Blair we, would like to fly."

"I will stop by later to drop off all the info you would need. You and Willy will be flying with all the rest."

"Thank you so much, Brother Blair, see you later."

With that Olivia, hung up the phone, "Brother Blair will drop off the information we need."

"That sounds good," was Willy's reaction.

Chapter Eight

It was eight o'clock when Brother Blair stopped by with all the information. Willy and Olivia would be picked up the day of the event at seven o'clock in the morning, they would be taken to the Albany Airport. Then on to New York's J.F.K. Airport. From there, they would be driven to the Empire State Building.

"They got this event on a pretty tight schedule," Willy said.

"I can't believe someone is handling all the cost. He must be a good Christian," Livy added.

The phone rang, Olivia answered, "Hello!"

"We have to start looking for a place to live," Betsy said.

"Sis, you are going to move here, we are moving downstairs."

"Really, I'll have Louie and his friends get you moved."

"The only thing we need to move is our clothes. Downstairs is completely furnished, Buck bought all new furniture a week before the event."

"Do you think Buck would be okay with this?" Betsy asked.

"You know, when I told Buck you might have to move. He just smiled and said, 'This will all work out fine.' Now I know what he meant."

"I feel so blessed, knowing what happened. I'm glad he was a sparkle in God's eyes," Betsy stated.

"Before Buck went to Heaven, he changed our lives for the better. We are just spreading his love a little further," Olivia added, "Oh! we will be going to New York City in three days, I don't know if we are coming back that same day. When I find out, I will call you and let you know."

"Willy and I will start getting our stuff downstairs. You can move in, in a couple of days. I don't think you will need to move anything, except for your clothes and stuff like that."

"Sis, I really appreciate all of this. I will keep you both in my prayers."

"Thanks, Betsy, we couldn't ask for anything better. See you soon. Love you!"

"Love you, too, sis," with that said the call ended.

"Willy, I'm going to start putting our clothes in bags and bring them downstairs. Betsy needs to move. The only thing we need to move is our clothes."

"I was hoping we would do that soon."

"Why would you be hoping about that?"

"The giant T.V. is going to waste," Willy said with a smile on his face.

Olivia just shook her head in a no motion and smiled back. Willy and Olivia have found more time for each other than ever before. They were aware that it was because of Buck and the love he shared.

The following morning, Olivia had all of their clothes in the closet and dressers downstairs. She called Betsy to let her know she could start moving in anytime. Betsy said she would stop over in about an hour.

Willy was returning from the store when he saw Betsy walking towards the house. "Glad to see you're going to move in," he said.

"You and Livy have saved my life, I don't know what I would have done if it weren't for you two."

"We are just sharing the blessing that Buck shared with us."

"We need to talk about the rent," Betsy stated.

"No rent, you are family and I don't know if Livy told you, but we are leaving you everything we have when we pass."

"We can't except your generosity for free."

"You are the only family we have left. You have Louie and two grown daughters. We will need to have you sign a paper to inherit everything. Olivia has the paper ready, she will mail them, after you sign."

"But—"

"Buck wanted it this way. He left everything to us, so we could leave it to you. Somehow, I believe Buck knew all of this was going to happen."

Olivia was sitting on the sofa when Willy and Betsy walked in. "Hi, sis," was Olivia's greeting.

"Livy, I told Willy, I don't know what we would have done without your help."

"It really was all Buck's doing. Let's go upstairs, so you will know what you need to move. But, first, step in the kitchen and sign the papers that Mr. Templar needs. I will mail them before our trip to New York City," Olivia looked around, "This is my dream house, which I think Buck picked out all the furnishing because he knew I would love it all." Betsey signed the papers and thanked Olivia for everything. With that said, they headed upstairs, Olivia sat in the stair lift. When they reached the top, Olivia reached in her pocket and retrieved the two sets of keys, "Here you go, sis."

Betsy loved Olivia and Willy's new apartment, she knew they have only lived there a few months, but she loved it from the first time she saw it, "I'm going to give Louie the bedroom off of the living room."

She checked out the other two bedrooms off the kitchen, "This place is beautiful," Betsy said, then she turned and hugged Olivia.

"This is all Buck's doing, he loved everyone."

"I really wish I spent more time around Buck, I would have learned so much," Betsy added.

"The only thing you would have learned was that Buck loved Rose. He lived his life with love and hope and charity. I look forward to seeing him and Rose in Heaven. Willy feels the same way," Olivia said.

"When are you leaving for New York City?"

"Tomorrow morning."

"Please call me when you're traveling back," Betsy added.

The next morning, Willy and Olivia got up and began to get ready for the trip. Olivia cooked a light breakfast. When they finished, they cleaned up and headed outside to catch their ride to the airport. The small bus was waiting, everyone except Brother Blair was in the bus. As they boarded, they were greeted by everyone there. Willy and Olivia sat across from the Pope and Mohammad Elsah. The Pope smiled and said, "This should be a joyful day for all of us."

"Is there anything Olivia and I will have to do?" Willy asked.

"Your presence is enough for all of us. If you would like to read the message from God with us, we would like that very much."

"We would love that," answered Olivia.

As they arrived at the airport, Willy and Olivia was still uncertain if they would be returning that same day. Willy didn't know who to ask. Everyone seemed to be occupied with their own thoughts. Willy thought he would wait until they were aboard the plane and then ask someone. He also thought they might not know either.

Everyone left the bus and walked through the airport right to the plane. Within minutes, they were in the air, they would be landing in thirty minutes. Willy noticed everybody was reading the message from God. At that point, the Pope handed Willy and Olivia a copy. As Olivia read the message, her heart was being filled with grace, Willy felt it, too. They didn't realize that God was smiling at them.

***

God turned to Buck, "It's about to happen."

Buck just smiled.

"This is happening because of you. I want you to go down and be with them when they speak."

"Is there any other directions I should give them?" Buck asked.

"Your presents will guide them. They know you represent Me."

"How will everyone in the world understand what they are saying?" Buck asked.

God smiled, "Everyone will hear it in their own language. Those that are working in the fields or in tunnels will hear every word as if someone was whispering in their ear."

"Will I be alone? Or will someone else be there?"

"You won't need anyone. You are on a mission for Me. You will have all the guidance you will need. Because of free will, the outcome may be different than he had hoped. At least, we will be on a track that we were never on before. You should go to Rose and spend some time with her. You will leave in a short while."

God looked at Buck and smiled.

Buck felt as if he would complete the task at hand. He turned to see Rose standing there. He walked over and gave her a kiss and smiled.

"When will you be leaving?" Rose asked.

"Very soon."

"We are all praying that God's dream will come true."

"I am, too. Even God is not aware of what will happen because of free will. But I will do my best to support those chosen for this task."

Buck heard God's voice, "It is time."

***

The plane was landing in New York City, Olivia looked at Willy and smiled. Willy smiled back. "I wonder if Buck will be here," Olivia asked.

"I hope so, he has guided us this far."

"No, God has guided Buck this far."

"You're right, this is all God." Willy remarked.

As they walked off the plane and entered the terminal, they saw Brother Blair standing at the entrance. No one said a word, they just smiled at one another. They all followed Brother Blair who led them downstairs to where a small bus sat by the curb, marked 'No Parking.'

A woman with a small baby in her arms approached the Pope and asked, "Holy Father, will you give my child and I a Blessing."

The Pope looked at his fellow travelers and said, "We all ask God to Bless and watch over both of you," then they all proceeded to the bus.

"When we get to the top of the Empire State Building, when should we start?" Rabbi Pearlman asked. Willy didn't know why he responded, "God will guide us."

Everyone nodded in agreement.

It was early morning still, but there was no traffic. The streets should be filled with cars, buses, trucks, and people. But everything was quiet. It was only a short ride. When they exited the bus, all they saw was a doorman holding the door opened. As they entered, a person escorted them to the elevator. As they entered, the escort pushed the top button; soon, they were on their way to the top lookout area.

"Isn't this a joyous occasion?" Olivia said, they all smiled and she said, "We need to talk and be excited as we can be."

"You're right!" someone said and they all began talking and laughing. "This has to be the most joyous occasion in all our lives," Brother Garcia stated.

The doors opened and they all stepped out. Willy looked out on the observation deck and it was empty. "Should we go out there?" Willy asked.

They all began to walk out, "I thought they would be microphones," Rabbi Lutz said.

"You won't need them," someone said behind them. They all turned to see Buck standing there, "You will read the message, everyone in the world will hear God's words. They will hear it in their own language, even the deaf will hear this message.

"God is with us and He is proud of all of you. After the message, there will be millions of people waiting for you downstairs. Don't be scared, they wouldn't hurt you, they just want to say, 'I saw them.'"

Buck walked over and gave Olivia a kiss on the cheek and hugged Willy.

He walked around and shook hands with every one of those present. Buck walked up to the Pope and said, "God loves your talk about abortion and how people will fight tooth and nail over the topic. But you stood up for the babies that are starving, that need medication, most of these same people don't think about them."

The Pope went to bow and Buck stopped him. Buck walked out in front of all of them, "I bow to you." He bowed and said, "We should begin."

Chapter Nine

The eighteen people stood in a half circle, they all held their two sheets of paper. Buck nodded.

"We have all witnessed a message from God. You can become righteous, you need to go an entire year without sin. It has happened recently with a man named Buck Thompson. We have never known what the requirements were before. If you work at being righteous and attain your goal, you will be escorted to Heaven by God. Buck Thompson was the first righteous man since Jesus walked this earth. There were a few before Jesus, but none for over two thousand years, let us rejoice and set our goal. You do not need to be righteous to get to Heaven. There are many good people on this earth that will be accepted.

"We need to work together and show God that we have a goal to work for. He is smiling down on us right now. Many of you have gotten close, but you didn't have any idea that you were close. Working together, we can help each other attain what is needed in the eyes of God. We were assured by God that every person in this world will hear these words and understand everything that is being said. We reassure everyone that God Loves each one of you."

As these words were recited, everyone heard them. A farmer working in his fields heard the word of God and shut off his tractor and prayed. People working in factories, which the noise level is so high they need to wear ear protection, stopped and heard the words of God.

Atheist stopped in their tracks, listened, and felt haunted. Some world leaders felt it was a plot to turn their people against them. Most rejoiced at the words they heard. They all heard God's words. Those in countries, which were in the dead of night, were awaken by these words. Love and righteousness were spread throughout the world and no one could say they didn't hear it.

Four terrorists in London were about to destroy a building and kill many people. They stopped what they were doing packed up everything they had and left that area. The reaction throughout the world was basically the same. Everyone felt love in their heart and a peace that set a calming effect in a world that was in array.

When the eighteen were finished, they began to leave. Buck shook every one's hand, except for Olivia and Willy, they were greeted with hugs and a whisper of I love you.

No one spoke, close to a million people were waiting for them to leave the Empire State Building. The streets were occupied by all races and denominations of every faith. They were not there to worship. They were there to see God's chosen speakers.

None of these people knew what was happening on top of the Empire State Building, they were drawn together by the words of God. As the speakers began to leave the building, no one stepped in their way. Most stood in awe of what they saw. Each member had a glow about them. True ambassadors from God.

After they boarded the bus, they pulled away. They waved to all the people they saw.

People felt blessed to be in their presence.

Buck reappeared in Heaven, standing next to Rose, who greeted him with a loving hug.

Buck felt God's presence and turned towards him.

"Today, the world is a better place because of you Buck."

"We all know this is because of You and the faith you have in Your people. I am honored to be a tiny part of it."

"The bus will take those who have also honored us to Madison Square Garden for a press conference. The fight is just beginning and there will be those who will fight us all the way. I may call on you again. You do not realize all you have done to make this possible. Most people believe in what they can see. They see an ordinary man who gives them hope, faith, and truth. Many will yearn for these qualities because of you. You have deserved some time with Rose and she, with you. You may do whatever you desire."

God then smiled and disappeared. Buck looked at Rose and hugged her very tight, she returned the hug, then they kissed. A joyful feeling filled them both.

"Let's go and be with our loved ones awhile," Rose said. Buck and Rose walked to their family mansion in Heaven.

The bus brought God's ambassadors to an underground entrance of Madison Square Garden. They were brought to a room where they would sit and eat before the interviews. A peaceful calm was instilled in them all. They had no idea that Madison Square Garden was packed and thousands of followers stood outside wishing to get in.

"Does anyone know if we will be traveling back to Albany today?" Olivia asked.

"We will be heading back at three o'clock," Willy replied. Olivia looked at him, "I don't know why I said that, it just came out."

Every one smiled.

After they all had something to eat, an escort walked them to an entrance, which would lead them to the main stage. They all took their seats and was amazed that with all the people no one made a sound. The press drew straws to see who would ask the first question and so on.

"Why were you the ones chosen by God to deliver his message?" one reporter asked.

They all answered at the same time, "We all have true faith, we believe the word of God and we do not doubt His word."

As question after question was asked and answered in unison by all eighteen ambassadors of God. People prayed and some prayed allowed. After two hours, the questions stopped. The eighteen stood and said in unison, "God loves all His creations and will help those who ask for His help. God asks that you listen to your heart and not the false prophets that will try to demean His words. He has given us a goal that is reachable and blessed. Sinners repent and ask for forgiveness. For your God loves you."

***

As God looked down, He smiled again joy filled His heart. This is the first time God saw billions of people start to regain their faith.

Buck and Rose watched the ambassador's leave to head home. "I am so proud of you Buck," Rose stated.

"It wasn't only me, you helped a great deal."

"No, it was you," Rose answered.

"No, my mind was always thinking about you and that is what prevented me from sinning. So, together, we have done this for God."

Buck was being called away by Jesus. Rose kissed him on the cheek and he left. Buck turned and saw Jesus sitting on a gold bench and he approached him. Buck had already noticed the scars on his wrist and feet and saw the faint scars on his forehead where the crown of thorns once sat.

"Lord, you wanted to see me."

"You know how you have changed the way the world was headed. You have brought our faith to the lives of God's children. You know how thankful we are."

"But God knows everything, he would have known this was to happen."

"God does know more than He wants to know, He knows the weather of every second of every day. He knows who will live and who will die. He can see the path that we may all take in our lives. But things can happen that changes the path drastically. His decisions sometimes haunt him."

"But how can that ever happen," Buck asked.

Jesus placed a finger to Buck's forehead. "What do you see?" He asked.

"I see two people standing near a bed where a boy is laying."

"The boy's name is Daniel; he is eleven years old and will die in one earth week."

"God can save him, I don't see a problem."

Chapter Ten

"Two weeks ago, Daniel was a healthy little boy, but his future was set. In two weeks, he would turn twelve. On his twelfth birthday, he accidently, blows up his house, killing his mother and father and his little sister. God saw how this occurrence will stain Daniel for life. He will suffer the torment of killing his family each and every day. He will try to kill himself by blowing up a house he lives in. He kills three more people.

"To save Daniel, God has given him cancer. I will be bringing him up here soon. His parents are good Christian people that don't blame God for his cancer. But how do you think God feels by the choice he had to make. God has talked with Daniel and told him what would happen and Daniel asked God to save him."

"No one has any idea what God does for all of us. How much He protects us from ourselves. He loves us so much and truly watches over all of us every day."

Buck felt his heart hurt and knew for sure that God is everywhere all the time.

"God will always deal with what he has to do. He knows Daniel's parents and little sister will cry for months about their loss. Everyday God will help them along. He will get them through this. But he cries when he feels their sorrow."

"I had no idea," Buck said.

"No one does. He doesn't want anyone to know the burden He bares for all of us. To everyone, he is the Almighty God. He knows all, He watches over everyone, and He prays for sinners. That is all we need to know. That's how He likes it."

Buck thought for a second and tears welled up in his eyes, "In all my life I prayed, but I never said a prayer for God Himself."

He started to cry.

Jesus placed his hand on Buck's shoulder, "You are the only one who has figured it out. No one thinks that God needs prayers. You are one of a kind.

"You know, no one has ever mentioned Judas betraying me. As the son of God, I also have the ability to know what will happen. No one has ever said why would Jesus select Judas as an apostle knowing he will betray Him? Judas was a part of my plan; he knew what needed to be done in order for everything to take place. We discussed it many times, he did what he did out of loyalty to me. He didn't want to do it. He knew everyone would hate him forever. He appeared in Heaven before I did. He was welcome by my Father. He did not take his own life, for that is a terrible sin. He asked me to make sure he got to heaven, so he wouldn't have to lie to anyone, about why he did it."

With that said, Jesus turned Buck towards Rose. Through his tears, he could barely make her out. He walked into her arms and remained crying. Rose held him tighter than ever before, she asked no questions, she just held him. A few moments later, Buck retained his composure. "Let's visit the children," he stated and they walked in that direction.

Buck and Rose watched the children playing and enjoyed the joyful noise. Then a girl, about six years old, walked up to Buck and Rose.

"Hi, Terry, how are you today?" Buck asked
"I am very well; can I sing you a song?"
"We would love that," Rose and Buck replied in unison.

"You are our sunshine. You are our light,
You guide us all in the dark of night,
You watch over us with joyful care,
We know our God is always there.

You make us happy and never sad.
Everything is joyous and never bad,
You watch over us with joyful care,
We know our God is always there.

We are the sheep that will never stray,
Because we know You made us this way,
You watch over us with joyful care,
We know our God is always there."

Buck and Rose started to clap, "That was the most beautiful song I have ever heard," Buck said.
"Thank you!" Terry said, she turned and headed back to the other children.
"That was so sweet," Rose stated.

"This is Heaven," Buck said. They both walked towards the children and watched them play. Buck saw no racism, nothing but love for one another, "Why can't we live on earth this way?"

***

After the interviews were done, the eighteen ambassadors embarked on their journey back to Albany.

"What are we to do now?" Olivia asked.

Brother Blair smiled and said, "God will let us know."

Everyone agreed, for they knew God was in -charge. Brother Blair walked to his car after departing the bus to drive back. Cardinal Burke had a driver ready to take him home. The rest boarded the plane. When they reached Albany, there were thousands of people just waiting to see them. All sixteen ambassadors acknowledged their presence and waved. The three Christian preachers and along with Father Chaffee, Olivia and Willy entered a waiting bus to be driven home. The Pope and the other Priest boarded the plane that would take them along with the Jewish and Muslim Ambassadors' home.

It was Friday evening about six thirty when Olivia and Willy got home. They were greeted at the door by Betsey and her son Louie.

"We heard God's words, I feel most of us received the grace of God at that moment. I will never forget this moment of our lives, and to think my sister and brother-in-law was a big part of it," Betsey stated.

"It was Buck who guided us all and God who gave us the words. We are really not in -charge. I want to visit Buck and Roses grave Sunday," Olivia added.

"The State of New York has asked people to not go to the Albany Rural Cemetery until the state builds parking lots and can handle an international crowd of thousands daily. Construction begins tomorrow."

"But that's a Saturday," Willy said.

"Donations have been pouring in to help provide a place for all the people to be able to see the place where the event occurred. The State has received nearly a billion dollars so far, that is why they are starting tomorrow," Betsey relayed.

At this point, the phone rang. "Hello!" Willy said as he picked up the phone.

"Hi, this is your honored governor. I wanted to tell you about the construction that will start tomorrow at the Albany Rural Cemetery."

"My sister-in-law just told us," Willy replied.

"You and your wife, Olivia, and any guest will always be allowed to enter during construction. We feel so blessed," The governor said.

"Thank you very much for the call, we do appreciate it. You have a blessed day," Willy said and hung up the phone, "That was the governor who said we will have access to Albany Rural Cemetery any time we choose during the construction."

"Thank you, God," Olivia responded.

"Then we will go Sunday. Betsey, if you and Louie want to go, you are welcomed," Willy said.

"We would love that."

***

Buck heard God calling him. He stood and kissed Rose on the cheek. "I'll be back soon," was all he said.

God saw Buck approaching, "It all looks very good. I hope it continues."

"What will be our next step?" Buck asked.

"I know that we have gained many followers that will always stay by us. I have some joyous news, all forms of religious services will be held this weekend all over the world. They shall all feel my presence and know that I love them.

"I have been thinking about our next move. We need to talk to all the world leaders.

"I will call for a Day of Divine Peace. On this day, no one will die. Everyone will know that this day is divine. On this day, I will provide rain to those who need it. I will provide food for those who suffer from famine. We will show everyone that I will always be there to help."

"How can we help those throughout the world to help one another?"

"I would like you to be our ambassador to the United Nations. Ask them how they think they could help one another. I would like you to go on the Day of Divine Peace. You will know what to say. No country will need an interpreter. They will all understand what you will say. We will talk later."

Buck left and went back to Rose.

Chapter Eleven

"Rose, God gave me a piece of fruit from the Tree of Knowledge and told me I was worthy. When I took a bite, I immediately knew it was the Tree of Knowledge."

Rose smiled and said, "I have heard many women in my life say my husband thinks he knows everything. My husband does."

"I have always wondered what were the answers to many questions I have had in my life."

"Like what?"

"I wonder why God didn't except Cain's sacrifice. I asked a preacher and he said because it wasn't a blood sacrifice. I never believed that. But now I know the answer."

"Can you share it with me?" Rose asked.

Buck thought for a second and replied. "Yes, I am allowed to share it with you. Unlike Abel who sacrificed an unblemished lamb, Cain worked at setting up his sacrifice with all the crops he grew. It took him three days. It looked so beautiful, it went from the ground up to five feet tall. Cain was so proud. When God told Cain to try it again, he didn't, he became very angry. If he did try to do it again, he would have seen the fruit on the ground started to spoil and he would have replaced them. But instead, he left the sacrifice and did what he did."

"That is very sad."

"When Cain found out the truth, He asked God to cast him into the fires of hell for what he did to Abel."

"Did God do that?"

"I don't know, that was not my question. I do not want to know. That is between God and Cain."

"You have become a remarkable man, not only a righteous man, but a true man of God," Rose said, then placed her arms around Buck. Buck placed his arms around Rose for this was truly Heaven.

"There were so many questions I wanted to ask God when I died. But I can't think of one."

"If you have the knowledge, you already know the answers, maybe that is why you can't think of any."

"God will have a Day of Divine Peace. He would like me to be His ambassador to the United Nations. On this Day of Divine Peace, no one will die, God will give water to those countries that are experiencing a drought, and food to those countries that are suffering from famine."

"When will this happen?"

"He said we would talk later. He is waiting to see what will happen next. He did say we gained many new followers that will stay with us from now on."

"That sounds great, this celebration is still going on and may continue for a while," Rose added.

"Let's check in on Willy and Olivia," Buck said.

As they walked to the edge, they looked down, they saw Willy, Olivia, Betsey, and her son Louie talking about their visit last Sunday at Buck's and Rose's grave site.

Buck and Rose listened and heard about some construction that was taking place at the cemetery.

***

"It looks like they are building two ten floor parking garages and a massive parking lot. Altogether, they would hold thousands of cars," Willy said.

"That is what we noticed last week. We should go this Sunday and see how their coming along with the construction," Olivia said.

"It's so nice that the governor allows only you and your guest to go anytime. No one else is allowed, to everybody else the cemetery is closed until after the construction," Louie stated.

Olivia stated, "I hope the State doesn't plan on making money from this. I don't think God would approve."

"The State wouldn't do that, all the money for the construction was donated," Willy added.

"You never know what politicians will do, if money is involved," Betsey said, then added, "Can we go with you Sunday?"

"Of course, any time you want to go, would be fine with us," Willy said.

***

Buck and Rose heard God's words.

"Faith on earth is growing, love is spreading. All religions are starting to organize. We still have a long way to go, but there is hope and faith spreading throughout lands that had no hope or faith."

All those in heaven cheered and began to pray. The brightness of heaven became brighter and God was pleased.

Buck heard God calling him. He released Rose' hand and turned, God stood before him with a heavenly glow.

"Soon, I will send you down to talk with those in the United Nations. I have halted those who call this a lie and try to persuade people not to believe. Most of them are religious leaders who feel they are losing their followers. I have instilled a path of repentance in hope they will change their ways."

"I am ready to go whenever you want me to go. I believe in You, and know whatever You want me to do is right," Buck said.

"Bless you, my son, I will be with you all of the time. Things may happen that will startle you, but I will be there."

God vanished and Buck turned and saw Rose.

"Well, are you going to God?" Rose asked.

Buck smiled and said, "We have had our meeting. I will be going down soon to relay God's messages. He told me some things may startle me, but He will be there."

Buck and Rose walked to the spot where they could see Willy and Olivia. They were getting ready for church and they would be going to the cemetery. Betsey and Louie were waiting to go with them.

"Their faith has grown, their love for one another show so lovingly," Rose said.

***

The Pope was on the phone with Italy's ambassador to the United Nations, "In two days, there will be an event taking place at the U.N. I don't know what it will be, but you must yield your time."

The ambassador agreed.

The Prime Minister of Israel was relaying the same message to his ambassador.

This event will travel through all countries across the world, even countries with no ambassador would attend. This was never released to the press. If it were, there would be millions of faithful followers trying to get to the United Nations.

All those who attended the blessed event knew something was about to happen. No one knew what it was or when it would happen.

Brother Blair started to receive calls from all kinds of Evangelicals. They all wanted to know what they could do to help. Brother Blair answered them all in the same way. Send money to those who need food or need medical attention. Use your money for good, not growth.

There were those who screamed foul, "This is a trick, God doesn't work this way." Most of their words fell on deaf ears. People believed what was in their hearts. God had faith in these people and knew He could help guide them and they would follow.

Two days later, all nations, big and small, attended a world meeting at the United Nations. As the meeting began, starting with Italy, "I yield my time," the ambassador stated. All countries followed this with their own release to yield their time. No one knew why they did this, they just did it. At the end when all countries stated their intentions, The Secretary to the United Nations hit his gavel once and took a seat. All members sat there looking around at one another. Then the brightest of light occurred. Everyone shielded their eyes. When the light vanished, Buck stood at the podium smiling.

Chapter Twelve

"Today is the Day of Divine Peace. Those countries that need water, it is raining there right now, those countries that are suffering a great famine have crops growing all around them and trucks of food being delivered. No one will die today. This is the word of God."

Fifteen people disappeared at that moment.

"Those were demons that attached themselves to the United Nations."

Two were members of the U.N., the rest were assistance.

"They were not here to help their countries. They had their own agenda, which would have destroyed half of this world."

As he spoke, all that were left, listened, no interpreters were needed. Everyone heard Buck's voice in their own language. "There are also four world leaders that are demons. You will have to draw them out."

"I am Buck Thompson, an ambassador of God. This is the only time you will hear my voice, for God wants to speak to you."

"Today, I address the world; some of you are here because you hold the fear of God in your heart. I want you to change that to the Love of God in your heart.

"Some are true believers, some became believers because of the blessed event that occurred here on earth. I would like to see this group work together to help one another. No country should thirst, there are too many countries that could help end this.

"No person on the earth should hunger, there are countries that throw away food. This could be shared. Those that have plenty, you can load the empty ships you send to pick up cargo. If we can spend a few days thinking about what to do to help those less fortunate than yourselves,, you have the skills and the tools needed to accomplish any of this. I will be with you to do whatever I see needed to be done.

"We need not only to help one another but to love one another. This will release a joy that will fill the world. You have many names for me. I would like you to all call me Father. For I will watch over you and protect you. But you have a great deal of work to do for yourselves. It won't be easy. Many of you hold strong resentments towards one another. If you are willing to work together, this will fade in time. I send a blessing to you all."

Then a silence filled the room. They watched as Buck ascended back to heaven. No one spoke, they all sat there.

The Secretary to the United Nations walked to the podium, "We will adjourn for two days."

Every one stood and departed the building. No one spoke.

***

Buck appeared before God.

"That went well, what do you think?"

Buck smiled and stated, "While you spoke, I looked out at all the people present. They seemed to be spellbound. I think you moved many of those who were on the fence."

"We have done our part. Many people will spend their lives thinking of what they heard. We have had a great number of those that belonged to occult religions turn towards us. They have heard the voice of God, they have never heard from their gods. Atheist are forced to believe because they witnessed what they always said didn't exist. I feel as if we changed the world. I was about to… I don't mean to say give-up, but lose a little more faith in mankind. I believe it was you who have brought this about. I will need you to do one more thing for Me, not now but soon."

Buck saw Rose, God smiled, and Buck knew their discussion was over. Buck walked over to Rose who embraced him in their loving way.

"That was wonderful to see and hear," Rose said.

"You saw everything?"

"God placed the event in all our minds. We watched everything. I am so proud of you and everything you brought about."

"It was God who brought this all about."

"No, it started with you, when you became the first righteous man since Jesus walked the earth. You have changed millions of lives and that is why God chose you for this mission."

"I still feel as if I am not worthy."

"You are a humble man who places everyone before yourself. You have set the path for those who will become righteous. You will always fill the hearts of those that think they are not worthy."

"Let's go and see what Olivia and Willy are doing."

As they approached the spot where they go to see Willy and Olivia, Buck turned to Rose and kissed her, "You will always be in my heart, I thank God all of the time for you."

"I know you do. God wants me to hear your words of love."

As they approached the spot, they looked down. Willy was sitting next to Olivia and holding her hand, "I can't believe that Buck was God's ambassador to the United Nations. He is truly the most righteous person the world of today has ever seen."

Olivia smiled, "He has always been one of a kind. Last Sunday, when we went to Rose's and Buck's grave site, I felt the presence of God. I always feel as if we are in the presence of God when we are there."

Willy thought for a moment, "I feel the same way. I tingle, I mean my whole-body tingles whenever we are there."

"I feel the same way, but didn't know how to explain it."

Rose and Buck left the site and began to walk. They stopped by where the children were playing and watched. The laughter they heard filled their hearts. Buck smiled, "There is never a sad face in heaven."

"Some when they first come are sad because they left their loved ones behind. But when they look down upon them, their sadness soon vanishes. God helps the family heal."

Buck heard Jesus calling him. Rose walked away. Buck turned and saw Jesus walking toward him. Buck still felt as if he should bow or do something. This soon vanished from his mind.

"You are a man of many wonders," Jesus said and then placed his arm around Buck's shoulder. As they walked, Buck knew that Jesus was leading him to a certain place. Buck saw a Gothic building with nine men and women sitting on the steps. As Buck looked at each one, he knew their names; Enoch, Job, Samuel, Daniel, Isaiah, Mary, and Joseph, Mary Magdalene, and Joshua.

"These are those who reached righteousness."

"I am honored to meet you," Buck said.

"No! it is our honor," Enoch said.

They all stood to hug Buck. Buck had tears in his eyes.

"Your heart is so beautiful," Mary said.

Joseph stepped forward and Buck hugged him and said, "You were always in my thoughts, you helped raise God's only son."

Samuel stepped forward. "I always loved reading your two books of the Bible," Buck said. Samuel hugged him tighter than anyone. Mary Magdalene stepped forward. Buck never did believe what the Bible said about her, he instantly knew that she was special to Jesus, he gave her a loving hug. Job stepped forward, "Your love of God is well known, your faith shined above most." They hugged. Daniel stepped forward, "You were a great teacher, you taught Gentiles about our God and proved he was the one and only God."

"It was God that proved Himself," Daniel replied.

Isiah stepped forward, "You were one of God's greatest prophets." Buck hugged him and then turned to Joshua.

"Moses picked you to deliver the chosen people to the promise land."

"You certainly know your Bible," Joshua replied.

Buck turned to Jesus, "My love for you will always grow. You saved us all."

"I had help," Jesus said, "I did it for my Father, for He so loved all those on earth. He started to lose some of that love. It was you who made his heart burst with joyful love. We are honored that you are with us."

"I am honored to be with all of you."

They all sat together and spoke of all they have seen in their lives. Buck was spellbound listening.

***

Chapter Thirteen

Willy picked up the phone on the second ring, "Hello?"

"Willy, this is Brother Blair, I am calling because in two weeks, it will be the first anniversary of the blessed event. Those of us that were there would like to go if that would be okay with you."

"Wow! It's been a year, of course, we would love that. We go every Sunday. I don't know if you been in that area lately. The State is building parking garages for the visitors. Olivia and I were the only ones who were allowed to visit during the construction and any guest that we would bring."

"Yes, it will be opened to the public that Sunday, about one o'clock."

"We always go about nine o'clock."

"I will let the others know."

"Keep us informed of the time and who will be coming."

"I will call you on the Saturday before, have a blessed day."

"Thank you and you also have a blessed day."

With that said, they both hung up.

Olivia entered the room, "Who was that?"

"It was brother Blair, he and the others that attended the blessed event want to go on the one-year anniversary. He also said that is the same day they will open the site to the public. They will open the site at one o'clock. I told him we always go about nine o'clock."

"That would be sweet," Olivia stated.

"I can't believe a whole year has passed; it seems like it was only a couple of months ago."

"You know I think I actually feel younger than I was the day it happened," Olivia added.

"Come to think about it, me, too."

"God has made a difference to all of us. We have all heard Him speak. We have witnessed many people turning to God again. Not directly, but in some way, I feel we have been a part of all this," Olivia said with a beautiful smile.

"I think Buck was a part of that," Willy said.

"Me, too," Olivia added.

After a great discussion among the righteous, Buck heard Rose calling him. He excused himself and walked towards the bench they used to watch over Olivia and Willy. He saw Rose sitting there. When she turned towards Buck, he saw the smile she wore that always melted his heart. She started to stand, Buck touched her shoulder and she sat back down and Buck sat beside her.

"I saw Olivia and Willy discussing a meeting they will have with the others that attended the blessed event, they're all returning for the one- year anniversary. The one- year anniversary, it still seems that I have only been here a month."

Rose smiled and kissed Buck on the cheek. Buck placed his arm around Rose and gave her a loving squeeze. They sat there for what seemed like hours. Rose and Buck both heard God call him.

Buck smiled at Rose and stood to leave. Buck appeared before God who wore a loving smile, also.

"Soon, will be the one- year anniversary of the blessed event. You will watch it from here. But I want you and Rose to go back down the week after the blessed event. You will have your final mission to do."

"What will that be?" Buck asked.

"I will shield it from you until that day."

Buck would never question God. He felt it was time to leave. He returned to Rose who was still sitting on the bench, "God said he has one more mission for me and you."

"What is it?" Rose asked.

"God will shield it from us until the week after they all gather for the anniversary of the blessed event. We will watch that from here."

"God has a mission for both of us. I am really proud to be a part of this," Rose replied.

Rose and Buck stood up and began to walk. Buck felt some one tug at the back of his shirt. He turned to see Elizabeth smiling.

"Hi, Missy,, how are you today?"

Elizabeth smiled and said, "I am a bundle of joy according to my father."

"That is so true," Replied Buck.

"Can I introduce you to my father?" Elizabeth asked.

"We would like that very much," was Buck's and Rose's reply. Buck and Rose saw Elizabeth's mother and father approaching. Elizabeth's father had tears in his eyes.

"I want to thank you with all my heart for letting me see my Elizabeth and Martha again."

Buck and Rose hugged Elizabeth's parents.

"It is our pleasure to see you all together. It was God who afforded you this comfort."

"We know, but it was your wish. This is the reason God brought us back together."

"It is so good to see the love in all your eyes. It warms our hearts to know we may have had a part in this," Buck said. With that said, Elizabeth and her parents walked away, holding one another's hand.

***

Willy and Olivia, Betsey and Louie walked up to Buck's and Rose's statues. They bowed their heads and said a prayer.

"Next week will be the one- year anniversary of the blessed event," Willy stated as he looked at Buck's glorious figure, "We will be coming with those who were witnesses to the event. I know you may not be able to attend with everything that is going on with God. But we will be here to represent you."

Olivia stepped forward, "We saw and heard your talk as ambassador to the United Nations. God has watched over all of us. I know he will continue to do so."

Betsey didn't know what to say. Louie said, "We love you both, you have changed our lives, also."

They stayed about two hours, most of the time spent just standing in awe at Buck's and Rose's statues. Willy looked at the statue of Elizabeth and remembered the argument they had with the authorities who wanted to remove it to make more room. Willy argued that this little girl was Buck's friend and the first statue that Buck talked to. He knew that Buck would object to any graves being moved.

The State, with permission of those involved, did move some graves a few feet to make a cement path for the visitors to walk on to view the site of the blessed event. It also worked out to keep the crowds moving.

Willy, Olivia, Betsey, and Louie left and headed home. Olivia had a dinner set to go when they got home.

***

Rose and Buck did not witness what happened that Sunday. They spent time with family. After meeting with their family, they walked the golden path, which led to God. God was talking to Daniel, the little boy with cancer.

212

God was reassuring Daniel that his parents and little sister would be fine. You could see a heartwarming smile on Daniel's face.

God introduced Daniel to Buck and Rose, they were greeted with a hug. Daniel moved away, there was an aunt waiting for him to guide him to their mansion.

"It is all going better than I expected. I have witnessed hearts filled with hate become hearts filled with love. I see enemies hug one another. We are at the beginning of a new world, and it is all because of your selfless acts of love."

Buck didn't know how to respond. He smiled. God smiled back, "You're a good man, Buck, and your wife is a very loving woman. You have placed joy in the hearts of many, including Myself. You two should go and witness the one- year anniversary of the blessed event."

***

Chapter Fourteen

It was the Saturday before the anniversary of the Blessed Event. Willy picked up the phone on the first ring.

"Hello, how are you?" Willy said to Brother Blair.

"We are all in town for tomorrow's get together. Can we pick you up in the morning?"

"That would be fine."

"How about nine o'clock?"

"Sounds good to me, see you in the morning."

With that said, both men hung up.

"Who was that on the phone?" Olivia asked from the kitchen where she was washing dishes.

"Brother Blair, he said they were all in town for tomorrow's anniversary. They will pick us up at nine o'clock."

"Will they have room for Betsey and Louie?"

"I didn't think to ask."

"Brother Blair's number is in the book."

"I will call right now," Willy said.

After the second ring, Brother Blair's phone went to voice mail, "Hi, Brother Blair, would there be room for my sister-in-law and my nephew on the bus? Call me back and let me know. Bye and have a blessed night."

Willy walked in and placed his arms around Olivia, she was still doing dishes.

"I called and had to leave a message."

"Louie said he was going to be busy next week, so we will have to take a taxi," Olivia stated.

At this point, the phone rang. It was Brother Blair who stated there would be enough room. Willy thanked him and they both hung up.

"No problem, there will be enough room for Betsey and Louie."

"That's great, I'll call her and let her know," Olivia responded. It was an hour later that Olivia remembered to call Betsey.

"Hi, sis, we are all going to be picked up in the morning and then head to the cemetery."

"Will they be enough room for all of us?"

"Yes, they will send a bus."

"See you in the morning, sis, love you."

"Love you, too," was Betsey's reply.

The following morning, Willy and Olivia was sitting on the sofa they each had a cup of coffee.

"Do you think Buck will show up today?"

"I was asking myself the same question," Olivia said, "He may, I guess, then again, he might be doing something for God."

"You are right; he has been doing a lot lately."

Olivia heard Betsey and Louie coming down the stairs.

"Come in," Olivia said before they reached the door.

Betsey and Louie entered.

"The Bus will be here at nine o'clock," Willy said.

"We still have twenty minutes, would either of you like a cup of coffee?" Olivia asked.

They both declined. At nine o'clock, they headed outside to see a limousine waiting for them.

A man was standing there, holding the door open. Willy looked in, it was empty.

"Where are the others?" Olivia asked.

"They will be meeting us at the gate," the man replied. After Louie got in, the man closed the door and headed for the driver's seat.

"Wow, I hope they didn't have to do this because Louie and I came," Betsey said.

The driver spoke up, "I was reserved a week ago by the governor. He has had all the others picked up also."

"Today is the opening to the public, that's supposed to happen at one o'clock," Willy stated.

As they pulled up, they noticed five limousines parked at the gate, each holding one person. One had Brother Blair, one had Rabbi Lutz, one had Father Chaffee, one had Mohammad Elsah, and the final one held the governor. They all approached Willy and Olivia. Betsey and Louie stood next to them. Brother Blair approached them, "You must be Olivia's sister and you are her nephew. It is a great pleasure to me you."

At this point, Olivia introduced Betsey and Louie to the others.

The governor explained that he would be at the opening ceremony at one o'clock, but wanted to be there with them for the first anniversary. Willy and

Olivia welcomed him to join them. As the nine present approached Buck's and Rose's grave site, Willy was waiting to see Buck and Rose appear. Of course, this did not happen. Buck and Rose were watching from their special spot in heaven.

They all walked up to the statues of the two most famous people at this time in history. Olivia spoke first.

"We all, except for the governor, remember what happened a year ago. We were so blessed to be a part of this blessed event."

Rabbi Lutz spoke next, "To see Buck, Rose, Moses, and General George Washington and the others that came down from heaven to witness what we witnessed was a great gift from God."

Father Chaffee stated, "I am so proud to be a part of all of this. We actually stood in the presence of God."

Mohammad Elsah, "It shouldn't have taken Buck or God to bring us together. We have learned so much in the past year. God has changed each and every one of us for the better."

The governor spoke up, "I can only dream of what you have all witnessed. I am proud to stand with you today, I am proud that New York State can pass along the blessed event to the public."

They stood gazing at the two statues, which beamed from the light of the sun. Two benches were installed. These were installed for Willy and Olivia. They would be the only ones who could spend more than a minute in front of the statues.

At this point they seemed to all be praying. When Willy opened his eyes, he saw the rest still had their eyes closed.

Olivia noticed the two benches, after her prayer, she tugged on Willy's sleeve and they both sat down.

"We provided the benches for you and your friends," the governor stated, "No one else would be able to sit, we will need to keep the crowd moving, there will be thousands of people a day walking through here."

"Thank you, that is very kind of you," Olivia said.

Rabbi Lutz pointed out the spot where Moses appeared. Then he pointed to another spot, "This is where Abraham appeared."

Willy looked at Rose' statue and pointed at the ground, "This is where Buck would sit every Sunday while he visited Rose."

They all recalled where certain spirits appeared, "George Washington was here and Philip Schuyler came from over there."

Father Chaffee pointed out.

"With your help, I will have these areas marked and have plaques placed in these spots. This will help provide the believers with more information," the governor said.

The group stayed for almost two hours. The governor invited them all to lunch at the governor's Mansion. They all accepted.

While lunch was being served, Mohamad Elsah said, "I sort of thought Buck would be here today."

"Me, too," they seem to all reply.

"Buck has been doing a lot of work for God, he may be on a mission," Willy said.

They all seemed to agree. They finished lunch about twelve thirty. The governor excused himself he had to head back to the opening ceremony.

After he left, the group still discussed the blessed event; they all had glorious memories of what happened. Shortly, after one o'clock, they headed to the limousines for their ride back to where they were staying. They all hugged each other and this included Betsey and Louie. It was not a goodbye. It …was a; 'see you later' type of departure. One by one, the limousines left the governor's Mansion.

Willy and Olivia, along with Betsey and Louie, arrived home a few minutes later.

"Sis, I can't explain how grateful I am to be a part of today," Betsey said as she hugged Olivia. Louie followed saying the same thing to Willy as they shook hands.

"It was great having you both with us," Willy said.

***

Rose and Buck watched as Willy placed his arm around Olivia and they walked into their home.

"That was beautiful," Rose said.

"It was nice seeing that group together. I hope they do periodically meet. You can see that they all have a great love for one another," Buck stated.

Rose stood up first, Buck followed her lead.

"Let's visit the children," Buck said.

Rose guided him along the way. They heard the laughter that always welcomed them to this wondrous place. They noticed immediately that Daniel was with the group. It warmed their hearts to see Daniel laughing and playing with the other children. Daniel spotted Buck and Rose and he waved, they waved back, still wearing their beautiful smiles.

A little girl named Emma ran over to them.

"I have something to say," she stated.

Buck and Rose smiled, "Then say it," Buck said.

"I love you is what she had to say," then ran back to the others.

"Rose, have you ever thought that anyone would walk up to you and say, 'I Love You'?"

"This would only happen in heaven," she replied.

"Because of you two, it is happening on earth, also."

They heard God's voice say.

Chapter Fifteen

They turned to see Jesus with a flock of children behind him, "Because of you, My Father says my escorting children to heaven will become less and less. He can foresee the help people are starting to provide for one another. He sees a love growing that will never die. Thanks to both of you."

The children standing behind Jesus all ran to play with the others. In a blink, Jesus was gone.

"He meant you did all this," Rose said.

"No, without you occupying my mind, I would have never become righteous."

With that said, they both kissed each other.

They began to walk and noticed Jamie sitting on a bench, she wore a beautiful smile. Even at the age of ninety-nine, she emitted a beautiful glow which made her shine.

"How are you today?" Buck asked.

Jamie smiled and said, "I am in love with the world. I see the changes that are happening. I see my family getting along so lovingly. Thank you both for all you have done."

She stood and Buck kissed her on the cheek and hugged her, Rose did the same.

"Have a blessed day," Buck said.

Jamie smiled and replied, "Time does not exist in heaven, but I will have a blessed time watching over my family."

Rose and Buck walked on.

"I keep forgetting about the existence of time in heaven," Rose said with a chuckle.

***

Willy was watching T.V. and Olivia was making up a list of groceries they would have to pick up in the next day or two. Willy spotted the list, "Are we going to buy enough food for the next year?" he said followed by a smile.

"I am also picking up some stuff for Betsey."

"We really are so blessed," Willy said. Olivia nodded her head agreeing with him.

"You know we should have invited Mr. Templar from S.E.F.C.U. and also Harley Davidson from Newburgh, they were both with us last year at the blessed event."

"You are right, we should have done that. Let's mark the calendar for next year and make sure we do invite them."

"That would be fine," Olivia responded.

"Sometimes, I like to close my eyes and picture Buck and Rose with us."

Olivia seemed a little startled, "I do, too."

They both began to remember things that happened before the blessed event.

"Remember that night at church, the preacher kept talking about righteousness."

"How can I forget, the next day when I went to visit him, he couldn't recall anything that happened. He thought I was losing my mind."

They kept bringing up the many episodes that entailed Buck's life.

***

Buck saw a man he knew, "Hey, Flynn," he said.

The man turned and looked at Buck.

"You don't remember me from when we were children in North Carolina," Buck added, "Rose, this man as a child walked a mile from his house to mine to give me his old pair of shoes."

"I remember that, my parents bought me new shoes and told me to throw the others in the trash. I remembered seeing you playing on the ground and I saw a hole in the bottom of your shoe. I thought you could use them."

"I thank you with all my heart, that was a kind and loving gesture."

"I have often wondered why God let me come to heaven. I turned out not to be a great person. I have prayed every day since I got here, hoping God didn't make a mistake."

"He never makes mistakes, he witnessed your act of kindness and knew you belonged here."

"That makes me feel a whole lot better."

"Let me thank you again for thinking about me," Buck added. As they departed, Buck noticed Flynn seemed to stand a little taller and looked a little prouder.

"That was beautiful to witness," Rose said.

"Many people really don't know how they have helped people throughout their lives. God never forgets those that help others."

Buck and Rose heard God calling them. They headed in his direction. God was sitting on His throne. He wore a beautiful smile.

"Buck, I mentioned I had one more mission for you."

"Anything for you, my God," Buck replied.

Rose started to walk away, letting Buck and God have their talk.

"Rose, I need you for this mission, also."

Rose froze and turned, "Anything for you my God," was her reply.

***

It was Sunday morning, Willy and Olivia were getting ready to head to the cemetery to visit with Buck and Rose.

"I'll call a cab," Willy said.

"Wait a few more minutes, I want to clean up before we head out."

Willy could hear Olivia in the kitchen putting stuff away. Then he heard her make the call for the cab.

"They said it would be about fifteen minutes," Olivia shouted.

Willy whispered to himself, "I was hoping to see you last week, Buck, but I know all you have been doing for God and understand why you couldn't make it. I love you and miss you both."

"Were you talking to someone?" Olivia asked.

"Just talking to Buck," Willy replied.

When they got outside the cab pulled up. Willy started to say Albany Rural Cemetery.

"I know, we have all drawn straws to see who will have the honor of taking you each week when you need us."

"That's really sweet," Olivia said.

They now had a state policeman standing at the entrance. It was a little after nine and Buck and Olivia saw the people already crowding the rope line next door. They would be standing there for hours before the cemetery opened. The state policeman was about to open the entrance when Olivia and Willy got out of the cab. Willy always tried to pay the taxi driver, but they would never except any money.

Willy and Olivia waved to the crowd, then walked into the cemetery. The state policeman shut the gate behind them. Willy had his arm around Olivia's shoulder as they walked. When they reached the grave site, they sat down on the bench closest to the statues.

"What were you talking to Buck about this morning?"

"I mentioned that I missed them both."

"We miss them both."

"Buck knew what I meant."

As they looked up to their left, watching the statues gleam from the sunshine, in front of them about ten feet away, Buck and Rose appeared.

Willy and Olivia jumped up and ran to them. Willy was hugging Buck and Olivia was hugging Rose, then they switched partners. When the hugging stopped, Willy asked in a low voice, "Are you here on a mission from God?"

Buck and Rose smiled and answered in unison, "Yes, we are, we are on our final mission"

Again, in a low voice, Willy asked, "Can you tell us what it is?"

Again, in unison, they replied, "We are here to take you home."

A puzzled look appeared on Olivia's and Willy's faces.

Buck pointed behind them, when they turned, they saw themselves slumped together in a loving embrace on the bench. They knew this was what they have been waiting for.

As the four hugged together, there was a great flash of light. They ascended up to Heaven. The flash caused the state policeman to investigate.

He discovered Willy and Olivia's bodies on the bench in a loving embrace.